PRAISE FOR THE NOVELS OF

MAYA BANKS

"A must-read author . . . her [stories] are always full of emotional situations, lovable characters and kick-butt story lines."
—*Romance Junkies*

"Definitely a recommended read . . . filled with friendship, passion and, most of all, a love that grows beyond just being friends."
—*Fallen Angel Reviews*

"Grabbed me from page one and refused to let go until I read the last word . . . When a book still affects me hours after reading it, I can't help but Joyfully Recommend it!"   —*Joyfully Reviewed*

"I guarantee I will reread this book many times over, and will derive as much pleasure as I did in the first reading each and every subsequent time."   —*Novelspot*

"An excellent read that I simply did not put down . . . a fantastic adventure . . . covers all the emotional range."
—*The Road to Romance*

"Searingly sexy and highly believable."   —*Romantic Times*

sweet persuasion

MAYA BANKS

Berkley Books / New York

THE BERKLEY PUBLISHING GROUP
Published by the Penguin Group
Penguin Group (USA) Inc.
375 Hudson Street, New York, New York 10014, USA
Penguin Group (Canada), 90 Eglinton Avenue East, Suite 700, Toronto, Ontario M4P 2Y3, Canada
(a division of Pearson Penguin Canada Inc.) • Penguin Books Ltd, 80 Strand, London WC2R 0RL,
England • Penguin Ireland, 25 St Stephen's Green, Dublin 2, Ireland (a division of Penguin
Books Ltd) • Penguin Group (Australia), 707 Collins Street, Melbourne, Victoria 3008, Australia
(a division of Pearson Australia Group Pty Ltd) • Penguin Books India Pvt Ltd, 11 Community
Centre, Panchsheel Park, New Delhi–110 017, India • Penguin Group (NZ), 67 Apollo Drive,
Rosedale, Auckland 0632, New Zealand (a division of Pearson New Zealand Ltd) • Penguin Books,
Rosebank Office Park, 181 Jan Smuts Avenue, Parktown North 2193, South Africa • Penguin China,
B7 Jiaming Center, 27 East Third Ring Road North, Chaoyang District, Beijing 100020, China

Penguin Books Ltd., Registered Offices: 80 Strand, London WC2R 0RL, England

This book is an original publication of The Berkley Publishing Group.

PUBLISHING HISTORY
Heat trade paperback edition / June 2009
Berkley trade paperback edition / January 2013

Berkley trade paperback ISBN: 978-0-425-26696-0

The Library of Congress has catalogued the Heat trade paperback edition of this book as follows:

Banks, Maya.
Sweet persuasion / Maya Banks.—1st ed.
p.   cm.
ISBN: 978-0-425-22770-1
1. Sexual dominance and submission—Fiction.   I. Title
PS3602.A643S83   2009
813'.6—dc22
2008055290

PRINTED IN THE UNITED STATES OF AMERICA

10   9   8   7   6   5   4   3   2   1

ALWAYS LEARNING   PEARSON *sweet persuasion*

CHAPTER 1

"*D*o you know of anyone who fulfills sexual fantasies?" Serena James asked.

Quiet descended. The hands massaging her tense shoulders stopped. Serena cracked one eye open to glance over at Faith Malone, who was lying on the next massage table, and then she craned her head to look over her shoulder at her masseuse, Julie Stanford, who owned the all-inclusive beauty salon Serena and Faith went to on a weekly basis.

"Uh, honey, you're the fantasy fulfiller," Julie remarked in a dry voice. "And do you have to talk about sexual fantasies while I'm giving you a rubdown?"

"Quit your bitching and keep massaging," Serena grumbled.

She closed her eyes and relaxed back onto the table. She should have known better than to bring up what was occupying her mind lately. A quiet sigh escaped her lips when Julie began kneading her muscles again.

"The time to talk sexual fantasies is when I'm giving Nathan Tucker a massage," Julie said in a dreamy tone.

Faith laughed next to Serena. "Is he a regular now?"

"Yep. Twice a month," Julie said cheerfully. "Now *that* is a job I'd do for free. I have to be careful not to drool on his back."

"Not the front?" Serena mumbled.

Julie chuckled. "He only lets me do his back. Pity. I'd pay him to massage that chest."

"Only his chest, huh?" Faith said.

"Why only his back?" Serena asked.

Julie's hands shook as she laughed. "He's embarrassed, I think. Doesn't want me to see his hard-on."

Her hands moved more firmly over Serena's back, and Serena groaned in pleasure.

"But enough about my obsession with Nathan Tucker. I want to know why you're asking about sexual fantasies."

"Yeah, me too," Faith piped up. "Thinking of expanding Fantasy Incorporated?"

Serena chuckled. "Uh, no. Paying people to fulfill other people's *sexual* fantasies is called prostitution, no?"

"Then why do you want to know about it?" Julie persisted. She patted Serena's shoulder to let her know she was finished and then moved over to Faith.

Serena sat up and reached for a bathrobe, wrapping it around herself as she perched on the edge of the massage table. She stared over at Faith as Julie started her massage. Why *was* she asking about it?

It was a slip of the tongue, one made by her ever increasing frustration that her life's work was all about fulfilling other people's fantasies—some frivolous, some the culmination of lifetimes of hope.

She was proud of her work. She made other people happy. And maybe that was why she was frustrated by her own lack of contentment.

"Maybe I just need to get laid," Serena muttered.

An amused grin split Julie's lips. "Don't we all. Well, except Faith here. I'm sure Gray is giving her all she needs in that quarter."

"Hey, no hating," Faith protested. "I can't help it if I'm irresistible."

Serena threw a hand towel at Faith's head, and Faith reached up, snagged it from her hair and threw it back.

"When are you getting married anyway?" Serena asked Faith.

"Oh, no, you don't," Faith said as she cracked her eyes open to stare at Serena. "We were talking about *your* sexual fantasy question."

"Yeah, we were," Julie said pointedly.

Serena let out an exasperated breath. "You two are worse than a dog with a bone."

"Yep," Julie said with a grin. "I have no life, remember? I have to live vicariously through my clients. Now spill."

Serena bit her bottom lip then shrugged her shoulders. What the hell. Nothing ventured, nothing gained.

"I have some pretty . . . interesting fantasies."

Julie snorted. "Don't we all."

Serena could see Faith's blush start at her feet and creep up her body. She grinned. "Apparently Faith does, judging by that blush."

Faith gave a mortified squeak and hid her face. "We're not talking about me," she said in a muffled voice.

"No, but I wish we were," Julie muttered. "I bet that sweet, innocent exterior shields a twisted mind."

"Serena. We're talking about Serena," Faith pointed out.

Julie turned back to look at Serena. "So spill, honey. What's so interesting about your sexual fantasies, and why would you want to know if someone we knew could fulfill them? As gorgeous as you are, you wouldn't have to walk far to find any number of men more than willing to take directions."

Serena gave her a dark look. "I haven't told you what my fantasies are."

"Ooohhh," Faith exclaimed. "Hurry up, Julie. This sounds like it'll be good."

"My magic hands are being dumped for her demented fantasies?" Julie asked in an exaggerated hurt tone.

"Like you aren't every bit as eager to hear as she is," Serena drawled.

Julie grinned. "True. Okay, Faith, all done. Better get dressed. You have no idea what Serena's fantasies involve, and I have to think Gray would object to a lesbian threesome."

Faith blushed bright red, and it looked like her insides were squeezed to the bursting point.

Serena rolled her eyes. "You're way too easy, Faith."

"You only think I'm all sweet and innocent," Faith mumbled as she pulled on a robe.

"What was that?" Julie asked, pouncing on Faith's statement.

"Serena. We're talking about Serena. Remember?"

The phone rang, and Julie held up a finger for them to wait as she walked over to answer. Serena sat there with her feet dangling down the side of the table. In the weeks the women had been meeting for massages and then lunch, they'd discussed a lot of outlandish topics, but never had those included the personal details of Serena's deep, dark fantasies, and she honestly wasn't sure she was prepared to unveil them. Even to her two closest friends.

But if not them, then who?

Exactly.

She sighed. Maybe she should just forget about them and continue on fulfilling other people's hokey fantasies.

Julie returned, a look of apology darkening her pretty features. "I'm sorry, guys. I can't do lunch today. That was one of my clients in need of an emergency overhaul."

"That's too bad," Faith said with an unhappy grimace.

"Overhaul? That doesn't sound good," Serena remarked.

Julie grinned. "It's her own fault. She went to another stylist to get her hair done, and now she's ten sorts of sorry and is crawling back to me."

"Just like you like them," Faith said as she hopped off the table.

"You two go on without me. But," she said, pinning them both with a glare, "I'll expect a *full* report later. As in nothing left out. Don't make me hurt you."

Serena rolled her eyes and got down off the table to go dress. "Trust me. It's not that juicy, Julie. As if anything in my boring-ass life would be."

Julie studied her with a speculative stare. "Oh, I don't know, Serena. It's always the boring ones who turn out to have the most shocking secrets."

Again, a rosy blush stained Faith's face, and Serena and Julie both burst out laughing.

"Obviously we haven't been pressing Faith enough for hers," Serena said dryly.

"Make her tell you at lunch," Julie suggested. "Then you can call me later with the dirt."

"Oh, she won't do that," Faith said innocently. "Because then I'd have to give you the dirt on her."

"Somebody had better give me the scoop on both you deviants," Julie warned. "I'll withhold all services until I get it. And you, my dear, are due for a wax soon."

"Crap," Faith grumbled.

Serena linked her arms through Faith's and started to drag her toward the dressing room. "We could always find a new salon, you know."

Julie snorted. "Sure, if you want to look like a scarecrow."

"She's arrogant, isn't she?" Serena said in a loud whisper as they exited the room.

Julie's laughter followed them into the changing area.

Serena veered off into her cubicle to dress, and a few minutes later she met Faith out front where Julie was already soothing her distraught client. As Serena and Faith headed for the door, Julie caught their gaze and rolled her eyes heavenward. Serena blew her a kiss.

"The usual?" Serena asked as she and Faith walked out to the parking lot.

Faith shook her head. "If we're going to have a down and dirty conversation, I don't want to go to Cattleman's."

Serena lifted her brow. "Why not?"

"Because any one of the guys might be there," Faith said.

"Good point," Serena mumbled. The men that Faith worked with, gorgeous specimens of men all of them, regularly haunted Cattleman's, a local pub and grill. The last thing Serena wanted was an audience. Although if one of them wanted to step up and volunteer to man her fantasies, she wouldn't complain.

"Where to, then?" she asked as they stopped at their cars.

"How about my apartment?" Faith suggested. "It isn't far, and I can warm up some leftovers."

Serena sighed. "And there's plenty of privacy for the juicy conversation you're going to make me have."

Faith grinned impishly. "Exactly."

Serena followed Faith into her apartment. She'd only been inside Faith's home once before, right after Faith's fiancé, Gray Montgomery, had moved the majority of his things in.

"Excuse the mess," Faith said as she stepped around a box on the floor.

"Moving?" Serena asked.

Faith's smile lit up her entire face. "Gray and I are buying a house. We hope to move in as soon as we get married."

"Julie is still mortally offended that you aren't having a huge church wedding so she can make you look like a million dollars for the occasion," Serena said as she settled onto a stool at the bar in the kitchen.

Faith made a face. "Neither Gray nor I was crazy about a big fuss. Not after everything that happened." Her smile faltered as pain flitted across her brow. "Pop wanted a big wedding too so he could give me away, but honestly, Gray and I just want to be together. The sooner, the better."

Serena smiled. "I think that's great, Faith. You deserve to be happy after all you went through."

"Enough about me," Faith said brightly as she began taking containers out of the refrigerator. "We're here to talk about you and these deviant fantasies of yours."

Serena groaned. "Who the hell says they're deviant?"

Faith chuckled. "The best ones always are. So what gives,

Serena?" Faith's expression became more somber as she gazed at her friend. "You haven't been yourself lately. You seem withdrawn, like you're unhappy about something."

Serena plunked her elbows on the counter and cupped her jaw in her palm. "I've just been doing a lot of thinking."

"About?"

"The fact that I put so much time and effort into making other people's fantasies come to life, but I ignore my own. And then I realized that I wouldn't have the first clue how to make them come true anyway. Other people's fantasies are so . . . normal compared to mine. My mother would have heart failure if she knew the girl she'd raised to be a self-sufficient, depend-on-no-man-for-your-security, successful businesswoman secretly fantasized about being a man's sex slave."

Faith choked then coughed delicately to mask her reaction. "Sex slave?" she squeaked.

"Yeah, knew you'd get a real kick out of that one," Serena said glumly.

"Uh, no. I mean it's just that's the last thing I expected you to say."

"Go ahead and say it. I'm crazy as a bat."

Faith set a plate of lasagna in front of Serena then settled onto the stool across the bar. "You're not crazy, Serena," she said calmly. "But sex slave? Are you talking one night of hot sex where you play the slave to the master, or is this something else entirely?"

Serena felt warmth invade her cheeks. Damn it. Unlike Faith, she was not a blusher.

"Well, preferably it would be longer than one night, but not permanent or anything. I mean, I think I'd like it. The idea turns me on, but I might hate it too."

Faith was silent for a long moment, and Serena fidgeted uncomfortably as she picked at her food.

"You're wondering where on earth I came up with this, aren't you?" Serena mumbled.

"Quit being defensive, and don't apologize for your desires," Faith scolded. "God, don't women do that enough? I'm just trying to figure out how serious you are about this. I mean if you just want to play out a fantasy, you could always hire a . . . What do they call a male prostitute anyway?" Faith asked with a giggle.

Serena closed her eyes. "I'm not hiring a damn gigolo. I want someone halfway normal. Preferably someone who hasn't already made it with half the women in Houston. And I'd like more than one night. I don't know, maybe a month. I won't be able to discover anything about the reality if it's only one night."

Faith gave her a thoughtful look. "I know someone who might be able to help you."

Serena's mouth gaped open. "You?"

Faith stuck her tongue out and scowled. "I'm not as innocent as you and Julie like to think."

Serena laughed. "Oh, I know, girlfriend. It's always the sweet, shy ones who are the real dirty birds."

"Dirty birds?" Faith sputtered. "Need I remind you of who is plotting to become a sex slave?"

Serena grinned. "It has such a forbidden quality, doesn't it?" She put a forkful of lasagna in her mouth and closed her eyes. "You're a wonderful cook, you know? I can't even boil water. I bet Gray thinks he's in heaven."

"He's not marrying me for my cooking," Faith said dryly.

"Admit it. You're a total dirty bird," Serena coaxed.

Faith flashed an unrepentant smile. "I can give you Damon Roche's phone number."

"Damon Roche? Is he the guy you think can turn me into a sex slave?"

"Not him personally," Faith corrected. "But he owns a . . . hell, I'm still not sure what to call it. I suspect Damon wouldn't appreciate me calling it a sex club."

"Sex club?" Serena raised one brow and stared at Faith in surprise. "What the hell are you doing hanging out in a sex club?"

"It was only once," Faith muttered.

"Clearly you've been holding out on me."

"It didn't exactly come up in conversation," Faith said with a laugh. "Anyway, back to Damon. If you called him and told him what you wanted, I bet he could help. There seems to be something for everyone at his . . . establishment."

"Is it safe?" Serena asked doubtfully.

"Extremely. Damon has very tight security, and he screens his members very thoroughly."

"Does Gray know about this Damon guy?" Serena asked, more to make Faith blush than any real curiosity.

Instead of blushing, Faith smiled broadly. "Gray knows all about Damon. Damon is flying us to our honeymoon on his private jet."

"The sex club business must be lucrative," Serena murmured.

"Oh, The House is a side diversion. Damon's a businessman." Faith frowned. "You know, I don't think he's ever told me what it is exactly that he does."

"Oh, great. He's probably a drug dealer."

"He's not a drug dealer," Faith said in exasperation. "Call him. Tell him what you want. He's very easy to talk to."

"You're not going to try and talk me out of my insanity?"

Serena asked. "You're my friend. You're supposed to be mean and give me lectures so that later we can go on *Oprah* and talk about what soul sisters we are."

"Or I could go on *America's Most Wanted* after I kill you and dump your body in the gulf," Faith muttered.

Serena shoveled more lasagna down and followed it with several gulps of tea.

"All right, I'll call him. Provided I don't go home and chicken out. You were supposed to talk me out of this, not provide me the name of someone who can help me down the road to debauchery."

"The debauched ones have more fun," Faith said with an evil twinkle in her eye.

"So says the voice of experience."

Faith walked over to one of the drawers and took out a notepad and pen. As she returned, she scribbled on a sheet of paper and then tore it out.

She slid it across the bar toward Serena. "Go home and call him."

CHAPTER 2

Serena walked into her office and paused by the window to stare over the Houston skyline. She was dressed smartly. Business suit, moderate heels. She knew she looked good. Efficient.

With a sigh, she turned around to face her desk. And the phone. The piece of paper with Damon Roche's number was crumpled damply in her hand. She unfolded it and smoothed the edges as she sat down in the executive chair.

No, she couldn't call from home the day before. She needed to do it here, where she could pretend it was just business. Here in her comfortable environment, she wasn't nervous. It didn't have to be about her. She could play it cool and pretend she was acting on the behalf of a client.

She picked up the phone and glanced down at the number again before punching it in. For several tense moments, she listened to the ring. About the time she decided no one was going to answer, a distracted voice muttered a terse hello.

She swallowed quickly. "Am I speaking with Mr. Roche?"

There was a distinct pause. "Who is this and how the hell did you get my private number?"

Shit. Damn Faith for not telling her this was his private line and apparently one he guarded closely. She'd managed to piss him off before she ever got to the hard part.

"Faith Malone gave me your number," she said as calmly as her pounding heart would allow.

"Faith? Is she all right?" he demanded.

She hastened to assure him. "She's fine. She gave me your number about a . . . business matter. I'm sorry to have bothered you. I hadn't realized this was a private number."

Before he could answer, she gently replaced the receiver and backed away from the desk.

Bad idea. Definitely a bad idea.

Her pulse raced, and she struggled to get her nerves back under control. She certainly wasn't the assertive businesswoman today. With a rueful shake of her head, she turned her attention to her list of tasks for the day.

Her office door opened, and she looked up to see her personal assistant, Carrie Johnson, walk in, a warm smile on her face.

"Serena, I just got a call from Mr. Gallows. He was very satisfied with the work you did on his job."

Serena sat back in her chair and smiled back at Carrie. "Oh, thank goodness. He was such a hard sale."

Carried worked to keep a straight face. "It doesn't help that his fantasy involved being head chef at Riganti's."

"Don't remind me," Serena said with a groan. "I may have lost my favored patron status with Carlos forever. He's probably banned me from the restaurant over this."

"I have it on good authority that the staff at Riganti's loves you, and that Mr. Gallows's short employment there actually went quite well. Mr. Gallows hinted that he was applying to culinary school in Paris, as a result of his experience."

Serena sighed. "Oh, that's lovely. It's so nice when there's a happy outcome. About half the time, the client figures out that some dreams are better left in the realm of fantasy and not ever brought to light. Reality is harsh, unfortunately."

Carrie's eyebrow lifted in surprise. "That doesn't sound like you, Serena. Something going on that I need to know about?"

"No, not at all." Liar. "I can't be Pollyanna all the time. There is a certain risk in what we do. We have the power to make someone's dream come true, but we also have the power to crush it forever."

Carrie shrugged. "Sometimes a healthy dose of reality is needed. You can't live in fantasy land indefinitely. I'd say you've done a lot of people a favor by making that clear."

Serena shook her head. "That's not my job. People don't pay me to give them a wake-up call. They pay me to fulfill a fantasy. To give them something no one else can."

"And you do it very well."

"Maybe."

Carrie cocked her head. "You're in a strange mood, Serena. Maybe you should take the day off. Come back when you're not so . . . morose. Or at least let me talk to clients today."

A smile cracked the corners of Serena's mouth. "I'm fine, Carrie. Really. I promise not to scare away potential clients with my dose of reality. Besides, today we have to outline the details for Michelle Tasco's fantasy."

Carrie's expression softened, and Serena smiled in satisfaction. Carrie really was the perfect assistant. She had a heart of gold and an undying commitment to making people happy.

"Her parents called a few minutes ago to thank you," Carrie said softly. "This means the world to them. I think it was wonderful for you to make the arrangements at no charge."

Serena shifted uncomfortably, her cheeks tightening under Carrie's scrutiny. "Yeah, well, it'll make a nice tax write-off."

Amusement glinted in Carrie's eyes. "You can't fool me, Serena. You're a big ole softie, even if you won't admit it."

"Did you arrange the tour?" Serena asked impatiently.

Still grinning, Carrie plopped a folder onto Serena's desk. "All done. You just need to call Michelle's parents with the final dates and times after you've touched base with the cruise line."

"Okay, I'll do that now," Serena said. "Then we can mark one more fantasy off our list."

"And don't forget to eat lunch," Carrie called over her shoulder as she walked out of Serena's office.

"Yes, Mother," Serena muttered.

She glanced down at the file that Carrie had dropped on her desk. Michelle stared back at her, a waiflike little girl who'd seen way too much horror in her young life. If Serena could make her smile, even for a short while, it was worth every penny.

She picked up the phone and dialed her contact at the cruise line. A few minutes later, she rang off, satisfied that all the arrangements had been made for Michelle's once-in-a-lifetime trip. She hesitated as she started to dial Michelle's parents' number then changed her mind and buzzed for Carrie instead.

"Can you call Michelle's folks and let them know that everything has been taken care of? I'm going to go grab lunch."

A light chuckle worked over the intercom. "Chicken. Yeah, I'll call them. You can't avoid them forever, Serena. They'll want to thank you in person."

Serena grimaced and broke the connection. This was why she had an assistant. Meeting grateful parents was much more Carrie's forte than it was Serena's. Serena could make decisions, run the business, but Carrie had a natural affinity for people that made her a better choice as the company's spokesperson.

Stretching her feet to feel around for her shoes, she snagged them with her toe and then slid them on. After grabbing her handbag, she tossed her cell phone inside and headed for the door. As she walked by Carrie's office, she heard her assistant's cheerful voice as she passed on the information to Michelle's parents.

A smile crept over her mouth despite her attempt not to become involved in the more personal details of Michelle's trip. She stepped into the hot summer air and closed her eyes as the sun brushed across her face.

It was muggy and hot, but she loved the weather in Houston. Even the perpetual haze that hung over the city in the summertime didn't bother her.

As she reached for her car keys, her cell phone rang. With a sigh, she fumbled for it and looked at the LCD. She frowned when she didn't recognize the number. It could be a client.

"This is Serena James," she said by way of greeting as she continued on to her car.

"Miss James, this is Damon Roche."

His deep voice crawled up her spine and hit her right at the base of her skull. She hadn't expected to hear back from him.

"How did you get this number?" she demanded, then winced when she realized she sounded exactly as he had when she'd first called him.

His chuckle rolled through the line. "It's my turn to intrude. Your number didn't register when you called me so I had to track you down using other methods. You're a hard lady to find."

"Not too hard, apparently," she murmured.

"I called Faith," he said simply. "I apologize for my earlier rudeness. It was uncalled for, particularly as you are a friend of someone I care a lot about. Now, what can I do for you?"

Serena grimaced. "Faith didn't tell you?"

"Of course not," he said smoothly. "She only told me that you needed my help. Have you had lunch yet?"

She blinked at his abrupt shift in topic. "Uh, no, was on my way right now, as a matter of fact."

"Perfect. Why don't we meet so we can discuss your . . . problem."

Hell. She drew in a deep breath. She'd already chickened out of her grand plan to seek out her fantasy. It was absurd to think she could go through with it. She hadn't counted on him calling her back after she'd hung up on him.

"Miss James?"

"Call me Serena, please."

"Very well, Serena. Would you like to have lunch?"

"Uh." Crap. "You see, Mr. Roche, what I wanted to talk to you about isn't something I wished to discuss in a public setting."

"I can guarantee we'll have the utmost privacy. Are you there at your office?" he asked.

"Yes—"

"I'll send a driver over to collect you. Say fifteen minutes?"

"But how on earth do you know where my office is?" she protested.

He laughed softly, the sound husky in her ear. "Research. Fifteen minutes?"

Her head was spinning, and yet she found herself saying okay. "I'll wait in the parking lot."

"I'd feel much better if you waited inside where it's safe. My driver will come up to collect you. I look forward to our meeting, Serena."

Before she could respond, he cut the connection, leaving her standing next to her car, openmouthed. Still, she found herself reentering the building and punching the button for the elevator.

"Back so soon?" Carrie asked when Serena passed her office a few minutes later.

"Last-minute appointment," Serena said. "A driver is coming up for me in a bit."

Carrie raised her eyebrows in question. "Sounds intriguing."

Serena ignored her and continued to her own office. Once there, she sank onto the couch in front of her desk and kicked off her shoes.

She'd officially lost her mind.

She closed her eyes. Sweet Jesus, but how was she ever going to have a normal conversation with the man on the topic of sex slaves?

Client. She'd pretend she was acting on the behalf of a client. Then it wouldn't seem so personal, and if this Damon guy reacted like she had a couple of loose screws then she could shrug it off as the oddities of her line of work. If he researched her, he probably already suspected she was asking to see him for a client.

Feeling marginally better about the sheer idiocy of her plan and the terror it invoked, she leaned back and tried to relax. Several long minutes later, her intercom beeped.

"Serena, Damon Roche's driver is here for you," Carrie said.

Serena scrambled up and hastily straightened her clothes. She slipped into her shoes again and collected her purse before striding out of her office and down the hallway.

A large man with a stocky build stood next to Carrie. When he saw Serena, he dipped his head in acknowledgment. "If you're ready, Miss James, the car is waiting."

She nodded in return and followed the man to the elevator. They rode down in silence. He held the door to the office building open for her as she stepped out then motioned her toward the street.

A sleek Bentley was parked in front, the metal glistening in the sun. "Nice car," she murmured.

The driver merely nodded and opened the backseat door then gestured for her to get in. A few moments later, they glided into the busy traffic.

She ran her palms over the soft leather of the seat, enjoying the supple feel of such luxury. She still wasn't convinced Damon Roche wasn't a drug dealer.

"Is the temperature to your liking, Miss James?"

She glanced up at the driver, who was regarding her in the rearview mirror. "I'm fine, thank you."

He returned his gaze to the street, and she turned her attention to her window to watch the flurry of traffic zip by. Finally, they pulled into the parking lot of the restaurant and came to a stop under the awning covering the entrance.

Her door opened, and one of the men working valet reached in to help her out. Before she made it to the entrance, she was greeted by the maitre d' and swiftly escorted inside.

Now, this is the place Mr. Gallows should have chosen for his head chef fantasy. It looked exclusive and obviously catered to a very upscale clientele.

"Mr. Roche will receive you in here," the maitre d' said with a bow as he opened the door to an opulent private dining room.

She walked in on trembling legs and saw a man rise from his seat at a table set for two. Good Lord but the man was gorgeous. He screamed wealth and breeding from the tips of his Italian loafers to the top of his meticulously groomed hair.

"Serena," he greeted as he came to meet her halfway. "I'm so glad you could join me."

He tucked her hand under his arm and guided her to her seat. It was all she could do not to gape as she settled into the comfortable chair.

First rule of business: Never let the opponent realize his advantage.

She straightened and shook off the awe he inspired. Okay, maybe it wasn't awe as much as a huge bolt of unadulterated lust.

Focus, Serena. For God's sake.

Reclaiming her poise, she relaxed gracefully in her seat as a waiter poured wine into her glass.

"I hoped you'd join me for a glass of wine since you aren't driving. I hope I wasn't too presumptuous in choosing the label or having the waiter pour you a taste."

"It's fine," she said easily. "I love wine."

"Excellent."

He gestured once before taking his seat across from her, and the waiter produced two menus.

"I hope you're hungry," Damon remarked. "The food here is quite superb."

"I am, actually," she admitted. Her nerves had prevented her from eating much the day before. "This was all quite unnecessary, Mr. Roche," she said as she swept her hand around the room. "I got the impression you were quite busy, and my request is . . . unimportant."

"Please call me Damon," he said with a smile. "And it was no trouble at all. As for the matter you wish to discuss with me, perhaps we should talk about it before you dismiss it so readily."

She took a sip of her wine as she studied the menu. She'd hoped he'd viewed her phone call as an irritation and would embrace her eagerness to drop it entirely, but he was quite insistent that she relate why she had called. It was all she could do not to let go of a huge sigh.

"Perhaps we should order first," Damon suggested.

"I've decided if you're ready," she said as she laid aside her menu.

Again Damon motioned, and the waiter appeared. Serena placed her order and watched Damon smile his approval. A giddy little tingle shot down her spine. Then she frowned. Why the hell should it matter if he approved of her choice?

"I'll have the same," Damon said as he handed his menu back to the waiter.

The waiter collected hers as well, then backed away from the table. As soon as he disappeared, Damon turned his gaze on her. His warm brown eyes were appraising as they flickered with interest. He was sizing her up every bit as much as she was him.

"So what did you wish to discuss with me, Serena?"

She took another sip of the wine before setting her glass down. "Was your research very detailed?" she asked. "How much did you discover about me before you called?"

His lips quirked into a half smile. "You're in the business of fulfilling fantasies. Very admirable. Your clients speak highly of you."

"How the hell would you know what my clients have to say?" she asked sharply.

"The internet is a wonderful tool. Amazing what will turn up in a Google search."

"I wouldn't know," she muttered. "I'm not in the habit of searching for myself using Google."

"So what can I do for you?" he prompted. "Perhaps a donation for the clients you waive charges for?"

Her cheeks tightened in mortification. "No! I don't ask for donations. This isn't about money. I wouldn't—"

Damon held up a hand to interrupt her. "I'm sorry. I had no desire to offend you. Let's start over. Why don't you tell me what you wanted to discuss?"

Serena squared her shoulders and bolstered her flagging courage. "I have a client whose fantasy is a bit different from my usual requests."

He remained silent as he waited for her to continue.

"Most of my clients want an experience, something they've dreamed about but feel they'll never accomplish on their own. I think perhaps in this case, it's more a lack of knowledge rather than an inability to achieve satisfaction."

Damon nodded. "Makes sense."

She drew in a breath. "Her fantasy is to be owned by a man."

He didn't outwardly react at all. He merely sat there, watching her, waiting for more.

"I'm unclear as to the precise name for it, but perhaps a sex slave would most suit," she added in a low tone after a quick glance around to make sure they weren't overheard. "This presents me with a rather unique problem," she continued. "Obviously this isn't something I can set up for her or pay for. I'm not looking for a legal quagmire nor do I fancy spending time in jail for solicitation of prostitution. Faith told me about your . . . The House, and suggested you might be able to help in finding someone suitable for this woman's . . . fantasy."

Damon rubbed his jaw thoughtfully. "I see."

If she'd expected him to be shocked or amused even, she wasn't prepared for him to take her so seriously.

"Tell me more," he said as leaned forward in his chair. "You say fantasy. I assume this isn't a permanent situation she's seeking."

"Um, no. Maybe a period of a month. She wants it to be long enough to experience it fully and all the nuances, but it's purely a fantasy."

"And Faith thought I would be helpful," he said with an amused smile.

"Not you personally," she said hastily. "She mentioned The House and thought you would know someone suitable who wouldn't mind a temporary arrangement."

"And what would this man receive in exchange for his . . . service?"

"Well, that's the hard part," Serena said.

They were interrupted when the waiter returned with their food. Serena broke off and waited until he'd settled their plates and left before she resumed. She picked up her napkin and laid it across her lap as she glanced back up at Damon.

"I can't pay him for sex, obviously. I'd draw up a contract outlining the non-sexual aspects of the arrangement. Anything beyond that would purely be left up to the parties involved."

"But sex would be expected," Damon said.

"Well, yes, unofficially, of course," she said hastily.

She tasted the grilled fish and sighed her contentment as the flavor burst in her mouth.

"You're right. The food's excellent."

"I'm glad you approve."

They ate in silence for a few moments before she peeked back up at him to find him watching her.

"So what do you think?" she asked hesitantly.

"It's not an unreasonable request," he said simply. "I could probably find a number of candidates for you to review. I do extensive background checks on all the members of The House but I would, of course, scrutinize a short list of men even further before providing you a list. With their permission, obviously."

She nodded. "I would want to do my own background check in addition to the information you provide."

"Of course. I would also ask that you provide me the name of your client so that I can do an appropriate security check on her as well."

Her eyes widened in surprise.

"If I'm to allow her access to my facilities and ask that one of my members participate in this elaborate fantasy, I have to be assured she is suitable. I understand if she is uncomfortable revealing her identity, but I would require it if I'm to offer my services."

This was so not going the way she'd envisioned. No, it wasn't as though she'd be able to keep it a secret forever, but there certainly wasn't a need to reveal her identity if no suitable candidate could be found.

Buck up and quit being such a wimp.

Clearly she needed a new motivational speech because as inspiration went, that one wasn't terribly effective.

"I'll . . . talk with my client and e-mail you the information this afternoon," she hedged.

"An outline of precisely what she's wanting would be helpful as well. I'd need her to be as specific as possible so that disappointment isn't met on either side."

Serena nodded. "I agree."

She looked up and locked gazes with Damon. He really was handsome. He looked arrogant but not obnoxiously so. Assured. Confident. Comfortable in his skin.

Subtle power surrounded him like an aura, and she briefly allowed herself to fall into the fantasy of what it would be like to belong to him. Owned.

Just the word sent a shiver straight down her spine. Her groin tightened, and her clit tingled and pulsed until she had to shift in her seat to alleviate the pressure.

His fingers tapped absently at his wineglass, and she watched in fascination as one slid gently over the surface. He had beautiful hands. Long, lean fingers. How would they feel on her skin?

"Is the food not to your liking?"

She blinked and shook her head before staring down at her half-eaten entrée.

"No," she said hastily. "It's excellent. Sorry, was just collecting my thoughts."

They ate the rest of their meal in relative silence, only breaking it occasionally for idle chitchat. When she was finished with the last bite, she checked her watch and grimaced.

"Lunch was lovely, but I really do have to go."

Damon rose and nodded toward one of the waiters. "I'll have the car brought around at once. Can I walk you out?"

She stood as he offered his arm, and she smiled at his gallantry.

"Your mother must be proud," she said as they walked toward the door.

"Well, she is, but why do you say so?" he asked in an amused tone.

"You have impeccable manners."

He laughed. "My mother would have no compunction about tracking me down and beating me if I ever forgot my manners, especially around a lady. She is a southern belle from the tips of her toes to the top of her head."

When they reached the entrance, the maitre d' opened the door, and Serena saw the Bentley parked a few feet away. Damon walked her to the door and opened it before handing her into the backseat. He leaned in, his hand holding the top of the door.

"It was a pleasure, Serena. I look forward to hearing from you."

She smiled as he withdrew and offered a small wave as the car started in motion. He stood watching her for a long moment before tucking his hands in his pockets and returning to the restaurant.

Nervous little bubbles popped in her belly, and she wilted against the seat like a deflated balloon.

It wasn't so bad. It wasn't so bad.

She'd survived, and he'd made it surprisingly easy to talk to him. As they drove back toward her office, a thought occurred to her. Damon owned The House, an establishment that catered to sexual fantasies, which begged the question: What was his?

CHAPTER 3

*I*nstead of returning to his downtown office, Damon drove into North Houston, where the private estate he'd turned into The House was situated. He'd given Serena his e-mail address, and he found himself curious as to the details of her client's request.

Serena James was intriguing. Stunningly beautiful. Sleek and long-legged with wide, exotic eyes and black hair that fell like silk around her shoulders. His fingers positively itched to touch it, to stroke it and wrap it around his knuckles.

What were her secrets? Her eyes shielded many, with a mysterious aura that enticed a man, beckoned him to come closer, to discover what lay beneath the cool exterior.

Fantasy Incorporated. Interesting business. He wasn't a big fan of role-playing and pretending, but it was a major part of the goings-on at The House. People liked to escape their reality. Slip away and step outside themselves for a little while. He understood it and encouraged it, but after a while, the façade wore on him.

There were quite a few men he could think of who would be more than happy to guide a woman through an elaborate sexual fantasy and be willing to walk away when it was all said and done. Temporary. An important word and one that held a wealth of meaning in the world of sexual fantasies.

Damon didn't want temporary, though. He'd long stood back and watched and waited, thinking that if he were patient, the right woman would come along, that the things he wanted would come together. He'd learned patience at a young age, but now he found himself fast running out.

Finding a woman wasn't the problem. There had been many women—beautiful, intelligent women—who had walked through his life. He'd enjoyed their company, given pleasure and taken it in return, but in the end, they weren't willing to give him the one thing he wanted most: themselves. Wholly and completely. Into his keeping and care.

He could have settled long before now, but that was the one thing he'd promised himself—that he'd never settle for anything less than what he truly wanted.

The security gate eased open when he inserted his card, and he drove up the winding drive to The House. He parked and got out, blinking as the bright sun flashed over his face. Squinting, he headed for the door. He stepped into the cool, darker interior, enjoying the chill of the air-conditioning as it touched his skin.

The house was empty. None of the staff came in until later in the day. He enjoyed the silence and the solitude that coming in early gave him. His office was comfortable and welcoming, and he was surrounded by things that gave him pleasure.

It was decorated in an old-world style with various models of clipper ships dotting the surfaces of antique end tables. An antique globe rested on his desk, and decorating his walls were paintings of ancient ships, fishing boats and yellowed treasure maps.

He smiled, as he did every time he entered his office, because this was where he felt at home. On his desk were several pieces of mail, but on top was a pale yellow envelope that looked as delicate and feminine as the sender.

He sat down and picked up the envelope, his smile becoming broader. His mom. Who refused to stride into the twenty-first century and use more modern methods of communication such as e-mail or a text message, God forbid. No, she clung stubbornly to her snail mail and said there was no substitute for receiving a handwritten letter in the mail.

And maybe she was right, because he looked forward to her letters. They were always filled with warmth and love, and her voice rippled off the pages as though she were sitting across from him, giving him a motherly lecture.

He'd have to call her later. They could sit and talk on the phone while they enjoyed a glass of wine. The image of her sitting on the wooden deck that overlooked the cypress-knobbed bayou in the Louisiana home he'd grown up in filled him with homesickness.

He hadn't returned home but once since his father's death two years ago, and it had been brief. It had been too hard to face his childhood home without his father's larger-than-life presence.

It was time to go back.

Usually, he embraced the silence of the afternoon and early evening hours, but today, he found it smothering and unsettling. He reached for the remote lying on his desk and punched one of the buttons.

The gentle strains of classical music filled his office, swelling and reverberating off the walls with a soft echo. He relaxed into his chair and leaned back, sliding his hands behind his neck to cup the base of his head.

He closed his eyes and allowed the music to soothe him. Why he suddenly felt restless and agitated, he couldn't say. But it didn't alter the fact that he felt as cagey as a lion in captivity.

After a moment, he leaned forward to glance over the letter one more time before folding it carefully. He opened his desk and placed it atop the other pastel-colored envelopes from his mother.

Straightening in his seat, he toggled the mouse to make the screen saver on his desktop monitor go away and then clicked to open his e-mail.

He spent several minutes working down the messages in his in-box. Most were minor issues easily dealt with. The few that required further attention, he forwarded to his personal assistant.

A new message popped to the bottom, and he saw Serena's name in the sender field. Intrigued, he clicked to open it.

Damon,

Below is a detailed letter outlining the requirements of the fantasy. Feel free to forward this on to your prospective choice.

Serena James

Damon scrolled lower to see the letter embedded within the e-mail itself.

To be honest, I feel embarrassed to be revealing my deepest secrets to a stranger, even more embarrassed that I am relying on you to fulfill a fantasy I am barely able to admit to myself, much less anyone else.

How can I explain the urge that overcomes me when I imagine being owned by a man? Possessed. Cherished and cared for. I have nothing missing in my life to suggest such a radical desire for sexual slavery. No deep psychological reasons that feed the appetite for submission. Some things just are, and for me, this is one of them.

I think often of my fantasies. Usually late at night in the quiet of the dark, they come to me, seductive and alluring. I imagine the scene well, how it all starts.

I'm in a room filled with hungry men. The appetite for carnal pleasures lies heavy, like a fog. I am naked save for the ropes binding my hands behind my back. And I wait. For you.

I am to be purchased this night, but by whom? Many men are eager to pay a high price for the pleasure of owning me. It thrills me and frightens me all at once. I wait with trembling legs, my eyes cast downward, for I hear the excited murmurs around me.

And then you enter. I don't see you, but rather I feel you the moment you come into the room. There is a subtle shift in power, and the others sense it as well. I can feel them holding their breath as they look to you. And then I lift my gaze.

You are staring at me from across the room. The first glance is a shock to my system, for I see the promise in your eyes. You want me and you will have me.

There is arrogance in your manner as you stride with

purpose toward me. You stop a few feet away and speak with my keeper. I strain to listen. I am eager to hear what you are saying, but you keep your voice too low.

And then you move toward me once more, and I shiver as each step brings you closer until you stop mere inches from my naked body. You reach out and tangle your hand in my hair, tilting my head upward until my neck is exposed and vulnerable to you. There is satisfaction in your eyes, as if you find me pleasing, a fact that brings me great satisfaction. I find myself wanting to please you more than anything I've desired before.

You lean closer still until your lips hover precariously over mine, and then you whisper, "You will be mine."

As you let me go and ease away, I swallow back the surge of excitement. But more than eagerness, it is need that fills me. A need to belong to you. I want it with my every breath.

A foreign hand tugs at my bound wrists, and I silently protest as I am guided away from you. But your gaze follows me, and promise burns brightly in your eyes. You will own me.

I stumble toward the front of the room as someone in the distance announces that the bidding will begin. My back is to everyone until I am ordered to turn around, and I do so, shyly.

I scan the men assembled and take in their lustful stares, but it is you I search for, you I want. My breath catches in my throat and tiny bubbles of panic fire in my stomach. I don't see you anywhere.

One man bids and then another, and still I don't hear you. For several tense minutes, the calls are heard and the price is increased. Then a pause. Silence falls. I hear my keeper as if there is not another as he prepares to close the bidding.

My eyes close as disappointment tightens my chest.

And then I hear you. Your firm voice carries above the quiet murmurs of those gathered. You state an impossible sum, much higher than the bids before, and it is clear that you have no intention of letting go of your prize.

Joy explodes in my soul, for I realize now that I will belong to you. My skin comes alive, itchy, and I'm barely able to contain my excitement. I am reprimanded by my keeper, but it is you I will answer to and no other.

There is a flurry as the bidders processes your offer, but no one comes forward to top it. My keeper smiles, for he has fetched a handsome price for me this night.

He calls an end to the bidding, and you start forward. The crowd parts for you as you stroll to the front. My keeper pushes me to my knees and reminds me to show you proper respect. I need no reminder and go gracefully to my knees as I await your command.

"Look at me," you say in a gentle tone, but one that brooks no argument.

I tilt my head upward as you stand over me, strong, powerful. Your hand caresses my cheek, and I close my eyes as I nuzzle into your palm. Your touch is magic. Warm and sensual, it begins a fire deep in my loins.

You pull your hand away, and your fingers go to your pants. You unbutton the fly and ease the zipper down. For a moment, your hand disappears as it dips inside. You pull your cock out of confinement. It bobs free in front of my face. You're long and thick, rigid with arousal and your musky scent surrounds me.

You stroke once and then once again, up and down the length as you guide yourself closer to me. My mouth waters, and I eagerly part my lips, my need to taste you overwhelming.

One hand slides into my hair and firmly cups my head, holding me in place. Sharp tingles dance down my spine and spread chill bumps over my skin.

"Open for me," you command.

I obey. There isn't a single thought of disobedience in my mind. I want only to please you and to be pleasured by you. You hold your cock with one hand and slide deep into my mouth as you pull my head to you with your other hand.

Your taste explodes on my tongue. All male. So rugged and earthy. You are firm and yet soft in my mouth. The contrast fascinates me and makes me hunger for more.

I suck you in deeper and run my tongue over your length, but you withdraw and squeeze my jaw as a gentle reminder that you are in control, not me. I relax and give myself over to your authority. I allow you to set the pace and to use my mouth as you wish.

Deeper you thrust, sinking to the back of my throat and pausing. I swallow around you, and I feel the pleasure it gives you. That pleases me.

My body is no longer my own. It sings sharply to a tune that only you play. My breasts are swollen, my nipples painfully erect. When you reach down to pluck one stiff peak, it nearly brings my orgasm crashing around me.

I gasp for breath and for control, for I have not brought you to completion yet. My pussy burns as if someone holds a fire to it. Each nerve is so tightly held that any stimulation will be unbearable, I fear.

You fill me again and again, your cock sliding so elegantly across my tongue. Then you become more urgent, your thrusts more forceful. You are close. Both of your hands grip my head, tangled in my hair as you pull me to meet each forward movement.

Your heated whispers fall on my ears, warm like honey and just as sweet. And then you flood my mouth with your release. Your hands become more gentle as they cup and stroke my face. Tenderness is in your touch as you murmur that I have pleased you.

I lovingly coax every drop from your erection before you finally pull away.

My body screams for yours. Your pleasure is my own. You lean down and kiss me softly on top of the head, and then you help me to my feet. Your hands trail down my body and up again as you explore my softness.

You take a nipple between your fingers and roll experimentally. With just a look, you command my keeper, and he puts his hands around my shoulders to steady me as your hands drift lower.

My breath draws sharply in when your fingers delve between my legs to the wetness at my entrance. You rub across my clit, and I moan. My legs tremble and threaten to collapse, but my keeper holds me up for you.

"You will come for me," you tell me.

Oh yes, I will come.

I try to breathe, but it's like inhaling fire. The air scorches my lungs and catches in my chest.

With your other hand, you pluck at my nipples, first one, and then the other.

"Do not let her fall," you caution my keeper, and his hands tighten at my shoulders.

You slide your fingers through my wetness, back and forth over my aching clit and then to my opening, where you tease unmercifully.

"Do you fantasize about having my cock buried inside you?" you ask in a silky tone.

"Yes," I gasp. "I want it more than anything."

You smile and increase the pressure of your fingers. "Soon. Soon you will have all of me. For now I want you to come with your keeper holding you for me, for it is the last time another man will ever touch you. You are mine now."

Your words more than your touch send my orgasm racing through my groin. It is frightening and splendid in equal parts as I shatter. My keeper's hands are firm around me as I buck and writhe. My knees threaten to buckle but you both hold me upright.

When the last waves of my release have broken, you command my keeper to release me. There is formality to your actions as you see to the change in ownership. I am not as of yet untied, but you take my arm and lead me away.

Outside the room, you gently untie my arms and then wrap a robe around me to shield my nudity from other eyes. Though you say nothing, I sense your possessiveness when it comes to me.

As we leave, you tell me once again that I am yours, and I am happy to hear it, for I am yours now, and glad to be so.

Damon sat back, stunned at how affected he was by the letter. Rarely had he seen anything so honest and raw. There was no hemming and hawing, no discomfort evident. Just a true and earnest accounting of one woman's most intimate desires.

His gaze continued down the e-mail where the woman's personal information was listed. His brow furrowed, and he leaned forward abruptly in his chair.

The name, address and birth date listed for the client was *Serena James.*

A smile curved Damon's lips upward. So it had been a ruse. The client was her all along, but she had waited to reveal it when she wasn't facing him.

Something potent surged in his veins. Excitement? Desire? Or was it something else altogether? Anticipation. It licked like greedy flames over dry wood.

Suddenly there was no question as to who he would find to fulfill Serena's fantasy. Hell would freeze over before he'd hand her over to another man. If she wanted to be someone's damn slave, then she would be his.

CHAPTER 4

*S*erena got out of her SUV and jogged toward the baseball field, aware that she was late. When she rounded the bleachers and scanned the mostly empty seats, she saw Julie look her way and wave. Faith turned as well and offered a smile in greeting as Serena headed up to where the women sat away from the handful of people sitting on the opposite side.

"Wasn't sure you were going to make it," Faith said when Serena plopped on the seat beside her.

"And miss our favorite pastime of ogling gorgeous men in shorts and sweaty shirts?" Serena asked in mock horror.

"Amen, sister," Julie muttered as she stared over the field.

The men who worked with Faith at Malone and Sons Security played in a four-week-long mini-league, or what the guys referred to as old farts reliving the glory days. Mostly it was an excuse to horse around and drink lots of beer afterward.

"I never can figure out which one is my favorite," Serena

mused as she took in Connor Malone and Micah Hudson. "Your brother is pretty hot, Faith, but then so is Micah."

"What's wrong with Nathan?" Julie demanded.

Serena grinned. "Nothing other than you've already pissed on the guy and marked him yours."

Faith choked on her laughter until Julie had to beat her on the back.

"When are you going to make your move on the man?" Serena asked.

"I don't know," Julie grumbled. "He's . . . difficult."

"Try nudity," Faith said solemnly. "It works wonders."

It was Serena's turn to laugh. "God, like we need the image of sweet little Faith in the buff enticing her man. I already see the way Gray looks at you clothed. Don't even want to know how he looks at you naked."

Faith smiled serenely and clapped enthusiastically as Gray came up to bat. "Shhh, you two. Gray is up."

Julie rolled her eyes but complied.

Faith stood up and squealed like a girl when Gray hit a double against the centerfield wall, driving Connor home. As she settled down again, Julie looked around Faith and pinned Serena with her stare.

"I'm still waiting to hear all the juicy details I missed out on the other day."

"You mean you haven't bludgeoned poor Faith to death for the dirt yet?"

Julie snorted. "She may look sweet, but she's like a frickin' bulldog when it comes to being stubborn. She informed me that it was your story to tell, not hers."

"Why, thank you, Faith," Serena said sweetly. "I appreciate that."

"Shhh, Micah is up to bat."

"Oh for the love of God," Julie said as she got up to move to Serena's other side. "Faith, honey, we don't actually come here to watch the *game*. We come to gossip and ogle."

She settled down beside Serena and flipped her brown hair over her shoulder. "Now, dish, Serena, and don't leave anything out or I swear I will retaliate and the results won't be pretty."

"You're totally not going to let me enjoy the scenery, are you?" Serena said with a disgusted sigh.

"You can watch them and talk at the same time."

Serena rolled her eyes then leaned in, and in low tones, related the conversation she'd had with Faith and her subsequent meeting with Damon.

"Holy shit," Julie breathed. "Now that's what I call a shocker."

"I'm not sure I like where you're going with this," Serena said in a dry voice.

"I get the fantasy bits, but Serena, a *sex slave?*" Julie asked in disbelief.

"Shhh!" Serena hissed. "For Pete's sake, I'd rather the entire greater Houston area not know about this."

"You're really going to do it?" Julie asked in a lower tone.

Serena paused for a minute then turned to her friend. "Yeah, I think I am."

"Wow. You've got balls, girlfriend. My hat is totally off to you. I'm such a chicken shit. I can't even work up the nerve to ask Nathan out, and here you are taking on your darkest fantasies."

There was a rueful gleam in Julie's brown eyes. Admiration shadowed her expression and a tiny bit of envy as well.

"If I can discuss sexual slavery over lunch with a guy who

looks like the cover model for GQ, then I think you should at least have the guts to ask Nathan out," Serena said.

"GQ, huh. This is Faith's friend, right?" Julie glanced sideways at Faith who kept her lips pressed tightly together although her eyes glittered with laughter. "I think she's been holding out on us, Serena. Not only does she work with a horde of hot guys, but now she's cultivating friendships with hot sex club owners?"

Faith heaved an exaggerated sigh. Then she leaped to her feet as Gray ran home.

"Girl needs to learn to share," Julie grumbled.

"Hey, I hand-delivered Nathan to you. What more do you want?" Faith demanded as she plopped back down beside Serena.

"She's got you there, Julie," Serena pointed out. "She took him to you when he wanted to get his ear pierced and you got him hooked on those massages."

Julie sighed unhappily.

"Bet if you showed up naked to massage him, he'd notice you," Faith offered.

"Make him roll over," Serena said with a snicker.

"He's not a damn dog," Julie said darkly.

Faith muttered a curse when one of their guys got thrown out at first, ending the inning. Then she turned to Serena, her expression serious.

"Are you sure you know what you're getting into, Serena? I mean, have you thought this through?"

Serena inhaled sharply then nodded. "Yeah, this is something I want to do. And hey, it's not like I'm making a major life change. It's a temporary fantasy. If I hate it, I'll just put an end to it early and go dream up something different."

"I trust Damon," Faith said. "He'll take good care of you, I know it."

"Just how is it that you know Damon anyway?" Julie interjected. "Seems like that has to be a juicy story."

Faith blushed and glanced down at her hands. "Let's just say I had some fantasies of my own, and Damon was very helpful in directing my path."

"Get out!" Julie exclaimed as she all but pounced on Faith. "Does Gray know about this?"

Faith laughed softly. "Gray hauled me out of Damon's club, so yeah, he knows."

Serena gave a small shiver. "Girl, you have all the fun. What I wouldn't give for a gorgeous man to go all he-man on me."

"So, um, what were these fantasies of yours, Faith?" Julie prodded.

Faith blushed again. "They weren't so different from Serena's, which is why I sent her to Damon."

Julie arched an eyebrow then glanced between Faith and Serena. "Don't get any ideas about me, chicas. I don't have a submissive bone in my body."

"We aren't out to convert you, Julie," Serena said in mild exasperation.

"We're just owning our sexuality," Faith said firmly.

Serena nodded. "Exactly."

"Well, damn, I want to own mine," Julie muttered. "Just as soon as I get it all figured out."

"You mean you're secretly a lesbian?" Serena teased.

Julie elbowed her in the gut. "Very funny. A girl can't get any straighter than I am. In fact, I think my fantasy might be to take on Nathan *and* his buddies."

Serena coughed and then she burst into laughter.

Julie's eyes narrowed. "Hey, I wasn't joking."

"Come on, Julie. More than one guy? What the hell would you do with them all?"

"Oh, you'd be surprised," Faith murmured.

Both Julie and Serena whipped their heads in Faith's direction, but she stared out at the field, a look of supreme innocence on her face.

"Tell me you haven't," Julie said in a low voice. "Because if you have, I may gut you in my envy."

Faith just smiled and continued to watch the game.

"Hell, she has," Serena said. She followed Faith's gaze to the field where the guys were lining up for handshakes. Then she glanced back at Faith, whose cheeks were a delicate shade of pink. "With them?"

"Not with Nathan," Julie groaned. "Tell me it wasn't with Nathan."

"Eeewww!" Faith exclaimed. "I mean not that he isn't hot, but he's like Connor, for God's sake."

"Who?" Julie demanded. "Was this before or after Gray? It had to be before. Gray doesn't strike me as the type to appreciate another guy screwing his woman, and he is extremely possessive of you."

Faith's grin widened.

"Okay, you made me spill the goods, Faith," Serena said. "No fair holding out. If I can admit that I want to be some man's sex toy, for crying out loud, then you can at least tell us who you had a threesome with."

"Oh God, was it more than a threesome?" Julie asked in sudden shock. "What would you call that anyway?"

"A gang bang?" Serena interjected sarcastically.

"It was just two," Faith said in a strangled tone. "Good Lord, what do you think I am, a porn star wannabe?"

Julie pounced. "Which two?"

"Gray and Micah," Faith mumbled.

Serena looked at her friend with newfound admiration. Sweet, shy Faith Malone was clearly a chick in charge of her sexual destiny. Suddenly she felt good about her decision to plunge forward with her own desires, and it made her feel even better to have shared her plans with her friends. It made her feel not quite so alone.

Julie made a forlorn noise and did an exaggerated frowny face. "I'm so freaking jealous. I could totally be down with a Connor and Nathan sandwich."

Faith closed her eyes. "Julie, please. I don't need images of you and my brother burned into my eyeballs. Let's stop this conversation while we're still in the realm of decency."

"Decency," Julie mimicked. "Who the hell wants decency? I want decadence. Hedonism. Clearly I need to be introduced to this Damon guy."

Serena frowned. "You stay away from Damon."

Julie glanced up at her in surprise. "Sheathe the claws, girlfriend. Are you staking a claim on Mr. GQ?"

Serena's cheeks tightened in embarrassment. What the hell was she thinking? And why did it irritate her that Julie would want to elbow in on Damon? It wasn't like Damon was anything to Serena. He was just the conduit between her and whatever man she ended up with for her fantasy.

Still, the idea of the way-too-pretty Julie batting those gorgeous brown eyes up at Damon made her want to search for sharp objects.

"You can have him after he's done what he needs to do for

me," Serena said. "Until then, why don't you stop pretending you're some shrinking violet and go after Nathan? You're acting like you had a brain transplant, for God's sake."

Julie scowled but Faith nodded in agreement and nudged her as the guys headed in their direction.

Poor Julie, she looked so hopeful as Nathan approached, but he and Connor were deep in conversation, and neither so much as looked in their direction as they walked by, equipment bags slung over their shoulders.

Micah, on the other hand, was more than happy to stop and flirt. And he was a gorgeous specimen of a man. Serena had to admit that.

"Hey, baby doll," Micah called up to Faith.

Armed with the new knowledge of Faith's sexual escapades with Micah and Gray, Serena watched the interaction between the three with interest.

To her surprise, they acted very naturally. Gray reached up for Faith as she stepped down the bleachers. She smiled and said hello to Micah but wrapped her arms around Gray's neck as he lifted her down and kissed him with a heat that Serena could feel several feet away.

Stop being such a jealous whore.

Faith deserved to be happy and she deserved a man who worshipped the ground she walked on. Serena just wanted one too.

Micah stared at Julie with undisguised interest in his gaze, but Julie was watching Nathan walk away with what could only be described as a kicked puppy look.

Serena laughed and shook her head, which drew a curious glance from both Micah and Gray. She grinned mischievously and accepted Micah's outstretched hand. He helped her down

the last step, and she landed on the ground next to him, Gray
and Faith.

Julie wasn't even looking at Micah's offer of a hand as she
snapped her gaze from Nathan's retreating back and finally
stepped off the bleachers to stand with the others.

"Would you ladies like to join us at Cattleman's for a drink?"
Micah asked with a lazy smile.

It was charming, that smile, but for some reason, Serena was
having a hard time getting rid of Damon's features. He was
stuck in her mind and refused to budge.

"Yes, let's all go over. It'll be fun," Faith said as Gray tucked
her against his side and wrapped an arm around her shoulders.

"I'm going to head home," Julie said glumly.

Faith shook her head in exasperation, and she and Serena
exchanged rolling eye glances as Julie walked away.

"Was it something I said?" Micah asked as he tucked his
unruly, dark hair behind his ear.

Serena grinned and patted Micah affectionately on the arm.
Hmm, nice arm too. "Nah, it wasn't you. She's pouting."

"I love it when a woman pouts," Micah said. "It's such an
opportunity to give them what they want."

Faith laughed. "You should never admit that, Micah."

He shrugged. "What can I say? I love pleasing women."

"There is something to be said for pleasing a beautiful
woman," Gray murmured as he nuzzled Faith's ear.

"Oh, for the love of God," Serena said in disgust. "Would
you two cut it out?"

Micah laughed and slid an arm around Serena's shoulders.
She settled in against his side and enjoyed the warmth and

power that emanated from him. He smelled nice even with the sweat dampening his shirt.

"Why don't you and I ditch the lovebirds and go back to my place?" he asked with a wicked grin.

Serena smiled. He was playful and sexy as hell, but for some reason, he just didn't do it for her. Damn shame too because she just knew he'd be awesome in bed.

She leaned in close and whispered next to his ear, "You couldn't handle me, honey."

His grip tightened around her as his body tensed against hers. He touched her cheek and turned her face up to meet his gaze.

"I wouldn't be so sure about that, baby doll."

She almost groaned. God, she needed to get laid in the worst way.

"I also won't be used as second best when the woman you really wanted took off on you."

"What woman?" he asked innocently. "Is there any other woman here but you?"

"Ahem," Faith interrupted.

"Hush, Faith, he's about to stroke my ego," Serena reprimanded.

"I'd stroke more than that if you'd let me."

Serena laughed and then moved even closer until her body was flush against his. Not embarrassed in the least, she slid her hand down his body until she boldly cupped his groin.

"When I let a man take me, it's going to be because he's so hard for me he's about to come in his pants," she whispered close to Micah's neck. "As flattering as your offer is, unless you've got some serious size issues in the dick department or you're just talking to hear your head rattle, it's clear to me I don't do it for you."

With that she pulled away, winked saucily in Faith's direction, fluttered her fingers in a wave good-bye to her, Gray and Micah and then she sashayed off, leaving Micah there gaping like an idiot.

"Damn it, I just fell in love," Micah said in a loud voice to Faith and Gray.

Serena laughed and kept walking.

CHAPTER 5

$\mathcal{D}$amon stepped from the small crowd of people he'd been conversing with, nodded politely as he passed another couple on his way to the hall. He was usually content to make the rounds at The House and make sure his guests were happy, but instead Serena occupied his thoughts. He was eager to begin the process of turning the upper level into an auction house for Serena's fantasy. His reality.

As he started to duck into his office he saw Micah Hudson walk out of the common room and head for the exit.

"Micah," he called.

Micah paused and turned around to look at Damon. "Hey, man."

"You heading out so soon?" Damon gestured toward his office. "Want to have a drink?"

There was a brief hesitation before Micah ambled forward. "As long as you have something decent. That pussy shit you drink is way too fine for my redneck taste buds."

Damon cracked a grin. "Your taste buds could use some refining. Leave it to me."

He motioned inward, and he and Micah entered the office. Damon flicked the lights on and headed for the liquor cabinet while Micah slouched into one of the leather chairs near the desk.

Micah fumbled in his pocket and took out a nearly empty package of cigarettes. He got up and leaned over Damon's desk for the wooden ashtray that Damon kept more for decoration than for actual use and dragged it back toward him.

"You mind?" Micah asked even as he put the end of the cigarette between his lips and flicked the lighter.

Damon shrugged. "Your lungs. I take it you've had no luck quitting?"

"I'm down to one or two a day," Micah said with an air of indifference. "Pop nags me. I'll quit. Eventually."

"So why were you heading out so early?" Damon asked as he touched each of the tops of the bottles. Finally he settled on a very nice aged scotch. Way too sophisticated for Micah, but it gave Damon a reason to make fun of him.

Micah grunted in response. He took the glass that Damon handed him and eyeballed it suspiciously. Before responding, he sniffed it cautiously and put his lips to the rim.

Damon settled into a chair across from Micah. "So? How is it?"

"Not bad," Micah mumbled as he took another drag of his cigarette.

Damon smiled. "And why were you checking out early? Hot date?"

Micah snorted. "Like I've had one of those in a long time."

"By choice, I'm sure," Damon said.

A shadow crossed over Micah's face. "Yeah, man, by choice."

Damon raised one brow but didn't press the point. There were other things he wanted to discuss anyway. He watched Micah inhale, savoring the hit for a moment before exhaling a long plume of smoke. "So," he said casually. "What do you know about Faith's friend Serena James?"

"Besides the fact that she's hot?" Micah flicked his cigarette at the ashtray then took another swallow of the scotch.

"Her hotness is a given. Any guy with eyes can ascertain that much," Damon said dryly.

"You interested?"

"In a manner of speaking."

"Not your type," Micah said with a shake of his head.

"What makes you say that?" Damon asked with only mild curiosity. "I think she might be exactly my type."

"What do you know that I don't know?" Micah asked. "You've got one of those smug, shit-eating grins. Serena . . . she's hot. Infinitely hot. Strong willed and well, hot. I've flirted with her, and she's given as good as she gets for sure."

"Not to mention she's driven, intelligent, motivated, honest and confident in her sexuality."

"But not *submissive*," Micah said. "Don't go knocking on doors closed to you, man. Wasn't once enough?"

Damon smiled. "Do you know what sort of business Serena runs?"

"Yeah, fantasy fulfillment, and not the fun kind."

"Well, she wants her own fantasy fulfilled. So she came to me."

Micah leaned forward in interest. He snubbed out his cigarette and fixed Damon with a keen stare. "Are we talking sexual fantasy here?"

"She wants to be owned," Damon said. "A slave. She wanted me to arrange for her to be sold in an auction at the house."

"And of course you didn't think of me," Micah grumbled.

"No one else will have her but me," Damon said quietly.

Micah studied him for a long moment. "Staking your claim, huh?"

Damon nodded. "She intrigues me. I want her, and she wants what I can give her. I'm willing to see where it leads."

Micah was already shaking his head. "I can't believe you signed on for this. Not with the way you view role-playing."

"Who says it has to be a role? I'll give her the real thing—"

"And she'll give you fantasy," Micah cut in.

"Your concern is touching," Damon said with amusement. "I have doubts that the woman I want exists, or if she does, I don't have a prayer of finding her. For now I'll take what I can get."

Micah's expression sobered. A spasm of grief flickered in his eyes before they became cold and unreadable. "She exists, Damon. There are women out there who crave what we can give them. Once you taste it, you can't ever let go of it," he said with a note of sadness in his voice.

Damon studied him oddly, but Micah looked away and drained the last of the alcohol from his glass.

"I hope it works out for you," Micah finally said. "Serena seems to be a very passionate woman. Not someone I would have pegged as slave material, but she is indeed beautiful and spirited. I know you'll take good care of her."

"I plan to," Damon murmured.

"Am I invited to the auction?" Micah asked in sudden mischief.

"Fuck off," Damon said crudely. "You'd only outbid me and complicate the issue."

Micah grinned. "A beautiful naked woman being sold can certainly add to a man's insanity."

Damon set his now-empty glass down on the desk and hesitated before finally deciding to say the next thing on his mind. It was forward, and it wasn't usually his style to be so intrusive with friends. But that was just it. Micah was someone he counted as a friend.

"When are you going to quit living in the past, Micah?"

Micah turned sharp, angry eyes on him, and just like that, the mild, amused mood vanished. He transformed into someone dark and angry. Tormented. Damon regretted his impulse even as he recognized the need to prod Micah from his status quo.

"Maybe when you do?"

Damon shook his head. "I'm moving on. I'm taking Serena as my slave."

"You're fulfilling some hokey fantasy for a woman who wants to play at having a master to spank her ass a little and throw around some authority. You and I both know it ain't real, and you pretending won't change that."

The words came out angry and clipped, but Damon didn't take offense. He was probably the only person Micah had ever confided in about the events that had brought him to Houston to begin with—a fact that Micah was probably regretting about now.

"Let's just drop it," Micah said when Damon started to respond. "Before we both say things we'll regret."

"Consider it dropped," Damon agreed.

"And for what it's worth, I hope you find what you're looking for," Micah said.

"I've already stopped looking," Damon said quietly. "It's kind of hard to look for something you've stopped believing in."

CHAPTER 6

$\mathcal{S}$erena read over the file of a prospective client with a frown of concentration as she assimilated all the information in her head. The fantasy was doable, and she loved the challenge of figuring out the details. She was already setting it up in her mind as she finished the last of the questionnaire.

The middle-aged gentleman wanted to be a whale for an evening. He wanted the guise of an ultra-wealthy player, someone sought after by the casinos and his every whim catered to. He wanted an expensive car, a gorgeous woman on his arm. Serena rolled her eyes a bit at that, but hey, arm candy was part of his fantasy and so she would do what she could.

Her mind was already racing. An appointment to have him appropriately attired. Expensive suit, all the necessary accoutrements to polish the façade. She could arrange for a limo to take him over to Lake Charles, Louisiana, where one of her casino contacts would meet him with all the panache afforded their regular gamblers.

She'd need to call and arrange it for a time when the casino wasn't already accommodating their *real* high rollers. The money the client gambled would be his own and it would be his choice whether to spend it, but the glitz and bowing and scraping would be arranged by her.

It was a win-win situation for the casino because they could in reality gain a new regular, and, in turn, she would benefit by making her client very happy.

If only everyone could be this simple.

She was interrupted when Carrie buzzed the intercom.

"Serena, Mr. Roche is on line two for you."

Her heart fluttered and slammed against her chest as she reached for the phone. Had he only just now gotten around to reading her e-mail? Would he have anything to say about the fact that she'd presented herself as the client? Oh, why hadn't she just come out and been honest and straightforward from the beginning?

"Mr. Roche," she said smoothly as she put the phone to her ear. She was proud of the fact that her voice didn't come out in a croak.

"I thought we'd agree you'd call me Damon."

His lazy drawl gave her a warm buzz, and she immediately relaxed. "All right . . . Damon. What can I do for you?"

"Well, I hope it's what *I* can do for *you*. Are you free for lunch?"

She smiled and loosened her grip on the phone. Maybe this wouldn't be so bad after all. He didn't act any different now that he knew it was her looking for a man to make her his slave.

A cringe worked over her shoulders. She was really going to have to find a better descriptor for her fantasy.

"I'm intrigued," she said. "I'm free. Now what is it you're going to do for me?"

A light chuckle sounded in her ear. "Meet me for lunch, and I'll tell you."

"A man who teases," she mused. "Okay, I'll bite. Where would you like to meet?"

"I'll send a car."

"No," she said after a moment's thought. "Why don't I pick *you* up this time? We'll eat on my turf."

There was a slight pause.

"Ahh, you're a man used to getting his own way."

"Always," he said in a husky growl.

A shiver worked uncontrollably down her back, and her nipples puckered against the silk of her bra.

"I like to give a man his way in appropriate circumstances," she said lightly. "I tell you what. You come pick me up and we'll eat at my choice."

"I'll be there in half an hour," he said silkily.

"I look forward to it."

She was smiling as she replaced the receiver. She leaned back in her chair and flexed her toes under her desk. What the hell she was doing flirting with Damon Roche when he was lining up another man for her was beyond her, but the devil just took over when it came to the man.

Had he found someone already? Nervousness scuttled around her stomach and gave her a slightly nauseous feeling. Could she go to bed with a complete stranger? More than that, could she place her well-being, her trust, her entire self in his hands?

Maybe she hadn't thought this through adequately.

A worried frown tugged at her lips, and she rubbed her face

with her hands. It wasn't too late to back out. She could meet Damon and tell him she'd changed her mind, right?

Of course you can, moron.

It wasn't as if this was some make-or-break business deal. It was sex, and she could say no at any time.

Feeling better about her options, she slipped her shoes back on and stood. A quick trip to the bathroom would tell her if she had any major repairs to do on hair and makeup.

Twenty minutes later, she walked into the lobby and was glad she'd chosen dressier heels today. They directed attention to her legs, which she knew without false modesty had drawn a man's stare more than a few times. Her skirt clipped the top of her knee, so she had plenty to show.

To her surprise, Damon was striding toward the door of the office complex. She smiled in greeting as he entered. He was dressed casually, as casual as a man could look in expensive slacks and polo shirt.

"You're early," she said as she checked her watch.

"I try to never keep a beautiful woman waiting," he said with easy charm.

"Good philosophy. Are you ready then?"

He offered his arm but didn't wait for her to take it. He reached with his other hand and enfolded her fingers in his firm grip before tucking it securely under his elbow.

They walked into the warm air, and she looked around for the Bentley. Instead, he guided her toward a sleek, black BMW parked in front of the entrance.

He opened her door and settled her inside before walking around to the driver's side. As he slid in beside her, she glanced appreciatively at the interior.

"You drove yourself," she said unnecessarily.

"It would appear so," he said with an amused smile. "So, where are we going?"

"Cattleman's. Do you know where it is?"

He grimaced. "Why beautiful women like you and Faith hang out in that place is beyond me."

"It has character," she said with a straight face. "But if you hate it, we can go somewhere else."

He pulled into traffic and maneuvered down the busy street. "No, I agreed to go to the place of your choosing, so Cattleman's it is."

"You're a snob," she said smugly.

He cast her a surprised glance and then evidently saw she was teasing him.

"Not a snob. I just enjoy . . . let's just say I enjoy the finer things."

Serena nodded. "Nothing wrong with that, but I have to tell you, I'm a beer and onion ring type girl."

"Barbarian," he said in mock horror. "I have nothing against some greasy finger food and a good beer, but I don't turn down a well-aged steak and a good glass of wine either."

"Mmmm, steak. I love steak. I love meat. I'm a total carnivore. Cattleman's has great steaks."

"I'll be amazed if you don't order a girly salad. What is it with women always ordering salads, anyway?"

She pretended to consider. "Well, I'll order a salad if it has steak in it."

He laughed. "Then I guess we'll have steak for lunch."

They drove into the parking lot, and when Serena reached to open the door, Damon stopped her with a hand to her arm.

"Let me," he said.

He got out and walked around to open her door. Then he

extended his hand down to her. Tiny little sparks shot up her arm when she slid her fingers across his palm. He pulled gently, and she stepped out to stand beside him.

"Thank you," she murmured.

Again, he tucked her hand under his arm and walked her toward the entrance. When they walked inside, the hostess greeted them, and Damon leaned in to murmur quietly to the young woman. She smiled immediately and nodded. Then she motioned for him and Serena to follow her.

They were seated across the room from the bustle of the lunch crowd. Serena settled in and raised an eyebrow as the hostess left.

"Bribery?" she asked. "This area is usually closed for lunch."

Damon smiled. "Let's just say I'm used to getting my way."

Serena snorted. "We've already ascertained that."

"I wanted a place we could speak privately," he said. "I have something for you."

"Oh?"

Her heart slammed against her chest when he slid an envelope across the table toward her. She hadn't even noticed that he'd carried it from the car, but then her concentration had been on other things. Like how damn good he looked.

With trembling fingers, she opened the envelope. Before unfolding the pages, she looked up at him in question. She was fairly certain that this was what she'd asked for, but now that it was here, in front of her, she was a little frightened and a whole lot unsure.

"You hesitate," he said quietly.

"I'm nervous," she admitted.

"Quite natural. Are you having second thoughts?"

She flushed. "You never said a word about the fact that it was me . . ."

He shrugged. "I figured you had your reasons. You don't owe me an explanation."

She stared down at the paper then slowly opened it. Age, address, physical details, appearance, characteristics were all listed first. Her eyes flickered over the sheet as she tried to take in as much of the information as she could at once.

No criminal record, stable job and income. Her gaze shot back up the page, and it was then she saw the name staring boldly back at her. Damon Roche.

She gasped sharply, and she yanked her head up to stare at Damon. "I don't understand."

He raised one brow as he studied her intently. "Don't you?"

"Why?" she demanded.

If he'd intended to catch her completely off guard, he'd certainly succeeded. She was so rattled that her hands were shaking, and sweat beaded her forehead.

"Why not?" he asked calmly.

"Don't play with me. This wasn't our agreement."

"Our agreement was that you wanted me to find a suitable man for a sexual fantasy situation. I'm that man. I don't see the problem." He leaned forward in his seat and pinned her with his stare. "Would you prefer a complete stranger take you and possess you? If we had not met as we did, if someone else had set up our meeting, would you object to my being the man who controls your fantasy?"

"But why?" she whispered. "Why didn't you volunteer from the get-go?"

"I didn't know you were the woman," he said simply. "When I found out, I knew I had to be the one to have you."

She gawked like a moron, her lips parted in shock. "You want me?"

"Why does that surprise you? You're a beautiful woman, Serena. I wanted you from the moment you walked into the restaurant. After I read your eloquent e-mail and saw who had written it, there was never any question as to whether I would step forward. No other man will have you."

Warmth sizzled through her abdomen, burning a path to her groin. Her clit pulsed and throbbed, and her nipples hardened until they ached. His vow whispered through her ears until it rebounded and echoed, seductive and alluring.

There was raw arrogance in his expression. Confidence. More than that, there was knowledge. Power. She craved it with her entire being. Wanted it and him more than she'd wanted anything else, and all she had to do was reach out and take it.

"Tell me, Serena. Do you want me?" he asked softly. "Do you ache for me? Do you want my possession? Do you lie awake at night wanting a man strong enough to harness your sexuality, stroke it until the fire rages and then unleash it, set you free?"

"Yes," she whispered, her voice catching in her throat. "Yes."

"There is much we should discuss," he said. "But not here. We'll iron out the technicalities and lay the groundwork, but for the more intimate details . . . we'll meet in a much more private setting."

As he said the last, he reached over and trailed a finger down her cheek and then pushed a tendril of her hair away from her face and tucked it behind her ear.

"I very much look forward to that conversation," he murmured.

Heat surged to her cheeks, and she leaned into his touch before she could think better of it. "I don't know what to say."

"There's nothing to say but yes. Unless you've changed your mind? I can, of course, find another suitable candidate, but I can't be the only one who has felt the spark between us, Serena, and after reading your e-mail, I don't take you for a coward."

She was quite simply overwhelmed.

He reached across the table once more and captured her hand in his. His thumb rubbed absently over the top of her knuckles, sensual and distracting.

"Let's get the nitty-gritty details out of the way," he said. "We can set a date to discuss the more . . . personal aspects after you've had time to digest it all."

"Nitty-gritty?" she croaked.

He picked her hand up and brought it slowly to his lips. Her breath caught in her throat and refused to slip from her lips as she anticipated the touch of his mouth.

A brush of electricity sparked along her veins. Currents, warm and vibrant, raced up her arm and sent prickles of awareness up the base of her neck until the tiny little hairs at her nape stood on end.

His lips moved softly up the crease of her fingers until they rested over her knuckles.

"The nitty-gritty being the unpleasant details, the not-so-romantic side of our arrangement. Sterile perhaps, but necessary."

She raised her eyebrow in silent question, because at the moment she couldn't have spoken if she wanted to.

He reached for a sheet of paper underneath the others and handed it to her. Carefully, she pulled her hand from his and regretted the loss of his warmth. She picked up the paper and scanned the contents.

It was a medical report. And then she realized.

"Oh," she said softly. "You must think me the biggest fool. I hadn't . . . God, what an idiot I am."

He smiled gently. "Not an idiot, Serena. Just nervous and wanting to forge ahead before you lost your courage. You would have thought of it, I have no doubt, and you would have demanded what I have just given you."

"But I haven't, I mean, I do see a doctor regularly, but I haven't gotten tests . . ."

"I can arrange it with my physician at a moment's notice," he offered. "It's important that you feel safe with me, and it is important that our good health is ascertained. I want to give you your fantasy, Serena, and I don't want any ugliness to intrude."

"I'll phone my doctor tomorrow," she said.

"Does this mean you're agreeing?" Damon asked.

She took in a steadying breath as she stared at the handsome man sitting across from her. Yes, he was gorgeous. He was confident, wore arrogance like a cloak, and God, she loved arrogant, assured men, but he didn't come across like an asshole. Was this man for real? Or was he just playing a role?

She wanted to find out so bad she could taste it.

She licked her lips and then nodded.

"I want to hear you say it," he prompted.

"Yes. I agree."

His smile was triumphant, and something dark and primitive flashed in his eyes. In that moment she imagined what it would be like to be his, and it filled her with a powerful longing.

"Have dinner with me this weekend," he said. It wasn't a request, and he seemed absolutely unapologetic that it was, in essence, a command. "That will give you time to see your doctor and think about me. And you. Us. Then we can meet to discuss the more intimate details of our arrangement."

Just the way he said *intimate* made all her girly parts tingle. And then it hit her that she was going to become quite intimate with this man. All fantasy aside, he was offering to give her reality. With him.

She would see him naked. He'd touch her, have his hands and mouth on her body. She quivered from head to toe and her knees knocked together until she had to put her hand on one of her legs to stop it.

Food? Completely forgotten. She had no hope of eating lunch. Not when all she was imagining was how he'd taste. Scorching flames burnt her cheeks when she remembered just how descriptive her e-mail had been.

"And I thought Faith was the only woman left on earth who blushed so vividly," he said in a tone tinged with amusement.

She groaned and closed her eyes. "I haven't a prayer of keeping it together. You've completely and utterly knocked my feet out from under me."

"As did you when I read your e-mail," he said softly. "I cannot allow another man to take what I already consider mine."

Her stomach clenched and a flush stole over her body. "You sound possessive already," she said faintly.

"And that's precisely the way you want me, is it not?"

She squirmed a bit under his scrutiny, but she wasn't going to lie or pretend to be bashful, even if she was ready to crawl under the table. Nothing about her approach had been shy so far, and there wasn't a need to start now.

"It is," she admitted. "I want . . . I want to belong. To a man," she added after a deep breath. "It sounds so crazy."

"Stop," he said with quiet authority. "I won't allow you to degrade yourself for voicing your desires. They're yours. That makes them important. Valid. There is nothing crazy about them."

"It's not just about possession." She paused for a moment but was determined to go on, to explain what beat so incessantly at her. "I want the security of knowing I am . . . owned. Oh, but that's such a terrible word and yet I can't think of a better one. I want to be cherished, protected, pampered . . . valued. I want the man to know me as well as I know myself. I want him to anticipate my needs and fulfill them but at the same time I want to be important to him. I want him to be strong. Capable. Dominant without being an asshole. For just a little while, I want to be in his hands. To give myself into his care and keeping and be able to trust in him to shelter me, pleasure me and teach me how to please him."

She suddenly felt so vulnerable, as if she'd exposed herself in the most brutal of ways. She felt naked, stripped bare by her own words.

"Look at me," he said gently.

Her chin came up and she met his gaze.

"You don't trust me yet, and you shouldn't as we've only just met. But you will come to trust me, and when that happens, you'll give yourself into my care and keeping. When you do that, I will give you what you most want. What you need. And I'm going to love every damn minute."

CHAPTER 7

*J*ulie scurried around her salon like a drunken salamander. Nathan was due for his massage in five minutes, and she was seriously reconsidering her mad seduction plan.

She stopped in front of one of the full-length mirrors and arranged her shirt for the tenth time. It was low-cut and cupped her breasts like a lover's hands. Her cleavage was plumped up like two ripe melons and it threatened to strain right out of her neckline.

Perfect.

"Oh hell," she muttered as she rearranged her shirt again. "I look like a whore on the make."

Worse than that, she looked desperate.

With a glum look at her reflection, she sighed and turned away to get the oils ready. She'd chosen them especially for Nathan because all her other stuff was too girly. Nathan . . . mmmm, he was all rugged man. He needed something that wouldn't make him smell too soft and flowery.

She pushed her cleavage up one more time before she headed into the massage room. A few times leaning over Nathan, a brush or two against him, maybe an accidental shove of her bosom into his face as she leaned across to get a towel.

Surely he couldn't continue to ignore her. She just needed to be brave. More forceful. Own her sexuality. Yep, that was it. Faith had owned hers (and then some), and Serena was well on her way into sexual slavery.

She rolled her eyes and shook her head. Sexual slavery, for the love of all that's holy. What possessed the woman? Not that the idea of Nathan tying her up and having his wicked way with her didn't inspire some serious heavy breathing, but she had some wicked and wild fantasies and in half of them, Nathan was completely and utterly at her mercy.

A decadent smile curved her lips as her groin tightened and pulsed. Oh, hell yeah, did she have plans for one Nathan Tucker. He didn't realize it yet, but he was going to be hers. And he'd never know what hit him.

Her business line rang, and she reached for it even as she surveyed the massage table to make sure everything was in place.

"Julie's," she sang out.

There was a slight pause. "Hey, Julie, this is Nathan Tucker."

"Hi, Nathan, are you running late today?" Hell, even her voice came out all breathy like some sixteen-year-old crushing on some college guy.

"Uh, that's why I'm calling. I can't make it today."

Her heart sank. "Oh. Well, okay."

"Can we reschedule?" he asked.

"Uh, sure, let me just check my schedule."

She walked over to the counter where her appointment

book sat and rifled through the pages, though she knew every time slot by heart.

"When would you like to come in?" she asked.

There was another pause and she heard him talking in the background to someone else. And then she heard a very feminine voice float through the line. There was a light giggle and then, "Oh, I'll give you a massage, Nathan. No need to pay someone else."

She stood there feeling ten times a fool. She glanced down at her cleavage and laid a hand over her chest to shield the low-cut shirt.

"Stupid," she muttered.

"What was that?" Nathan asked.

"Nothing. Did you want to reschedule or not?" she asked through gritted teeth.

"I'll tell you what. Let me call you in a few days and we'll set up a time then."

"Sure," she said stiffly. "Have a nice day."

Before he could respond, she hung up the phone and blew out her breath with puffed cheeks.

"Look on the bright side, Julie. You were saved from making a huge ass of yourself."

Serena walked out of her apartment to the parking lot where Damon's driver waited for her. She had to stifle the giggle that threatened to emerge when she saw several of her neighbors openly gawk in curiosity.

Tonight's date with Damon was at his home. That fact made her a little nervous because they weren't meeting on neutral ground. But at the same time, she was looking forward to seeing him in a more intimate environment.

She'd dressed in jeans and a T-shirt, purposely not going for an overtly sexy look. He was already well acquainted with her desires, and she didn't want to pressure him, to make everything about sex. She wanted to feel comfortable around him and vice versa.

When she arrived, Damon greeted her in the circular drive of his large home. He opened the door and held out a hand to help her out.

To her surprise, he too was dressed casually, and if she thought he couldn't look any better than when he was outfitted as Mr. GQ with the expensively tailored slacks and silk shirt with the leather loafers, she was dead wrong.

The man was simply to die for in a pair of tight-fitting jeans and a T-shirt that molded to his muscled arms and chest. His loose clothing from before had disguised just what a tight body he had.

He kissed her cheek in a casual manner before turning to guide her inside. Cooler air washed over her when they walked into the house. She followed him into a luxurious sitting room where a fire burned in the hearth of a large stone fireplace.

She did a double take and then turned to him with an expression of surprise. "A fire? In this heat?"

"I like the ambience," he said. "It lends the room such a homey feeling, don't you think?"

It did at that. "I love it. It was just a shock to see at this time of year. Heck, it doesn't get cold enough down here in the winter for a fire most years."

"I very much like my creature comforts," he said with a smile.

"You might even say I'm spoiled, but my needs are few, and I like to see that they are met."

Oh, yes, he would take such good care of her. She could feel it, and God, she couldn't wait.

"Please, make yourself comfortable," he said as he gestured toward one of the leather couches. "Would you like something to drink? A glass of wine, perhaps?"

"That sounds lovely," she said as she settled in the soft comfort of the couch. "Whatever you choose will be fine."

He smiled that predatory smile, one that said he liked making her choices very much.

She kicked her sandals off and tucked her feet underneath her as she settled further into the couch. He was right about one thing. The room was homey and comfortable, and thanks to the rush of cool air being pumped in by the air-conditioning, the fire didn't warm things too much.

Damon returned a moment later and extended a crystal wineglass down to her. Then he retreated to the armchair across from her and sat down.

She took an experimental sip and let the flavor burst over her tongue.

"Good?" he asked.

"Perfect."

He nodded and smiled.

She drew the glass away after taking another small swallow and stared at him over the rim. "Did you get the fax I sent you this afternoon?"

"I did, but then I had no expectation of anything but a perfect bill of health."

A smile quirked the corner of her mouth. "Wouldn't you

have been surprised if I'd tested positive for some scary STD?"

He chuckled. "That would have been a shame, indeed."

"Are you a good lover, Damon?"

Even she was a bit stunned at how easily the question popped out. To his credit, Damon didn't so much as flinch. He lowered the wineglass to rest above his knee and his warm brown eyes found her own.

"I like to think so. I'm demanding but generous, though somehow I think the demanding part will mesh quite well with your desires."

Heat tinged her cheeks but she nodded.

"There are things we should talk about before we sign a contract," he said.

Again she nodded, but for the life of her, she had no idea where to start. Thankfully he didn't suffer any such difficulty.

"You've outlined quite well what you'd like, or at least where you'd like to start."

"Yes," she croaked.

"Then perhaps we should get to my expectations," he said levelly.

Her eyebrows went up in surprise, and he smiled.

"I know what you're thinking. This is your fantasy. You're in control. But your fantasy is to relinquish your power. You will submit to me and my wishes. My wants and desires will be your own. You will please me, and in return I will please you."

Her hand shook as she raised the wineglass to her lips again.

"For the times you are with me, I expect complete obedience and respect."

Her hackles rose at the way he stated obedience, but she

could see him studying her, waiting for her protest, almost as though he was waiting to call her a fraud.

"Does that bother you?" he asked.

"I assume you mean sexually."

His expression didn't change. "I mean in all aspects."

Her eyebrows shot up.

"Not sure how you feel about that?"

How did she feel about it? The independent decision maker in her balked at anyone expecting obedience from her. It was a ridiculous notion, or was that her feminist sensibilities screaming? And if so, why weren't they screaming louder?

It was more like an obligatory murmur of protest before they scuttled back for cover.

"It's important to you?" she asked softly. Because she could sense it was. He was testing her. Throwing down the gauntlet, so to speak.

"You don't have to choose me," he reminded. "You could always find a more . . . accommodating man."

"And how would he accommodate me?" she asked quietly. "By pretending?"

"Is that not what this is? A grand pretense? A scripted performance?"

He had her there. She had listed her conditions, but now he was listing his. No, she didn't have to agree, but damn she wanted him. She wanted him badly.

"It's important to you," she said again.

"It is," he acknowledged. "Even if this is a temporary situation, I want it to be real for as long as you choose to live it."

"And by real you want me to submit. To you. Completely."

His voice was like velvet, soft, fluttering across her skin as he uttered just one word.

"Yes."

She was bathed in want. Need burned in her heart, in her *soul*. She hadn't realized just how much she wanted this until now, until Damon had inspired such a desire in her.

"And if what you ask of me is unreasonable, what then?" she asked.

He propped one ankle on his knee and relaxed further into the chair. "In a lot of circles, indeed for most in this, shall we say 'lifestyle,' the use of safe words abounds."

She nodded because she knew what a safe word was.

"I won't use them," he said firmly.

Her eyes widened. "You're asking me to trust you that implicitly?"

He shook his head. "I won't use a word that encourages a man to disregard the word no coming from a woman's lips. If you say no, if you're even thinking no, then it ends for me. I won't indulge in silly little no-means-yes games. When that word crosses your lips? It's over. If I ever ask of you something that you won't give unreservedly, then all you need to say is no."

She wasn't even sure how to respond to that because he was absolutely, one hundred percent right. How moronic to ever discount the notion of a woman saying no.

He shifted his position again, setting his feet back on the floor as he leaned forward.

"Come here, Serena."

She glanced up in surprise.

"You've become tense, and I want you to relax. I want you to be comfortable with me or this will never work."

He held out his hand, and she found herself rising from the couch, her bare feet touching the wood floor. As she walked toward him, his gaze fell to her feet and he smiled.

"You like being barefoot."

She was mildly embarrassed that she'd made herself so much at home in the short time she'd been here, but she nodded as she slid her hand into his.

"Then you'll never wear shoes in my house," he said softly. "Your comfort is very important to me."

He tugged her downward. "Sit here at my feet and lay your head on my lap."

Awkwardly she lowered herself until she settled on the floor. His hands guided her head until it was nestled on his lap.

"I've dreamed of running my fingers through your hair from the moment we first met," he murmured.

As his fingers trailed through the strands of her hair, she closed her eyes and let out a blissful sigh. His movements were tender as he stroked and caressed.

"Now relax," he urged. "And we'll talk while I touch you."

He wanted her to relax when every single nerve ending in her body was on fire?

He played with the strands and alternated guiding his hands through the heavy tresses with light touches and caresses to the curve of her neck. Slowly she began to unwind, and she went limp against him.

"We need to discuss birth control," he began. "I don't like to make assumptions even given my preferences. You stated in your letter that part of your fantasy was for your new master to ejaculate in your mouth."

Oh God, now she knew at least why he'd let her hide her face, because sweet Lord, it was burning.

"Relax," he murmured. "There should be no shame in voicing your fantasies."

She forced herself to relax again as she realized she'd gone completely tense against him.

"It is my preference not to use condoms, but I'll use them if that is your wish. I love the idea of coming deep inside you and watching my seed slip from your pussy as I leave your body."

She shivered uncontrollably, and his hand tightened in her hair.

"You like that too."

She nodded.

"I'm not sure I can logically explain the desire I have to mark a woman. I'm sure it all has to do with the primitive male psyche," he added with a chuckle. "But the fact is, I want to come in your mouth, your pussy, your ass, on your breasts. I want to mark you mine in every conceivable fashion. You will be mine. Your body will be mine to do with as I wish."

Another soft sigh escaped her, and her entire body trembled as his erotic words brushed her skin, reached to her most intimate places.

Yes, she wanted it too.

His fingers worked through her hair and to her neck, lightly caressing. "Are you protected against pregnancy, Serena? Or do you prefer that I use a condom?"

"I'm on birth control," she said softly. "I—I don't want you to use a condom."

His hand squeezed her shoulder in approval.

"Now suppose we talk about your auction."

She raised her head to look up at him. There was something warm and vibrant in his eyes, something that went beyond simple sexual attraction.

"You'd do that for me?"

He touched her cheek and let a finger trail down to her jaw, and then he ran it over her bottom lip.

"Of course. It is your fantasy. I admit that it's a rather exciting scenario for me as well."

She frowned for a moment even as she leaned further into his touch.

"So this is your fantasy too?"

His expression became more serious. "No," he said distantly. "This isn't my fantasy."

"Then why . . . ?"

She let the question trail off as she looked intently into his eyes.

He continued to stroke her face, touching each part of her skin with inquisitive fingers as he stared back at her.

"Perhaps I'm tired of waiting for something I may never find."

"And what is it that you want?" she asked softly.

A faraway look entered his eyes and they turned almost wistful. "What you want as fantasy, I want as reality. A woman who will surrender to me, who will trust me to take care of her, provide for her, and who doesn't mind relinquishing control in all aspects of our relationship."

"And you haven't been able to find a woman who meets those requirements?"

She couldn't help the surprise that bled into her question.

"No, I haven't," he said quietly.

She laid her head back on his lap, and he resumed stroking her hair. "Then why are you agreeing to this?"

He stopped for a moment, her hair tangled around his fingers. "Because I'm tired of waiting, and so for a little while, I'd like to experience my own fantasy."

She nodded. That much she could understand. Fantasies were safe. It was a break from reality. A chance to act on desires for a short period of time.

"Now about the auction. You seem open to being nude in front of a room full of men, of even having them touch you, watch you and want you."

She squeezed her eyes shut but nodded wordlessly against his leg.

"And you want me to fuck your mouth in front of these men."

Again she raised her head to look at him and tried not to cringe over his bluntness. "Does that bother you?"

He smiled. "Does it bother me that a beautiful woman wants to pleasure me while every other man in the room is eaten up with jealousy?"

She let out a small laugh. "Stupid question, I guess."

"I was more worried that it would bother you," he said gently.

She tried to look down, but he wouldn't let her. He nudged her chin up with his fingers, forcing her to look directly at him.

"It's fantasy," she said. "I want, for a while, to do things that I wouldn't normally do, to be a person I'm not. I know this isn't me but I still crave it. Just a taste. When it's all over, I can look back without shame because . . . it's not real."

"You seem so sure this isn't you," he said. "And yet you articulate your desires so well. You know precisely what it is you want."

She shook her head. "No, this isn't me. I'm stronger than this. I don't want to be weak. I just want . . . an adventure."

His eyes flickered and became shielded. "Then that's what

you'll have. If you trust me to make the arrangements, I'll set up a night for your fantasy to begin at my establishment. I'll enlist the aid of some of the club members, but I believe the fantasy will be more powerful for you if you don't know every single detail."

"And after?" She asked the question uppermost on her mind. What happened after Damon claimed her?

He tilted her chin even further upward as his eyes bore into hers. There was latent power simmering in his gaze. A tightly held current just begging to be unleashed.

"After the auction, you are mine."

CHAPTER 8

"Julie, you're killing me," Serena said through gritted teeth. "This is supposed to be a massage, not a lesson in dough kneading."

Julie eased off and muttered an apology.

"What's wrong with you, Julie?" Faith asked from the next table. "Not like you to be so . . . grumpy."

Serena raised her head. "She hasn't gotten to you yet. Feel fortunate. I'm going to have bruises."

"Nathan stood me up," Julie said.

"Stood you up? You had a date?" Faith asked in an excited voice.

"Not exactly," Julie mumbled.

She continued massaging Serena's back, much gentler now, though Serena could still feel the tension in her fingers.

"What do you mean by 'not exactly'?" Serena asked as she relaxed on the table.

Julie sighed. "He rescheduled his massage after I sort of

plotted to begin my grand seduction scheme. Well, he hasn't exactly rescheduled yet. He just cancelled."

"Uh-oh. That doesn't sound good," Serena offered.

"Faith, is Nathan seeing anyone?" Julie asked.

"Not that I know of, but I don't keep up with his love life. Why do you ask?"

"I want to hear about this seduction plan," Serena spoke up.

"I wore a shirt that my tatas were damn near about to spill out of."

"Oh my," Faith said in amusement. "That had to be a glorious sight to behold. You have such, um, impressive tatas."

Serena sat up, and Julie's hands fell away from her back.

"I'm not finished, hon," Julie protested.

"Oh yes, you are. I want to hear all about this, and I hate having a conversation lying down unless it involves a gorgeous man."

Faith laughed. "You know we're getting to you next, Serena. Just so you know."

Serena rolled her eyes. "As if I thought I could escape you two." She turned to look at Julie. "So? You displayed the tatas, then what?"

"Nothing. That's what I've been trying to say. I'm here plumping my cleavage, planning how to plant it in Nathan's face, when he calls to cancel his appointment."

"Ah, gee, I'm sorry," Faith said, sympathy shadowing her pretty features.

"It gets worse," Julie said darkly. "Some bimbo in the background was informing him that he didn't need to pay for a massage because she'd be more than happy to give him one. Then when I asked him when he wanted to reschedule, he said he'd call me."

"Oh, ouch," Serena murmured. "The *I'll call you* line."

"Yeah," Julie grumbled. "Shot down before I ever got off the ground. Clearly I need to focus my attention elsewhere. I mean, I'm not a complete dog, right? I've never had a man want to put a paper bag over my head during sex or anything."

Serena and Faith both burst out laughing.

"I'm so sorry, Julie," Faith said as she wiped tears of laughter from her eyes. "I have no idea what Nathan's problem is. You're gorgeous!"

Julie rolled her eyes. "Spoken like a loyal friend talking to an ugly woman."

Serena snickered. "Well, you're not as pretty as I am, but you're definitely not paper-bag ugly."

Julie shoved at Serena's shoulder. "Gee, thanks, what a pal."

"Why don't you just ask him out?" Serena asked. "Stop with the hinting around—the plan to jump him while giving a massage, though that wasn't a bad idea at all—and just come out and ask him on a date. If he refuses then wipe his existence from your memory banks and go ask Micah or Connor out. They're both hot."

"I can't go out with someone who's slept with one of my friends," Julie muttered. "So thanks, Faith, for ruining Micah for me."

Faith chuckled. "If you knew how good he was in bed, you wouldn't be all holier than thou about going out with him."

Julie groaned. "For the love of God. Stop already. You're killing me. What I wouldn't give for a threesome with two hot guys. Hell, right now I'd take one hot guy. Or even a not-so-hot one. I just want to get laid, damn it."

"Toys not working for you?" Serena asked innocently.

"Fuck you," Julie said darkly. "So speaks the woman who is

assured of some killer sex now that she's signing on to be someone's sex slave."

"Which brings us nicely to the next topic of our conversation," Faith said. "Did Damon find someone for you yet?"

Serena bit her lip and looked between her two friends, wondering if she should tell them everything.

"He has, hasn't he?" Julie pounced. "Dish, Serena. We want details."

"He didn't exactly find *someone*," she hedged. "He sorta volunteered himself."

Faith's mouth fell open while Julie just looked confused.

"He did what?" Faith demanded. "Are you serious?"

Julie looked rapidly back and forth between Serena and Faith. "What am I missing? This is the GQ guy, right?"

Faith ignored her. "But he's so not into all the role-playing and games. I mean, he once told me that if he had his way, he'd have a woman collared and tied to his bed."

A delicious shiver started at Serena's toes and worked up until her entire body was bathed in goose bumps.

"Well, we don't need a rocket scientist to figure out where this is going," Julie said dryly.

Now it was Serena's turn to ignore Julie. "Well, he did sort of mention that. Not in such specific terms, mind you, but um, it works for me, at least on a temporary basis."

Concern shadowed Faith's eyes. "I never figured Damon would go for something temporary. He's very focused on what he wants."

"Maybe he'll talk you around," Julie teased.

Serena shot her a glare. "Come on, Julie. Can you really see me as someone's permanent sex slave? It's fine for some really hot sex and a scorching fantasy, but for real? So not me."

"Why isn't it for you?" Julie challenged. "Obviously it appeals to you on some basic level or you wouldn't be advertising for a man to tie you up and have his wicked way with you."

"Has anyone ever told you how obnoxious you are?" Serena grumbled. "It's a fantasy. Everyone has one even if it isn't something that would translate to the real world. I'm too . . . strong-willed to ever permanently submit to a man."

"Gray once told me that he would never go for a woman who wasn't strong enough to submit," Faith said softly. "It takes a strong woman. Don't ever doubt that."

Julie and Serena both turned to look at Faith in shock.

"Wait a second. Are you saying that you and Gray . . . that you have that sort of relationship with him?" Serena asked.

Faith shrugged. "I wouldn't classify our relationship as typical of anything but what we make it, but if you're asking if he's the dominant force in our relationship, then yes, he is."

"Oh, shit, and now I've gone and insulted you," Serena said as she frowned apologetically at her friend.

Faith smiled. "No, you haven't. I used to think as you do. That it made me weak to want a man to take care of me, that I was some lily-livered ninny for submitting to a man. But it was what I wanted, and I was tired of settling for second best."

"Owning your sexuality," Julie murmured. "I tell you, I'm going to have to get me some of that."

"Amen," Serena seconded. "Faith, I don't mean to pry, but you've simply got to give me more to work with here."

Faith grinned. "Well, I'm afraid that Damon is probably a little more hardcore than Gray, at least going by what he's told me. He wants . . . he wants a woman. In his own words, he wants a slave, although he did go to great lengths to say that he objected to the word, but for all practical purposes that's what he wants."

"Wow," Julie breathed. "It's getting hot in here, and suddenly I'm thinking about shit that's never before crossed my mind."

Serena rolled her eyes. "Julie, you don't have a meek bone in your body."

Julie grinned cheekily. "Nope. I don't."

Serena turned back to Faith. "Okay, so if Damon isn't into games or fantasies, why the hell is he signing up to be my . . . master? God, I hate that word. It just sounds silly."

Faith shrugged. "Maybe he's attracted to you? Maybe he's tired of waiting for the right woman?"

"Or maybe he just wants a few nights of hot sex with a slave," Julie added with a mischievous smirk. "I mean, come on, what guy is going to turn down a gorgeous woman begging for a man to own her?"

Faith's eyes glimmered with amusement. "Micah informs me that men go crazy for a submissive woman."

"Ah shit, not him too," Julie groaned. "Good lord, woman. So you let him and Gray both have their wicked way with you? What did you do, let them tie you up and fuck your brains out?"

Faith pretended interest in her fingernails and cast Julie a sidelong glance. "Pretty much."

"You are such an evil whore," Julie muttered. "And Gray was okay with this?"

"You've already asked that," Serena said patiently. "Obviously he was since they were both there."

Julie shook her head. "I just can't get past that. I mean, Gray is all forbiddingly possessive of Faith and yet he lets another man fuck her while he watches? That's seriously messed up."

Faith snorted. "Like you'd turn down a threesome with two hot guys?"

"Hell no, I wouldn't," Julie exclaimed. "I'm just stunned that your man let you get away with it."

"It was his idea," Faith said with a grin.

Julie closed her eyes. "Why are all the good ones taken?"

"Maybe you should rethink your stance on sleeping with men your friends have had sex with," Serena said. "Forget about Nathan and redirect your attention to Micah. If you just want to get laid, I bet he'd accommodate you."

"Oh, right, like I want him out comparing notes with the guys on mine and Faith's performance in bed. No thanks."

"Not that I'm encouraging you to go after Micah, but he'd never do that," Faith said. "He's not like that."

"So are you still sleeping with him . . . them?" Julie asked.

Faith shook her head. "I'm not saying it would never happen again, because it's a serious turn-on for Gray, but it's only happened once."

"Okay, I get why it's a turn-on for a woman," Serena said. "But for the guy? What's he get out of it?"

"Hell of a conversation," Julie interjected. "Thank God you guys are my last appointments of the day."

Julie leaned back against the massage table and looked between Serena and Faith. "You two are sitting here in the buff, and we're dishing about hot guys. There is something seriously wrong with this picture."

"We have towels," Faith corrected.

Julie rolled her eyes. "And they cover so much."

"So?" Serena butted in. "What's a guy get out of it, Faith? You've got me totally curious. I always thought a guy's fantasy was to get it on with two women, not to get it on with another woman and a man."

"Ohhh," Julie gasped. "The men don't . . . they don't do each other, do they?"

Faith dropped her face into her hands and let out a groan. "This conversation has seriously deteriorated. For God's sake, Julie."

"Hey, it's a legitimate question," Serena said.

"Thank you, Serena," Julie said as she folded her arms over her chest and glared at Faith.

"No, they do not get it on with each other," Faith said in a strangled voice. "They don't even touch each other."

"Then what's the point?" Julie asked.

Faith sighed in exasperation. "The point is that it's a turn-on for Gray to watch while another man fucks his woman. He likes to fuck me at the same time. You know, different orifices?"

Serena snickered. "She said 'orifices.'"

Faith threw a towel at Serena's head. "I swear, I'm sorry I ever said anything to either of you. I was trying to help a *friend*."

Julie rubbed her chin thoughtfully. "So you're saying it's a male primitive thing. Sort of like, 'Here's my woman. She's mine but you can have her for a little while.'"

Faith rolled her eyes. "I guess you could say that in a barbarian sort of way. I can't speak for anyone else, but in my situation, the men were focused solely on me. They weren't touching each other. They were too busy touching me."

"And fucking your brains out," Julie added.

"That too," Faith added with a grin.

"Lucky bitch," Julie said mournfully.

"So, if we can direct the conversation back to me and my impending slavery," Serena said.

"By all means," Julie said airily. "Don't let my fantasies about being sandwiched between two hot men interrupt you."

Serena looked at Faith. "Do you think I'm making a mistake by letting Damon fulfill my fantasy?"

Faith pressed her lips together for a moment. "Honestly, no. I'm not sure you could ask for a better man. I'm surprised that he agreed, or offered I suppose I should say, since you didn't exactly ask him, but I actually think he's perfect for you. And it certainly helps that he's so freaking hot."

Serena watched as Julie sent her eyes toward the ceiling. "Green isn't your color, Julie," Serena teased.

Julie sighed. "That's me. Jealous bitch."

"Why don't we take Julie out for a drink?" Serena suggested. "Maybe we can get her laid in the process and then God knows her mood would improve."

"I don't think you were supposed to look so hopeful, Julie," Faith said as she choked on her laughter.

Serena discarded her towel, slid off the table and wrapped her robe around her body. "Well, come on then. Let's get decent and go imbibe. Considering what I agreed to yesterday, I think I could use a drink or three."

"Yeah, well, just promise me you'll give me all the down and dirty details of your stint with slavery," Julie said. "If I get really desperate, I'll sign up to go a round with Mr. GQ."

"I thought you wouldn't sleep with guys who'd had sex with your friends?" Serena said with a raised eyebrow.

"It was very uncharitable of you to remind me of that," Julie huffed. "It would seem that between you and Faith and the bimbo that's hovering around Nathan, all the hunks are accounted for. It's damn sad when I'm actually contemplating leftovers."

"For God's sake, Julie, shut up," Faith said. "I thought only men objected to sloppy seconds."

"Honey, apparently your men don't," Julie said sweetly.

"Okay girls, enough. Let's go get drunk before the catfight starts," Serena interjected.

"Drunk and laid," Julie said as she performed a mock toast.

CHAPTER 9

When Serena, Julie and Faith walked into Cattleman's, Julie groaned and tried to turn around and walk back out.

Sitting at one of the tables was Nathan and a blonde bombshell.

Faith and Serena each grabbed an arm and hauled Julie forward. "Never let them see you run," Serena advised. "Walk in here like you own the place, bodacious tatas and all."

Julie glanced down at her chest and then glared across the room at Nathan. With a quick flick of her finger, she unbuttoned the top two buttons of her shirt and arranged it so the barest hint of her lacy bra was bared. Serena had to admit, Julie had some pretty fantastic cleavage.

An evil gleam entered Faith's eyes. Sweet, innocent Faith suddenly looked like satanic, scary Faith. She tightened her grip on Julie's arm then stared purposefully at Serena.

"Come on, we're going over there," Faith announced.

"What?" Julie all but screeched. She yanked her arm back, but Faith held tight.

Between Serena and Faith, they dragged her across the floor toward Nathan's table.

"I'm going to kill you for this," Julie hissed just before she pasted on a bright smile.

Nathan looked up and smiled warmly. "Hello, ladies."

His companion was not so pleased to see them.

"Hi, Nathan," Faith said sweetly. "Early day at work?"

Nathan laughed. "Yeah, just don't tell Pop. He and Connor are still at a job."

His gaze flickered over Julie and then Serena, and Serena could swear she saw interest in his eyes, especially when he got a good look at Julie's cleavage.

Julie smiled, but it was one of those calculating smiles that should have told Serena she was in trouble.

"Well, it was nice seeing you, Nathan. Call me and we'll reschedule your massage. We'd stay and chat, but we're heading over to the bar to discuss Serena's upcoming auction," Julie said.

Faith coughed, and Serena closed her eyes and groaned silently.

"Auction? What are you selling?" Nathan asked.

Don't say it. Don't you dare say it, Julie.

"Herself," Julie responded as if it were an everyday occurrence.

Nathan's eyebrows shot up, and he turned his gaze to Serena. Even the blonde bimbo looked surprised.

"Well now, that's an interesting auction," Nathan drawled as amusement crept into his eyes. "Is it open to everyone?"

"Julie's been drinking," Serena explained as she dug her fingers into Julie's side. She could feel the heifer shaking with silent laughter. "It was nice seeing you, Nathan. And you . . ." She glanced over at the blonde, who looked irritated that Nathan hadn't introduced her.

"Nice to see you ladies too," Nathan said. "Faith, I'll see you tomorrow."

Julie fluttered her fingers then tossed her hair and followed after Faith toward the bar.

"I'm going to kill you," Serena hissed when they slid onto the bar stools.

Julie laughed. "That's what you get for hauling me over there."

"Me? Hell, it wasn't my idea," Serena sputtered. "It was your *sweet* friend over there."

"Yeah, well, I'll get her back as soon as I come up with a way," Julie said as she threw Faith a dark glance.

"Well, he noticed your cleavage," Faith said. "Though I'd think you'd want him to notice more than that."

Julie rolled her eyes. "Oh boy, here we go. Faith's going to give us the *he should want you for yourself, not your attributes* speech. Which is nice, but at the moment, I'll take him noticing me any way it happens. I don't want to marry the guy. I just want to wrap myself around him a couple of times."

"She needs two drinks," Serena said as she motioned for the bartender.

"One for each hand," Julie said with a grin.

Faith turned around on her bar stool. "So why are we here again?"

"To get Julie drunk," Serena replied.

"And laid," Julie spoke up. "Don't forget the most important part of the equation."

Male laughter sounded behind them.

"Fuck me," Julie muttered as she closed her eyes.

Serena turned around to see Gray Montgomery standing behind them, a wide grin on his face.

"Interesting conversation. Am I interrupting?"

"No," Faith said.

"Yes!" Julie exclaimed.

Faith hopped off her bar stool and was immediately enfolded in Gray's arms. Serena and Julie exchanged eye-rolling glances but they both knew they were being jealous bitches.

"I take it you'll be here awhile," Gray said, amusement still heavy in his voice.

Faith smiled. "Uh, yeah, we're sorta plotting the demise of—"

Julie held up her hand to cut Faith off. "Don't you dare say his name, Faith, or I swear to God I'll choke you with your own hair."

Gray chuckled. "I don't know whether to envy the bastard or feel sorry for him."

He leaned down to kiss Faith again. "I'll leave you to your girl talk. I'm meeting Micah and Nathan for a drink. I'll see you at home later."

His hands slid possessively over Faith's body as he captured one last kiss, and Serena watched unashamedly. The chemistry between those two was tangible.

"I think you'll find Nathan otherwise occupied," Julie said snidely.

"Oh, you mean his client meeting?" Gray asked. "He's finished now."

Julie frowned and then she glared at Faith. "Client? The blonde chick is a client? Why didn't you know she was a client, Faith?"

Faith shrugged. "Contrary to popular belief, I do not know everything that goes on at Malone and Sons."

"Are all your clients so . . . clingy?" Julie asked Gray.

Faith frowned at that and then looked up at Gray. "Yes, are they? You don't have any business meetings with blonde bimbos, do you?"

Gray laughed and touched a strand of Faith's long blonde hair. "You're the only blonde I have eyes for, baby." Then he leaned in for one more kiss. "I'll see you later, okay?"

He drew away but then frowned at the drinks the bartender had set in front of the women. "Tell you what. I'll hang around and drive you ladies home when you're done."

"Fine with me," Julie said with a shrug. "I rode over with Serena."

"I wasn't planning on drinking anything," Serena said as she smiled at Gray. "It was sweet of you to offer, but I can drive Julie home."

"Yes, but now you can drink," Faith said. "I'm sure Nathan and Micah wouldn't mind helping to get our cars where they need to go."

Serena almost laughed at how transparent Faith was being.

"Okay, sounds like a plan to me," Serena said. "Drink up, girls."

Several drinks later, the three women were laughing, though for the life of her, Serena couldn't figure out what they were laughing about. Julie was doing an imitation of Nathan's blonde chick offering to do his massage while Faith tried in vain to get her to lower her voice.

"Do you think they know we're talking about them?" Julie asked as she leaned in and yanked a thumb over her shoulder to where Gray, Micah and Nathan sat several tables away.

"They probably have a good idea," Serena said dryly. "You aren't exactly the poster child for discretion."

Julie shrugged. "Oh well, fuck him."

"You're trying, remember?" Faith said as she stifled her laughter.

"Not anymore," Julie announced as she drained the last of her drink. "If he doesn't appreciate me and my massages, then I'll find someone else who will."

"Atta girl," Serena said.

"Oh, Serena, don't look now, but Damon just walked in," Faith whispered.

Julie whirled around in her seat and promptly sucked in her breath. "That's Mr. GQ? Damn, he's . . . nice. Very nice, Serena. I think I might be rethinking my whole stance on submissives and slaves."

"Turn around and put your tongue back in your mouth," Serena said. "You're getting drool on my shirt."

"He's coming this way," Julie reported as she swiveled in her chair.

Serena's heart beat just a little faster, and she looked to Faith for confirmation. Faith nodded just before she turned and smiled.

"Damon, such a surprise to see you here," Faith said as Damon approached.

Finally Serena turned calmly on her stool to see Damon standing a mere foot away. He was wearing jeans again and a T-shirt. Even casually dressed, though, he positively oozed raw sexuality. And confidence. He stood there like he belonged, as though there were no question that he would be welcomed.

"Quite a surprise," Serena agreed. "Came to mingle with us barbarians?"

Damon chuckled. "Some of my favorite barbarians hang out

here, but actually, I was looking for you. Your assistant said I might find you here."

"And here I am."

"Don't mind us," Julie muttered. "We can take our drunken carcasses elsewhere."

"Not at all," Damon said smoothly. "Can I buy you ladies your next drink? I didn't realize I would be interrupting girls' night out."

Julie motioned for Faith to move down a bar stool and then Julie hopped up and took the seat that Faith vacated. "Have a seat," she offered Damon. "If you're buying drinks, the least you can do is get comfortable."

"Damon, you've obviously met Faith, but this is our friend Julie Stanford. Julie, this is Damon Roche."

Julie put her hand out, and Serena silently prayed that Julie would keep her mouth shut about auctions and slavery.

"Very nice to meet you, Damon. I've heard so much about you."

"The pleasure is mine, Julie," he said as he took her hand in his.

Then he turned to Serena. "Do you mind if I sit?"

"Not at all," she said as she motioned to the stool. "Was there something you needed? Not that I mind you looking me up here," she hurried to add, "but was there something in particular you wanted?"

"You," he said simply.

Serena swallowed then swallowed again when the knot in her throat wouldn't disappear.

"If you don't already have dinner plans, I thought we could eat together and discuss . . ."

He went silent, but his meaning was clear.

Julie leaned forward. "Don't hold back on our account, Serena."

"But you rode with me," Serena protested. "I can't leave you here."

"I'd be happy to give your friend a ride home," Damon said. "I'll have someone take your car to your apartment, if that's okay with you, and I'll run you home later."

Julie leaned back and stared at Damon with interest and then she returned her gaze to Serena. "Okay, forget everything I said about a take-charge man, because I'm finding it very attractive all of a sudden."

Damon smiled, and Faith burst out laughing.

"Do you have a problem with Damon taking you home, Julie?" Serena asked. "Maybe I shouldn't go. I hate to run out on you guys."

"We can always have dinner another time," Damon interjected. "Or Faith and Julie are welcome to join us, although I see Gray scowling over there, so I rather doubt he's going to be thrilled with the idea of me walking out of here with not one, but three gorgeous women."

"Oh, I like him," Julie breathed. She blinked and seemed to snap out of her semi-drunken stupor. "You two go on ahead. Gray has promised to take care of getting me home."

"Are you sure?" Serena asked.

"It's no trouble to take you home," Damon assured.

Julie smiled. "I appreciate the offer, but I'm sure you two have plenty of stuff to talk about. You know, like auctions, slave collars, chains . . ."

Serena closed her eyes and prayed for deliverance, but Damon just laughed.

"Let's go," Serena muttered. "Before I kill her."

CHAPTER 10

$\mathcal{S}$erena stepped into the parking lot with Damon's hand lightly at the small of her back. She purposely kept stride with him so his hand wouldn't slide away.

Dusk had fallen, and a faint evening breeze blew through her hair. It was less humid than usual tonight, and the sounds of the city surrounded them.

After Damon settled Serena into his car, he walked around and got into the driver's seat. Instead of keying the ignition, he pulled out his cell phone, and she listened as he directed his driver to meet them at the restaurant to collect her car keys.

"Sam will drive your car to your apartment tonight after I've dropped you back home so that he can give the keys to you. I'll make sure he phones ahead so you're expecting him."

Serena laid a hand on Damon's wrist as he went to insert the key in the ignition. "You didn't have to do this, Damon. You could always just drop me back by here to get my car after we've eaten."

He started the car and then reached out to touch her cheek. "It's no trouble at all, Serena. Better get used to me taking care of you, because I assure you, while you are mine, I'll be seeing to your every need."

Her throat seized, and a thousand butterflies took wing in her stomach. He made it sound so enticing, so beautiful. Not at all like the stark image that the word *slave* invoked.

"I think I'm going to like it," she said softly.

"I intend that you will."

As he drove out of the parking lot, he reached over and slid his hand over hers. His thumb rubbed lightly up and down one of her fingers as he maneuvered the busy streets.

"I like touching you," he said as he saw her staring at his hand. "You have infinitely touchable skin."

"I don't mind," she said huskily. "Your hands are strong. I like them against my skin."

His eyes flickered in the glow cast back by numerous headlights. "Soon you will feel me on every part of your body, Serena. Are you prepared for that? Do you lie awake at night and think of me touching your breasts? Your lips? Between your thighs?"

Her senses came alive as if he commanded them. An exotic tingle scurried from her pelvis to her breasts, squeezing her nipples into taut points.

"Yes," she whispered.

"I find myself impatient to own you," he murmured. "It's why I sought you out tonight. I wanted to tell you that the arrangements for the auction have been made."

She trembled, and he tightened his grip on her hand as if to soothe her.

"We need to talk about what happens afterward," she said.

"Yes, we do. I'd like a week where I have you completely and wholly to myself. You mentioned a month's time frame for your fantasy, and I realize you can't take the entire month away from your business, but can you arrange to have a week off directly after the auction?"

She licked her lips and found herself clutching at his hand. "I'm sure I can. What happens after that week, though? When I go back to work?"

He smiled. "You go to work just like any other day. But at the end of your work day, you return to me and surrender to my care and keeping."

"And when I have obligations outside work?"

"You will, of course, keep them. I'm not a monster, Serena. All I ask is that when you're with me, your time is mine."

She nodded. "Okay. I can agree to your terms."

"They're your terms," he said calmly. "I'm only fulfilling your deepest desires."

"Yes, I know. And thank you. I think."

She smiled as her voice came out all quivery. He smiled back and squeezed her hand reassuringly. "Give me a chance to make you happy, Serena."

She cocked her head sideways to look at him. "You know, somehow I can't imagine not being happy with you."

He raised her hand and brushed his lips across her knuckles. "It is my goal for you to enjoy our every moment together."

She leaned back in her seat, hazy with contentment. Damon did that to her. Relaxed her and made her feel at ease. Like she could trust him. Which was absurd when she thought about it. She'd known him such a short period of time, but he got her. Without question, without reservation. He didn't judge her. He accepted her.

He kept her hand in his lap for the duration of the drive.

When he wasn't stroking her fingers, he ran his fingertips up and down her wrist and up the inside of her arm.

It was addicting. He was addicting, and the scary thing was that their relationship had yet to go beyond a simple touch, a light caress or a sizzling look. He could spell trouble for her in a big, big way if she wasn't careful.

He drove to the same restaurant they'd had their first meeting at, and they were ushered back to the private dining room. At night, it took on a whole different atmosphere. The lighting was dim and more intimate. The drapes were drawn back from the large picture window, and the city skyline twinkled brightly on the horizon.

"I feel decidedly underdressed," she murmured ruefully as she looked down at her jeans and T-shirt.

"I'm not wearing anything dressier," he reminded her. "Besides, we are alone, and there is no one to see us."

Her expression eased as she smiled. He made it so easy for her to relax and not worry about anything beyond the immediate moment.

He settled her into her chair and then took the seat across from her. A waiter hovered close by, and Damon ordered a bottle of wine.

"Would you like to see a menu?" Damon asked her.

She sat back in her chair, holding her wineglass to her lips. "You choose," she said softly. She knew it would please him to do so, and she didn't question her burning wish to accommodate his desires.

Damon related his choices to the waiter in a low voice, and in another moment, they were left alone.

"Tell me more about yourself," she said as she set her glass back down on the table. "I don't even know what you do for a living. Do you have family? Are you alone?"

He gave a self-conscious grimace, and it was the first chink she'd seen in the self-assured manner he always wore. "I was fortunate at an early age to have gotten in on the ground floor with what turned out to be very lucrative stocks. I love a challenge, and so I buy struggling businesses and turn them around."

"And have you ever failed?" Serena asked, though she already knew the answer.

He stared levelly at her. "No," he said simply.

"What is your latest acquisition?"

He tapped his fingers on the table, and an excited gleam entered his eyes. "I picked up two chip mills farther east that were on the verge of bankruptcy. I fully expect to have them showing a profit in under a year's time. It's all in hiring the right people and making sound financial decisions."

"You sound much more cutthroat than I am when it comes to business," she said. "I fully admit that I don't always make the best business decisions and let my heart get ahead of my brain. Carrie tells me that I'm way too soft and that I'll never wear brass balls."

Damon smiled as he leaned back in his chair to study her. "And yet your business is profitable, you have no debt and you have happy clients."

"You've been checking up on me again," she muttered.

"Not again. Just the once. I just made sure it was a very thorough investigation. I'm very curious as to how you ever got into this sort of business. I've never known of another like it."

She shrugged but couldn't contain the bite of excitement that gripped her when she talked about her business and what inspired the idea behind it.

"It started off quite fanciful, actually. I've always been some-what of a dreamer. Okay, a big dreamer. My mother used to swear that I spent ninety percent of my time with my head in the clouds."

"Dreamers never die," Damon said.

Serena smiled. "That's so true and such a lovely sentiment. At any rate, even at an early age, I loved to fulfill other people's wishes. If I overheard a friend or a family member express a desire for something, if it was in my power to give it to them, I did.

"After I graduated with my MBA, I spent a couple of years working in office management. Long enough to figure out I was bored stiff, and I hated working for other people."

"Ah, a rebel," he said in amusement.

She wrinkled her nose. "'Fraid so. It's not that I can't get along with people or that I buck authority. I'm just happier when I'm making my own decisions and I'm working in a job that motivates me. In short, I didn't love what I was doing. I do now, and that makes all the difference."

"I bet you get a lot of interesting requests."

She rolled her eyes. "That's an understatement. Some of them are obviously crackpots out for a laugh, but the worst are the insanely off-the-wall *serious* requests. These come from people who genuinely want and expect that I can fulfill their bizarre fantasies, and as weird as I may find them, they're still just people who are longing for something just out of their reach. It's hard to have to tell them that I can't help them."

"You have a soft heart," he said in a gentle voice.

She grimaced. "Coming from you, I doubt that's a compli-ment. My business decisions would probably horrify you."

He looked at her in surprise. "Do I come across so ruthlessly? I sincerely meant it as a compliment. And as your business is a success, and you've made so many people happy, I hardly think your decisions would horrify me."

Warm pleasure suffused her cheeks at the approval she saw in his expression. "I'm sorry. I didn't mean to imply that you were ruthless. It's just that, as you discovered in your research, I've subsidized more than a few of my client's fantasies when it was clear they couldn't afford the expense involved."

"And you think this is a weakness," he stated.

She shifted uncomfortably. "Maybe not a weakness, but I lecture myself on setting limits and then find myself unable to say no to a client because their fantasy doesn't fit their budget. Don't get me wrong; I'm choosy. I don't particularly feel sorry for a guy whose fantasy is to orchestrate the photo shoot for the *Sports Illustrated* swimsuit issue, but when a mother comes to me because her daughter is ill and wants to be a princess on a cruise ship, I won't tell her that I can't help her because she's several thousand dollars short."

"I think what you perceive as a weakness is your greatest strength and attribute," Damon said as he reached across to take her hand. "You have a generous soul, but you're also practical."

She let him turn her hand over so that her knuckles rested on the table. He touched a finger to her palm and traced a path across her skin. In turn, he stroked each of her fingers as if he savored the sensation of her flesh.

How she loved his touch. She could sit for hours and simply let his fingertips glide over her hands, her arms. She shivered as she remembered how his hands felt tangled in her hair, massaging her scalp and caressing her neck.

"You said—" She stopped and cleared her throat. "You said you had arranged the auction?"

He slowly withdrew his hand and sat forward in his chair so

that there was little space between them. "I have. Is next weekend too soon?"

Adrenaline spiked in her veins, surging like a flash flood. Excitement. Dread. Terror. All were accurate descriptors of the emotions battering her.

Her mouth went dry and she swallowed quickly.

"No. Next weekend is fine. I'll arrange my work schedule so that I'm off the following week. The auction. What do I need to do?"

Damon smiled. "Not a thing. I'll have my driver pick you up and take you to The House where your keeper will await you. He'll assist you in readying yourself for the auction. You'll remain under his care until I claim you."

Desire thrummed heavy in her veins. Liquid heat pooled in her loins and simmered there, waiting to be stirred to greater heights.

"Why are you doing this?" she asked. It was something she'd already asked, but she couldn't help the need to know more about this intriguing man.

"It's very simple," he said calmly. "I want you, Serena. I've wanted you since the moment we met. When I discovered that you were the one wanting a fantasy fulfilled, there was never a chance of me turning you over to another man."

"And so I will be yours," she murmured, liking the words—and their meaning.

"Yes. You will belong to me."

Satisfaction glimmered in his brown eyes. They were dark, and warm with promise.

"Tell me, Serena. Have you opened yourself to the possibility of new and daring experiences? Have you given thought to precisely what it will mean to belong to a man? And not just any man, but what it will mean to belong to me?"

She paused as she stared back at him. "I think I've prepared myself for new experiences. I'm a little nervous because I don't know how far a man—*you*—will take things. But I trust you. Maybe I shouldn't, but you make me feel very at ease."

"I'm glad," he said in a soft voice. "I wouldn't want you frightened of me."

"I find myself entertaining crazy thoughts," she admitted. "Some are so far out of the realm of my personal experience that I wonder if I should even entertain them in reality or if they are better left as fantasy."

"I hope that you'll explore your boundaries when you're with me and not be too swift to withdraw. I want you to open your mind and your heart. Don't judge. Don't think. Just feel. But," he added, "if there is ever a time you're afraid, I want you to be honest with me. I will never do anything to intentionally hurt you or frighten you."

"I know that," she said huskily. "I really do know that."

Deep down, she wanted him to push her comfort zone. She wanted him to take control, so that she wouldn't have a choice. She didn't want him to ask, rather she wanted him to take, to demand, to *give*.

"I wanted to see you tonight because it will be the last time we'll be together until the auction," Damon said.

She looked up in surprise.

He smiled. "I like the dismay that flashed in your eyes. It matches my own. And the arrogant part of me likes it that you enjoy spending time with me."

"Then why—"

"Because I want you to think of me all week. I want you to imagine the night of the auction when I lay claim to you. That first time I touch you and establish ownership. I want you to anticipate it."

"You're awfully sure of yourself," she said in a low voice. But he was right. She would think of him all week. She would think of nothing else.

"No, I'm merely hopeful. And regardless of what will be on your mind this week, you will be what occupies my thoughts. I haven't felt this degree of anticipation in a long, long time."

She smiled.

"Your arrogance matches mine," he said with a slight tilt to his lips. "I like it."

"The contracts?" she questioned.

"I'll courier them over first thing Monday morning. I want all the paperwork out of the way before the auction. I would have nothing intrude upon our time once we embark on your fantasy."

Her breath quickened and she nodded her agreement. Finally. This was it. She was actually doing it.

It amazed her that she was sitting across the table from a gorgeous, powerful man, making plans to fulfill a longing within her that had grown from an idle curiosity to a full-fledged need.

In just over a week, she would walk into Damon's club and be auctioned as a sex slave. That she knew who her master would be didn't lessen the adrenaline-laced fear and excitement that raced through her body. If anything, knowing that Damon would command her body heightened her anticipation all the more.

CHAPTER 11

"*What* do you mean, Nathan drove you home, you woke up naked in your bed the next morning and you don't remember what happened?" Serena asked in disbelief.

She propped her cell phone between her cheek and her shoulder as she fumbled for the paperwork she was trying to organize.

Julie groaned in her ear. "Faith set me up. The bitch."

Serena laughed. "Oh come on, Julie. She was just trying to help."

"I know," Julie said with a heavy sigh. "But she was way too obvious. She all but shoved me at Nathan and suggested he drive me home. I really don't remember how he reacted because I'd had too much to drink. I vaguely remember him driving me home, but after that? Nothing. I woke up the next morning in my bed, completely naked, and Serena, I don't sleep in the buff."

"Ah, and you're worried that you did the nasty with Nathan and don't remember it?"

"If I had sex with him and don't remember it, I'm going to kill myself," Julie said mournfully.

"Well, why don't you just call and ask him?"

"Oh yeah, that's what I want to do. 'Hello, Nathan, this is Julie. Would you mind telling me if we fucked the other night?'"

Serena laughed. "I'm sure you could be more subtle than that, sweetie."

"If we did sleep together, he sure hasn't got the part down where you're supposed to call the next day. For that matter, if we had sex, he sure hightailed it at the ass crack of dawn, which tells me I must not have been any good."

"Quit getting down on yourself, Julie. From all you've said, I have to think you didn't have sex. Nathan doesn't strike me as the type to take advantage of a woman when she's drunk."

"But what if I took advantage of him?" Julie squeaked.

Serena laughed again. "Nathan is a big boy. Chances are he put you to bed and left. Simple as that. What you ought to do is call him and tell him you appreciate the ride home then offer to make him dinner as a thank-you."

"You're a fucking genius. Why didn't I think of that?"

"Does this mean you're finally going to make a move on the man?" Serena asked.

"Uh, maybe."

Serena closed her eyes and shook her head. "For the love of God, Julie. You make me crazy. Faith and I are supposed to be the wimps, not you. Remember? You're Miss Brass Balls, take no prisoners. So start acting like it."

"You're right. I'm totally unworthy. I bow before your greatness."

"Shut up and go call him," Serena said in exasperation.

"I know this phone call has been all about me, but the

whole reason I called was to say good luck tonight. There's no doubt I think you've lost your marbles, but in a weird, twisted way, I'm insanely jealous and I hope you have a great time at, um, your slave auction."

Serena grinned as a tingle of excitement fluttered around her stomach. "Thanks, Julie. I'm going to be out of the office for the next week so I'll catch up some time after that."

"Oh wait, fuck no, you don't. You can't just disappear for a week after being sold in a slave auction," Julie sputtered. "What if he drags you off to his cave somewhere and molests and kills you?"

"Are you just trying to scare me?"

"Yes! Use your head. You'll call me the morning after the auction or I'll call the police and have them beat down Damon's door. I don't care how close he is with Faith or how gorgeous the guy is. For all you know he could be a serial killer."

"Thank you for that," Serena muttered.

"Sorry, hon. I don't mean to ruin your night, but someone has to beat some sense into your pretty head."

"Okay, okay, I'll call you the next morning."

"Good. Now off you go. I'll talk to you tomorrow and you can tell me how your first night in slavery went."

"Irreverent bitch," Serena muttered.

"You love me."

"Good-bye, Julie." Serena took the phone from her ear and punched the button to end the call.

She laid the phone on her desk and glanced over at the clock. If she wanted to get home and showered and primped, she needed to leave now. She needed the downtime to collect her composure before Damon's driver picked her up, because she was a mass of chaotic nerves.

She piled the paperwork into a bunch and shoved it all into her briefcase as her impatience to get home nipped at her. After a quick glance around her office to make sure she wasn't forgetting anything, she headed down the hall to have a quick conversation with Carrie.

Carrie had been delighted with Serena's decision to take a week off, even if she didn't know why. She assumed Serena was taking her first vacation in years, and in a way, it *was* a vacation. From reality.

After gaining Carrie's assurances that she'd call if anything came up she couldn't handle, Serena left the office building and headed to her apartment.

First she indulged in a long soaking bath as she tried in vain to calm her overwrought nerves. Faith had called her that morning and described her experience at The House so that Serena wasn't walking in totally blind, and after hearing Faith's account, she was that much closer to hyperventilating.

She wasn't sure what she was expecting, but Faith's description of the openness of the club goers' sexual activities made her feel like a fish out of water before she ever set foot there.

Hello, you are a fish out of water.

Fish out of water about to jump from the goldfish bowl into the freaking ocean.

Thanks to a trip to Julie's, she was waxed and buffed from head to toe and all parts in between. She was confident in her appearance and that she wouldn't scare anyone with her nakedness. She gulped at the mere thought of being nude in front of a roomful of men. It was just so . . . decadent. So very bad girl of her.

After a look at the clock, she put it in high gear. She didn't worry too much about what to wear since she'd be naked for most of the night, but she took special pains with her hair. Not that she did much to it, because she knew Damon liked it long and trailing over her shoulders, but she brushed it until it shone.

As for makeup? She got the giggles as she sparingly applied foundation and left off eyeliner, mascara and lipstick. If things went according to her fantasy, eye makeup and lipstick would be rather silly. Damon probably wouldn't appreciate bright red lipstick on his cock.

She sucked in her breath as she imagined taking him in her mouth. Would he take her e-mail literally? Would he replicate all aspects of her fantasy or would he use it for a general guideline? She didn't know, and that uncertainty added to her breathless excitement.

How would he taste? Would he be big or small? Would he be gentle or forceful?

She didn't want gentleness from him. She wanted to tap in to the power that she sensed was tightly held just underneath the surface. She wanted him rough and hard, demanding and forceful.

The doorbell rang just as she was reaching for her sandals. Her stomach lurched up into her throat as she thrust her feet into the shoes and nervously smoothed her hair with damp hands.

She reached for her overnight bag and headed for the door. When she swung it open, Sam stood there, his big body filling her doorway. He inclined his head.

"Miss James, are you ready?"

"Yes," she managed to croak out.

He reached for her bag, and she relinquished it to him. She quickly locked up and followed him to the Bentley.

The drive seemed to take an eternity. With each passing mile, the tension coiled and swelled within her. By the time they pulled into the winding drive of a large estate, she felt lightheaded, and her pulse pounded loudly at her temples.

Sam parked the car, and her door opened immediately. She found herself staring into the face of a handsome man. His expression was enigmatic, and he simply held his hand out to her.

She took it with trembling fingers and allowed him to help her from the car. She started forward, but the man tugged her back with a sharp pull until she stood at his side.

"I am your keeper," he said by way of introduction. "You will heed my instructions at all times."

She blinked and nodded.

"Yes, Keeper," he prompted.

"Yes, Keeper," she stammered out.

He nodded in approval. "I'll escort you in and prepare you for the auction."

He took her elbow in a surprisingly gentle grip as he guided her toward the door. Silence greeted her when they stepped into the darkened foyer. Before she could look around and absorb her surroundings, her keeper hurried her down the hallway. He paused outside a door then opened it and directed her inside.

It was a small room but was lavishly decorated. The furnishings were expensive, simple, but extremely tasteful. It looked to be a sitting room, or even a changing room, as there was no bed. Just two armchairs, a full-length mirror and a vanity. To the side, there was an open doorway to a half bathroom.

As she did a small circle, taking in the room, her keeper's hand touched her shoulder.

"It is time to prepare you," he said.

His fingers went to her T-shirt, and she almost batted his hand away. He paused for a moment and leveled his gaze at her. He didn't back down, but he also didn't barge ahead. He exerted his authority even as he gave her time to adjust to his touch.

"I'm sorry," she murmured. "I'm a nervous wreck."

He didn't reply, though a half smile niggled at his lips.

"I can undress myself," she offered, thinking to save him the awkward task.

He raised one brow and shook his head. "You are mine until another purchases you. It is my duty and my right to ready you as I see fit."

Her eyes widened, and her stomach knotted and convulsed. Oh hell, this was it. She tried to relax as he slowly lifted her T-shirt over her head. He directed her to raise her arms and she did so almost mechanically.

It took every bit of her will not to fold her arms protectively over her lacy bra. Instead, she let her hands fall to her sides even as her fingers curled into tight balls.

"You will fetch a high price, indeed," her keeper murmured.

His fingers trailed up her arms, raising goose bumps on her flesh. When they reached her shoulders, he hooked his fingertips under the straps of her bra and slowly tugged them downward.

She held her breath as the cups lowered until her breasts were free of confinement. She wanted to look at him, to get a better view of his appearance, but she was too afraid to raise her gaze so she kept her focus on his abdomen as his hands circled around to the clasp of her bra.

Deftly, he unhooked it, and he tugged until the bra fell to the floor at her feet.

Softly and sensuously, his palms grazed her waist as he

moved around to the button of her jeans. Her nipples were puckered and hard, standing taut as though begging for attention, for his touch.

His fingers slid into the waistband of her pants as he worked the zipper down and parted the fly. And then the denim rasped along her hips and down her legs until they too fell in a heap around her ankles.

There she stood in front of this stranger, her keeper, in just her panties, a mere wisp of material, transparent and hiding nothing of her femininity. Was she crazy for the surge of excitement that cut razor sharp through her veins?

Her keeper stood back for a moment, his gaze raking up and down her body with what could only be classified as pure male appreciation. No longer did she seek to hide from him, for she felt alluring and seductive, as though she held the power and not he.

He was handsome, and appealing, but *he wasn't Damon*. She nearly shook her head. Were it not for the fact that Damon had volunteered, this could well have been the man she'd give herself to for her fantasy.

Her keeper stepped forward and placed his hands at her slim hips. There was a moment's pause and then he slipped the thin string of her underwear down. The lacy scrap fluttered down her legs, lightly brushing the insides of her knees.

He held his hand to her and she took it as she stepped free of her jeans and underwear. She was completely and utterly naked.

He moved to the vanity and rummaged in the drawer until he drew out a brush.

"Come here," he ordered quietly.

She obeyed with no hesitation, and once she stood before him, he gestured for her to turn around.

He began brushing her hair, stroke after stroke, until the

strands lay soft and wispy down her back. His fingers alternated with the brush as he worked both through her hair from scalp to the very ends.

Finally he was done, and disappointment shuddered through her body at the loss of his touch. She wondered if he'd brushed her hair to comfort her and calm her, but then he grasped her arm in his commanding grip and turned her around, all hints of gentleness gone.

He took one of her hands and pulled it behind her, and then he claimed the other one, pulling it as well until he held her wrists together at the small of her back. Rope scraped across her skin, abrading her flesh as he bound her hands.

When he was done, he left her for a moment and returned a mere second later. He carried a leather belt of sorts. It looked more like a tether or a leash, though the circlet was far too large for her neck. Her unspoken question was answered when he secured the belt around her waist.

There was a hook in the front that the lead attached to, and it was then she realized that he was going to guide her with the harness. His hand cupped her chin, and he forced her gaze upward to meet his.

"You will speak only to answer a direct question asked of you. You will respect my authority and that of the man who ultimately purchases you. There will be many men watching you, wanting to touch the flesh that they would bid on. I will be at your side to protect you, and you are to trust that I will not let anyone go too far."

"Yes, Keeper," she whispered.

"Good, then we are agreed." He gave a slight tug on her leash as he started for the door. "It's time," he said, and she followed him with shaking knees.

CHAPTER 12

*H*er keeper led her down a darkened hallway lit only by sconces on the wall. There was a decidedly medieval feel to the house, and she wondered if it was always so or if Damon had arranged a more atmospheric setting for her fantasy. Surely not. He wouldn't have had time for such a venture, nor would he waste that kind of money, would he?

A slight tug at her leash made her redirect her attention to her keeper as he mounted the wooden stairs. As they neared the top, she could hear muted sounds in the distance. The murmur of male voices.

Her breathing shallowed, and her limbs went tingly.

At the top of the stairs there was another hallway with doors on either side. At the end there was another door, this one open with light spilling into the hallway.

Her keeper walked toward that distant doorway, and she followed behind, her fingers in tight balls behind her back.

The voices grew louder as they neared the room. Her keeper

paused just inside and turned back to her. He didn't speak. He just eyed her calmly, as though he was giving her a chance to prepare for her entrance.

She glanced down self-consciously at her nudity as embarrassment crept slowly over her body.

Her head came back up as her keeper tugged, none too gently, at her chin. His eyes bore into her, his expression stern.

"Do *not* look shamed. You will hold your head high."

"Yes, Keeper."

He nodded his satisfaction and then turned, and with a slight tug on her leash, pulled her into the room.

There were at least thirty men assembled, gathered in small clumps, others standing alone. They held drinks, sipping idly as they conversed, and waiters circled the room with trays of hors d'oeuvres.

It all looked ultra-civilized.

Her keeper conveyed her farther into the room, and it was then that the men took notice of Serena. They made no effort to disguise the blatant interest in their stares.

Serena and her keeper circled in and out of the throngs of men. Hands touched and caressed, sliding over her arms, her hips and her breasts. There were murmurs of appreciation as well as more overt compliments coupled with lascivious stares.

As promised, her keeper stood solidly by her side and allowed no more than the idle touch or gentle caress. When one of the men slid his hand between her legs, her keeper was quick to pry the man's hand away with a tersely worded warning.

Fingers touched her hair, separating the strands. It was all like a haze brought on by too much alcohol. Everything seemed in slow motion, like a dream world. She heard the men, heard their every lustful thought. Heard their promises, that if she were theirs, how they would pleasure her and take care of her every need.

As she and her keeper circled the room, lustful gazes followed in her wake. Such power made her heady when she should have already relinquished it. She had none. Or did she?

She hadn't expected to actually feel when Damon walked into the room. It was merely a product of her fantasy, her overwrought imagination. But she did indeed feel the shift in the air, the sudden rise of tension.

She looked to the doorway and saw him standing there, his gaze arrogantly searching the room. For her.

Her breath left her, and she swayed unsteadily. Her keeper put a solicitous hand to the small of her back and murmured a command for her to stand straight.

Damon found her and their gazes locked. Smoldering awareness danced between them. It was nearly tangible in the air. The room was thick with it.

Arousal sparked in his dark eyes, and a slow smile carved his sensual mouth. He strode toward her, and the crowd parted, leaving his path to her unimpeded.

It was as if the words she'd penned had jumped from the pages. Every nuance, every detail that she'd painstakingly written had come to life at Damon's hands. Which could only mean he'd carefully orchestrated every detail according to her e-mail. And that meant . . .

She swallowed and tried to calm her shaking nerves.

Damon stopped beside her keeper and murmured close to his ear. As she'd done in her fantasy, she strained to hear what Damon said, but her keeper pulled sharply at her leash. A reprimand.

She straightened and waited, though her entire body was strung so tight with anticipation that she feared breaking.

Damon came to stand in front of her and then reached out, cupping his hand behind her neck. The strands of her hair were wrapped around his knuckles, and he pulled her roughly to him, tilting her head so that she looked him straight in the eye.

Her neck was exposed to him, and she felt vulnerable standing there as he towered over her. There was a pleased look in his eyes, as if he found her satisfying.

Her pulse jumped and raced, for she knew what he would say as soon as his lips parted. They were close to hers, so close she could feel the warmth of his breath, smell the crisp mint on his tongue.

"You will be mine, Serena," he said in a silky voice.

She trembled, her body alive with need and desire. Damon stepped away and melted into the crowd, and it was all she could do not to call him back, to beg him not to leave her even for a moment.

Her keeper pulled at her bound hands and she stumbled as he led her away. She looked back over her shoulder, searching frantically for Damon, but he was lost in the crowd of men who were pressing close in anticipation of the auction's start.

In the distance she heard a man announce that the bidding would start. Her keeper turned her around and positioned her so that her body was displayed. His hands coaxed down her sides then around her abdomen and slowly glided upward until he cupped one breast in his palm. He ran his thumb over her taut nipple as the crowd urged him on.

Slowly he circled behind her, his hand still at her breast. He pressed in close, his chest molding to her back. She began to shake in earnest when his arms enfolded her and his hands molded both breasts, plumping them to their best advantage, showing each man what could be his if he was willing to pay a high enough price.

He tweaked her nipples, rolling them between his thumb and forefinger until they were tight and throbbing.

The bidding started and immediately, hands went up. For the first several minutes there was a flurry of bidding as the price increased. Then, as it grew higher, only a few men remained, each determined to outbid the other.

Where was Damon? She couldn't see him even though she searched frantically among the crowd. Forgotten was her fantasy, and that she'd penned this part and knew well how it should end. Her only thought was that she couldn't find Damon, that he'd somehow left her to the mercy of another.

Finally it was down to two men. As one raised his hand to raise the bid, the other remained silent. The announcer paused and then said, "Going once . . ."

Serena held her breath, her body rigid against her keeper.

"One hundred thousand dollars."

Damon stepped forward, his demeanor calm, but determination flashed in his eyes. How easy it was to forget this was a carefully orchestrated charade. It seemed so real. It felt real.

There were a few gasps and more than a few grumbles but no one stood forward to top the bid.

She shook with excitement, with relief. Her keeper pinched one nipple and uttered a command in her ear for her to be still.

"Sold to Damon Roche," the announcer said.

She sagged against her keeper, relief making her weak. At the same time, profuse joy flooded her. This was really happening! She had to blink to make sure she wasn't imagining it, that she wasn't indulging in her fantasy from the comfort of her dreams.

As her keeper walked around her, she could see the smile on his face. Damon walked forward to greet her keeper . . . and to claim his prize.

As Damon approached, her keeper pushed at her shoulders, forcing her to her knees.

"You will show your new master proper respect," her keeper murmured.

Serena sank to her knees, only too willing to please Damon. She forced her gaze downward, waiting for him to command her.

Damon's warm hand, so firm and strong, cupped her chin.

"Look at me," he directed.

She looked up to see him towering over her, strong, so powerful. He stroked her cheek, and she nuzzled into his palm. His touch lit fire to her insides. Her skin crawled with an itchiness she had no hope of alleviating. Only he could satisfy her needs now.

There was magic in his touch. Warm and sensual, it stoked the fires inside her, made her clit bead and pulse with an agony only he could soothe.

Her knees ached from her perch on the hard floor but she gave no thought to complaining or shifting her position. Damon slid long fingers along her jawline before retracting his hand.

His fingers fumbled at his fly as he undid his pants.

"You will look only at me," he said huskily as he kept his gaze connected with hers.

"Yes . . ." She wouldn't call him keeper, for she called another man by that name, but she wasn't sure what he wanted to be called. Master? She didn't like the word. It sounded silly. Juvenile. Not all in keeping with the very adult feelings and sensations that coursed through her body.

So she settled for a quiet acknowledgment of his command

and kept her gaze on him as he reached into his pants and pulled out his cock.

He was achingly erect. Hard. Thick. His cock filled his hand as he pumped back and forth. The hair at his groin was dark, but trimmed close to his skin. She loved a guy who took care of himself down there.

As his pants fell farther down his hips, she could see his sac bulge and flex with the movements of his hand. She wanted to touch it, feel him roll in her hand.

He guided the tip to her lips and gently brushed it against her mouth.

"Open for me, Serena," he commanded. "Take me inside your mouth."

She readily complied, and he immediately plunged deep into her mouth. Like velvet on her tongue. He tasted of salt, smelled faintly of musk and leather.

He worked back and forth and she sucked avidly at him, running her tongue from tip to base as he dragged his cock in and out of her mouth.

He stilled for a moment and tapped her cheek with his fingers. Then he tilted her head upward, his cock nearly sliding free of her lips. His gaze warned her as did his hand against her jaw.

She relaxed immediately and let him take over. Let him use her mouth as he wished in the manner he wanted. She was his.

His hands framed her face, and he pulled her closer into his groin. He slid deep until his hairs tickled her nose. A low groan worked from his chest, and her body tightened with pleasure. She was pleasing him.

Harder and deeper he thrust. He held her in place, fucking her mouth with ruthless abandon. If she had feared he would be too gentle, too soft, she'd feared wrong. There was nothing gentle about his possession. He took her with savage abandon, leaving her no doubt as to whom she now belonged.

His fingers crept deeper into her hair so that his hands were tangled in her tresses as he rocked against her. Several times she thought he was on the verge of his release, but it was then that he slowed, holding himself still in her mouth until he regained control. Then he resumed the deep strokes to the back of her throat.

The blunt crown of his dick nudged at the softness in the deepest part of her mouth. She swallowed convulsively, and she could feel the shudders working through his body.

Warm saltiness spilled onto her tongue, just a precursor to his orgasm. She lapped hungrily at it, wanting more, but he stilled and gave her a warning tap on the cheek again. Again she relaxed and relinquished control to him.

"I'm close, Serena," he said. His voice slid like silk over her ravaged senses. "I want you to swallow it all. Drink from me. Taste my pleasure."

She closed her eyes as his erotic words flickered over her hungry body. So hungry. She wanted him. Needed him like she'd never needed anyone else.

His thrusts became more urgent. Less measured and less controlled. He pounded against her mouth without mercy and still she wanted more. All of him. Nothing less.

The first jet of his release hit the back of her throat like a shock. For a moment she held it in her mouth, unable to swallow fast enough in her surprise. More spilled onto her tongue. Creamy and exotic. Wild tasting. Masculine and strong.

As she swallowed, he continued to work in and out of her mouth, his movements more gentle now as the last of his orgasm quivered through his loins. He sank to the back of her throat once more and stayed there, locked against her mouth.

"Swallow," he said in a guttural voice. "Swallow against me, Serena."

She obeyed, swallowing and listening to his moans of pleasure as she milked the last drops of his cum from his cock.

Finally he slid from her mouth and loosened his grip on her head. He gazed down at her, warm approval glistening in his eyes. With one thumb he wiped a trickle of his seed from the corner of her mouth and then slid it inside her mouth.

Dutifully she licked his thumb clean and he withdrew it. He reached down to grasp her shoulders and helped her to her feet. Her hands were numb behind her, but she offered no complaint as she stood before him.

He fingered one nipple and a soft moan escaped her. Then he plucked at the other, manipulating the bud until she shook from head to toe. He cast a pointed glance at her keeper, who then stepped behind her and grasped her shoulders in firm hands.

Her muscles twitched in anticipation as Damon's hands trailed down her body to the curls between her legs. There wasn't a word to describe the pleasure, the sharp agony, that tightened her body.

Carefully he breached the folds of her femininity with one finger. It glided easily over her slick flesh, over her clit and to the opening below.

When her keeper's hands slid over her shoulders and to her breasts, cupping them and tweaking the nipples, her knees threatened to buckle. He held her tight as Damon delved deeper between her legs.

"Do not let her fall," Damon cautioned her keeper.

His fingers slid over her clit, massaging and manipulating the bundle of nerves.

"You will come for me, Serena."

Oh God, yes, she would come for him. She tried to breathe, but it was like inhaling fire. The air scorched her lungs, burned her chest.

Harder and faster he worked her clit and then moved lower to her entrance, where he teased her mercilessly.

"Do you fantasize about having my cock buried inside you?" Damon asked silkily.

"Yes," she gasped. "I want it more than anything."

He smiled and increased the pressure of his fingers.

"Soon, Serena. Soon you will have all of me. For now I want you to come with your keeper holding you for me, for it is the last time another man will ever touch you without my consent. You are mine now."

His words more than his touch sent her orgasm racing through her groin. It was frightening and splendid in equal parts as she shattered. Her keeper's hands were firm around her as she bucked and writhed. Her knees threatened to buckle but Damon's free hand shot out to hold her upright.

When the last waves of her orgasm broke around her, Damon ordered her keeper to release her. There was a formality to his actions as he saw to the change in ownership. She listened numbly as Damon thanked her keeper for his care and promised to be a good master to her.

Her hands were still tied behind her back as Damon gently led her away. Dozens of male eyes followed her, their stares envious as they watched Damon take her from the room.

He stopped outside the doorway and tugged at the ropes around her hands. As her arms fell free, he reached down and took both hands in his then raised them to his lips. He kissed the red circle of flesh around her wrists and soothed the numbness away with tender fingers.

There was a robe thrown over a chair situated in the hall, and he picked it up. Carefully he wrapped it around her, helping her to put her arms in the sleeves. Then he secured the tie so that every part of her body was covered and she was comfortable.

He touched her cheek in a loving gesture and then tucked her securely against his side as he headed for the stairs. As they walked slowly down, he turned to her again.

"You are mine now, Serena."

"Yes, I'm yours," she whispered.

CHAPTER 13

*S*erena felt a bit strange walking out to Damon's car in just a robe and no underthings. Worse, his driver waited at the Bentley, standing beside the back door. When she and Damon neared, Sam opened the door and Damon directed her inside.

Damon slid in beside her and pulled her flush against his body. She curled into him, fitting perfectly under his arm, her head resting on his shoulder. He was careful to keep the robe securely fastened around her, and for that she was grateful. It was doubtful that Sam could—or wanted to—see flashes of her nudity, but she appreciated Damon's regard for her modesty.

And then she had to laugh. A giggle escaped her before she could prevent it, and her shoulders shook with the hilarity of her concerns.

"Something amuses you?" Damon queried.

"I'm such a moron," she said. "I was all worried about walking outside in just a robe and was so grateful that you were so careful to shield my nudity from Sam when I just spent the last half hour completely naked in a roomful of men. My absurdity knows no bounds."

"You are naturally modest," he said simply. "Once the auction was over, you reverted back to your true nature. I don't see anything absurd about it. Quite frankly, it pleases me that you are so careful about who sees your body. For the next month, only I and those I choose will be granted that privilege."

Her heart seized just a bit, and she hid her smile against his chest. It pleased her that he was so possessive. Whether it was an act or what he truly felt, it delighted her.

"What happens now, Damon?" she asked quietly.

They'd discussed it before, but all knowledge fled in light of her nervousness.

"We go home," he said simply.

"I need to get my things from my apartment," she said. "Your instructions were to bring an overnight bag but I'll need more stuff if I'm to stay with you a week."

He put a firm finger over her lips to quiet her. "First, you'll stay with me the entire month. The week we discussed was for the time you'd devote solely to me, away from your work. Even when you go back to work, you'll still return to me every day, sleep in my bed, be bound to me.

"Second, you have no need of your things. While you're mine, I'll provide for your every need. I will dress you, feed you, take care of the smallest of details. Are we understood?"

She nodded and then, remembering the whole confusion over what to call him, her cheeks warmed, but she looked up at him anyway.

"What do I call you?" she asked softly. "I couldn't call you keeper, not when I'd called another man by that name, but neither could I stomach calling you master, because it seemed so . . . silly, and silly is the last thing I feel when I'm with you."

His hand trailed through her hair, glancing off her cheek with the gentlest of touches. "You'll call me Damon. I see no need for dramatic titles. I, on the other hand, will call you beautiful . . . lover . . . *mine*. I'll call you mine."

She closed her eyes and leaned into his touch, rubbing her cheek along his palm.

"How prettily you do that," he murmured. "You remind me of a contented cat, so sleek and purring."

She made a low sound of contentment in her throat as she nuzzled closer to him. "If I could purr, I would, for you are so good to me, Damon."

"I'm glad you think so. I'll push you, Serena. I'm demanding. I expect obedience and compliance. But I will be so very good to you. That, I promise."

She stirred restlessly against him, her skin itchy and alive.

He smiled, an arrogant smile of male satisfaction. He knew damn well she wanted him. Wanted him badly. Still, she voiced it because she was compelled to do so.

"I want you, Damon. I'm going to go crazy if you don't make love to me soon."

With his thumb and the knuckle of his forefinger, he tilted her chin, angling her so that her mouth was inches from his own. She sucked in all available air. Would he kiss her? Would he finally kiss her?

He pressed his lips to the corner of her mouth. Soft and gentle. Just one kiss, so light, and yet it burned the tender skin. Her chest swelled and her stomach turned over, and just that quickly, it was over.

He pulled away, his eyes glittering as he smoothed his thumb over her bottom lip.

"Soon, Serena. Soon I will have you, and you will have me. Anticipation is half the pleasure. For this reason, I would not want our coming together to happen too quickly. It is to be savored, not rushed."

She snuggled back into his arms, holding his promise close to her heart. Yes, she was impatient. She wanted him desperately, but it went beyond sex. She wanted his care. His regard. She wanted to be pampered. She wanted to belong.

Exhaustion, spawned by too much excitement, crept over her body. The adrenaline rush had left her and on the heels of her explosive orgasm; she resembled a gelatinous puddle.

When the car stopped, she moaned her protest, and Damon chuckled low in her ear. "Stay still, Serena mine."

She relaxed in his arms as Sam opened the back door. Damon carefully extricated himself from around her and eased out of his seat. Then he reached back in for her, sliding his arms underneath her body and lifting.

A sigh of contentment whispered past her lips as he carried her up the steps to his house. As soon as they were past the doorway, he lowered her until her feet hit the floor. He turned her around until she faced him, and he reached for the lapels of the robe he'd adorned her with.

Her mouth opened in protest, but he silenced her with a stern look.

"When you're in my home, you'll stay undressed unless I've chosen to clothe you."

She stared dumbly at him as he pulled the robe over her shoulders and let it slide down her arms. Air from the vent above blew quietly over her skin, and she shivered. Her hands went to her arms in a protective measure, but he wouldn't allow it.

"You have nothing to fear from me," he husked as he pried her hands from her body. He caught her fingers in his and squeezed gently. "You are a beautiful woman, and I have no intention of allowing any of that beauty to remain hidden while you are in my keeping."

"I have to have permission to put clothes on?" she asked incredulously.

He stared wordlessly at her, telling her in no uncertain terms what he thought of that question.

"Okay, okay," she grumbled.

"Come with me," he ordered.

He put his hand to her back and urged her forward. Her bare feet padded across the wooden floor, and while before she had gravitated toward him, to the warmth and security of his body, she now kept a foot of distance between them. Self-preservation.

She wasn't sure why she suddenly quaked with uncertainty, but now that she was on his turf, doubt niggled at her.

They entered what was obviously the master bedroom. It was huge, a suite. In the center, a king-sized bed rested. It was a mahogany, four-poster frame that dominated the space. Everything else in the room was secondary to this centerpiece.

To the left a large armoire stood flush against the wall. The wood was a match to the bed, in fact, to all the furnishings in his house. Rich, dark woods. Masculine and warm.

"Sit there on the bed," he told her.

She walked to the edge and perched gingerly, hands clasped in her lap. He moved with grace and elegance that was a contradiction to the rough, animalistic way he'd fucked her mouth just an hour before. He was indeed a contradiction, one that intrigued her. Outwardly he seemed so civilized, so refined. He was the epitome of culture, a consummate gentleman. And yet there was a caveman buried under the polished exterior. A man driven by his needs and desires. A man who quite simply wouldn't accept less.

He opened the armoire, and she heard a slight rustle. A moment later he turned around, a small package in his hand. Curious, she stared as he opened the box and pulled out a gold circlet.

The bed dipped as he settled beside her, not one but two bands in his grip.

"Turn around and look at me," he directed.

She shifted and turned, bending one leg and dangling the other over the side of the bed.

"I opted not to use a collar on you."

Her hand flew to her neck as her eyes widened. She knew of the practice of collaring slaves, but it seemed so . . . barbaric.

"However, I am greatly pleased by the idea of you wearing the mark of my ownership, so I bought these."

He held up the cuffs, opening one. His free hand trailed up her arm and stopped midway between her elbow and her shoulder. Then he clasped the cuff around her arm, the metal cool against her flesh.

It was a beautiful piece of jewelry. Feminine and thin. Not thick or bulky. It was about two inches wide with intricate designs etched onto the face. And it fit her perfectly.

He reached down and caught her foot in his hand and raised it to his lap. Again, his fingers trailed over her flesh, sensual and soft. He opened the other cuff and secured it around her leg, just above her ankle. The anklet was a perfect match to the one on her arm, and it conjured images of a harem girl, adorned in gold, as she danced for her sultan.

"For as long as you belong to me, you will wear my mark," he said. "You won't remove them, not even to bathe."

She glanced at her arm and then down to her ankle. She felt exotic, not at all like herself, and wasn't that the purpose of this? To step outside herself and live a fantasy?

Another giggle threatened to escape, and she swallowed it back. How absurd was this? She was sitting naked on the bed next to a man who'd just shackled her for all practical purposes. Shackled her and commanded her to stay naked while she was in his presence.

Clearly she was loopy.

"First, a shower," Damon said as he studied her closely. "I'll have a tray brought up, and we'll eat in bed afterward."

"Tray brought up?" she croaked. Did he have servants who would be witness to her nakedness? To the fact she was acting as his slave? Good lord, would he want to have sex with her in plain view of anyone walking by?

"You're starting to panic," he reprimanded. "Relax and allow me to take care of you, Serena."

She inhaled deeply through her nose and then let it out in a long exhale. "I'm sorry. I won't question you again."

He smiled. "Yes, you will. Of that I'm sure."

She raised an eyebrow, intrigued by the satisfied glint in his eyes. "And what will you do?"

"I have my methods of punishment," he said in a silky, sexy-as-hell voice.

"You're not exactly encouraging me to be good," she murmured.

He shook his head. "No games, Serena. That isn't what this is about. If you want games of cat and mouse, disobedient slave to punishing master, you're better off with someone else. As much as this is a fantasy and not your reality, in the time you're with me, it will be real. In all ways.

"I want your obedience. I expect it—no, I demand it. I don't relish nor will I enjoy the idea of punishing you. So if you seek to bait me so that you enjoy the thrill of discipline, you're sure to be disappointed."

She nodded. "I understand." She glanced down at the band circling her arm again. Unable to resist, she raised her other hand to touch the beautiful designs. "Why did you choose this instead of a collar?"

"Because I want you to wear the sign of my ownership in public as well as private, and a collar . . . I don't seek to embarrass you, nor do I desire to make our relationship public. It's a private matter between the two of us and not open for speculation. All that matters to me is that you know that you belong to me. What others think or not is irrelevant. I'm not so insecure that I need you to overtly scream to the world that you are my slave."

Her chest squeezed, and without thinking, she leaned in and wrapped her arms around his shoulders. She buried her face in his neck and hugged him tightly.

"Thank you," she said, clearing her throat to get rid of the catch.

His hand swept up her arm to rest on the band. "You're welcome. I like seeing the evidence of my possession on your body. It pleases me and will please me every time I look at you and see my gift on your arm and your leg. I need no satisfaction beyond that."

Slowly he pulled her away and then stood, taking her hand with him. He tugged until she rose to stand beside him.

"Come now so I can see to your shower."

She looked at him in surprise, but he just smiled in return.

"In time you'll learn that I'm very serious when I say that I plan to see to all aspects of your care and keeping."

CHAPTER 14

Serena stood in the shower under the spray of water as Damon undressed outside the glass door. Her gaze was drawn to his muscular body. Lean, hard, perfectly tanned with not a single flash of whiter skin.

His cock was impressive even in its semierect state, set amidst the dark hair at his groin. This was a man who clearly took care of himself, and it didn't detract from his manliness whatsoever.

He was, in a word, beautiful. Rugged. All male. He wasn't a knuckles-dragging-the-ground he-man Neanderthal type with more muscles than brains. He was several inches taller than her, but not so tall that she had to strain to look up at him.

He stepped inside the shower, and before he ever touched her, her body went on alert. Her nipples beaded and strained outward as though begging for his touch. Her pussy pulsed and tightened. She wanted him. Her need was powerful and overwhelming.

There was nothing sexual about his ministrations as he gently set about washing her. His long fingers glided over her skin, spreading soap bubbles in their wake. When he'd covered every inch of her body, including her most intimate areas, he turned his attention to her hair.

Methodically, he lathered her hair, massaging her scalp with firm fingers. After he'd rinsed, he worked in conditioner and gently pushed her back away from the spray.

Then he handed her soap. "Now you will wash me. Use only your hands. I would feel your touch on all parts of my body."

Her pulse skittered and jumped like a drunk trying to play hopscotch. With trembling fingers she took the soap and worked it in her hands until she had a good lather. She set the soap aside and tentatively put her hands to Damon's chest.

He closed his eyes the moment she touched him. Emboldened by his response, and her own pleasure at touching him, she began to stroke her hands over his shoulders. Then down to his taut abdomen.

She skipped his groin and his now turgid erection and soaped both his legs. When she knelt on the floor of the shower to soap his feet, his hand touched her head.

She glanced up, worried that she'd done something wrong, but she saw approval shining brightly in his eyes.

"You kneeling at my feet, so sweetly, as you wash them . . . it's quite beautiful, Serena. You are beautiful."

She ducked her head, suddenly shy and self-conscious. She finished his feet and then worked her way back up to his groin. His cock bobbed in front of her, and when she would have stood, she remembered how pleased he'd looked when she went to her knees. And so she merely hoisted herself higher on her knees so that his cock was eye-level and she closed her hands around it.

It was hot against her skin, hotter than the water cascading over them both. It pulsed slightly against her palm as she rubbed back and forth. When she reached the base, she slid her fingers beyond to his sac. His balls rolled against her palm, and she marveled at the softness of the skin, the pliability, and how swollen they were as his cock jutted outward above them.

She wanted to take him in her mouth again and pleasure him. A light tap to her cheek made her blink and look upward. Was she so transparent?

"Use only your hands this time," he said in a raspy voice.

He reached up to direct the nozzle away from them and then guided her hand back to his straining erection.

She worked back and forth, moving the foreskin as far up the bulbous head as she could before pulling it away, revealing the smooth top again.

"Harder," he urged.

She readily complied, tightening her grip and moving more rapidly.

Then suddenly, he yanked himself from her grasp. With one hand, he shoved her arms down while he jerked at his cock with the other. She gasped when the first hot jet exploded onto her chest.

He continued to pull as he leaned closer to direct his cum onto her breasts. Some landed at the hollow of her throat and slid downward, slithering between her breasts and down to her navel.

One thick rope traveled to the tip of her breast, coated the rigid nipple and dangled precariously before dripping to the shower floor.

Damon pulled upward on his cock and leaned farther in, pushing at her mouth. "Open," he said hoarsely.

She complied, and he slid in with ease. His cum coated the head of his penis, and as he pumped deep into her mouth, she swallowed away the last of it.

"That's it," he whispered. "Clean me, Serena mine."

For several long seconds he rocked up on his toes, rhythmically fucking her mouth as his cock continued to soften. Finally, he pulled away and reached for her hand to help her up.

With an arrogant look of satisfaction he gazed at the trail of cum covering her chest.

"Bathe yourself with it," he murmured. "Rub me all over your body and know that you are mine."

Hesitantly, she raised her hands and then looked down at the sticky cream on her breasts and down her belly. She put one hand to her skin first and cautiously rubbed in a tight circle.

Damon's breath hitched and his cock bobbed upward, already recovering from his orgasm.

With growing confidence, she placed her other hand to her wet breast and began massaging the fluid over her skin. She swayed sensuously as she rubbed and caressed.

Her body was hypersensitive to her every touch. He'd driven her so close to her release just by attaining his own. He hadn't touched her to bring her to orgasm in any way, but yet she verged on the brink. Hovering. Aching. So close. So very close. If she could just get her hands lower . . .

Strong hands gripped her wrists, and he pulled her hands away from her skin. Without a word, he directed the water so that it poured over her body, and he began to rinse the conditioner from her hair.

Again, with no attempt to arouse, he washed her until her hair was clean and the remnants of his orgasm were gone from her skin.

"Stay here," he said as he turned the water off and stepped from the shower.

She watched as he quickly dried his naked body. He wiped the last of the moisture from his skin and then gave his hair a quick tussle before tossing the towel aside and picking up another.

He reached in to take her hand and drew her out of the shower. He started with her hair, squeezing the excess water from the strands. Then he worked down, patting her skin with the soft towel.

When he was finished, he dropped the towel and pulled her against the warmth of his body. He cradled her perfectly. They meshed so well, her softness conforming to his harder planes.

He just stood there, his heart beating softly against her throat. His hands smoothed deliciously over her back and down to her buttocks before traveling up her arms. His right hand came to rest at the cuff she wore on her left arm, and he stroked it for a moment, as if pleased by the ornament she wore. For him.

"Come, it's time to feed you and put you to bed."

She bristled the slightest bit because he made her sound like a pet or even a child. But as his hands moved sensuously over her shoulders as he turned her in the direction of the bedroom, those thoughts, and her irritation, fled.

To her relief, the tray of food was already delivered and sitting on a table by the bed, which meant she didn't have to face any hired help in the nude. The sheets and covers had been pulled back and the pillows repositioned at the head of the bed.

Damon, it seemed, did indeed like his creature comforts.

He gestured for her to climb onto the bed, and it was only after she crawled onto the plush mattress that she saw the rope and satin cuffs secured to the bedpost on her side of the bed.

She glanced back uncertainly at Damon, but his expression didn't change. He expected obedience, and his stance didn't offer any alternative.

He waited until she turned around and settled against the pillows before he reached for her left hand. She watched in shocked fascination as he pulled the rope with the cuff from the bedpost and secured the cuff around her wrist. Silently, he captured her other hand and brought it around to the small of her back where he secured it with the other cuff so that her hands were bound together behind her.

She wasn't even going to ask the obvious question of how the hell she was going to eat, because after his speech and countless reminders of how he would take care of her every need, she had a suspicion of just how she was going to consume her food.

"Are you comfortable?" he asked as he stood by the bed.

She nodded. And she was. The bed was wonderfully soft. Not too soft, though. It molded to her body, contouring perfectly as it cradled her. It would be heaven to sleep on.

Satisfied with her response, he walked around to the other side where the dinner tray sat, and he sat on the bed beside her. After spending a few moments preparing a plate from the dishes arranged on the cart, he then scooted back against the pillows and sat cross-legged, the plate resting on his lap.

It smelled wonderful.

There was roasted chicken with scalloped potatoes and a decadent looking chocolate dessert waiting on the side.

Damon cut into the chicken, arranging bite-sized portions on the plate. When he was finished, he forked one of the pieces and held it to her lips.

For a moment she simply stared at him, wondering why she

didn't feel ill at ease at what he proposed to do. He waited, patiently, the chicken resting lightly on her bottom lip. Finally she opened her mouth, and he carefully slid the fork inside.

How strange that he could make the act of feeding her, as though she were helpless, so intimate and loving. There was such tenderness to his actions, such regard for her, that she couldn't muster any discomfort over him feeding her while she sat there, bound and naked, in his bed.

Even more curious was the way he made her crave his attention. As soon as he gave her one bite, she hungered for another, not because of the food but because of his regard.

He alternated feeding her with taking his own part of the meal. She watched the bites slide into his mouth, watched his lips run over the tines of the fork that her mouth had touched. His warmth still lingered on the metal when he next placed it in her mouth.

When it slid from her lips, clean, he trailed it gently down her chin, down the column of her neck and to her chest. The tines were lightly abrasive, scratching along her skin, eliciting a shiver in their wake.

He topped the rise of her breast and ever so lightly skimmed the tip over her nipple. Her shoulders shook, making her breasts bob, which rubbed her nipple rapidly across the fork.

When he pulled it away, her breaths were coming in shallow bursts. How much more teasing could she take before the need for her orgasm drove her to insanity? She ached. Her pussy ached. Her breasts strained, so tight and sensitive that each brush across them was agonizing.

He returned to his plate, carefully picking at the remainder of the food. He fed her three more bites before pushing the cart away from the bed.

When he rolled back over to face her, he reached behind her back to free her hands. But before she could pull them in front of her, he merely repositioned her arms over her head and refastened the cuffs around her wrists.

"Find a comfortable position," he directed.

As best as she could, she shimmied down until she was lying on her back, her head nestled among the pillows. He tested her bonds and instructed her to roll right and then left. Satisfied that she could move freely, he pulled away and ran his hand freely down her body.

He rested on his side next to her, his head propped in his palm as he regarded her with contented eyes.

"Before we go to sleep, I thought I should acquaint you with more of my expectations so that you aren't taken by surprise," he said.

She raised an eyebrow at that. He'd been pretty darn clear in what he expected. What else could there be? But she didn't voice that thought, and she waited for him to continue.

He smiled. "You wanted to object. I admire your restraint, but more than that, I am pleased by your desire to please me."

Not knowing what to say to that or if he required a response, she remained silent.

"Sex," he said. "Your body is mine to do with what I want. This means that I take you when I want, how I want, sometimes with your pleasure in mind, sometimes with mine. It is at my discretion as to when you achieve satisfaction."

He waited as though expecting her to speak, but she was figuring this out pretty quickly. He wanted compliance, and so she would give it to the best of her ability.

Again, he looked pleased when she merely waited for him to continue.

"It is a particular pleasure of mine to have sex when I awaken, when my mind is still clouded with sleep but my body craves the sweetness of a woman. I'll mount you while you are tied to my bed, helpless to do anything but give me what I demand."

She closed her eyes and pressed her thighs together to try and alleviate the burn. He was going to make her come with no more than his voice.

A finger trailed over the swell of her breast and then circled her puckered nipple.

"You questioned me about why I wanted you nude at all times. Part of the reason is that I find the female body the truest form of art. I like to enjoy it. I like to gaze upon it, especially when I know it belongs to me. The main reason, however, is that I intend to enjoy unimpeded access to your body. I like the idea of being able to fuck you when I want, how I want. I can enjoy your mouth, your pussy and your ass with little more than the effort it takes to bend you over the couch, or my chair or my lap. As you walk by, I can reach out and take you. I can press you against the wall and take you from behind. You won't deny me. I won't allow it. Unless you are injured or ill. Or you say no. Once you say no, it ends.

"So you see, Serena, despite all the power you have ceded me, it still rests very much in your hands. You have complete and utter control over your fantasy because with one word, it all ends."

She was balanced precariously on the edge of the sharpest of orgasms. She was going to come despite the fact that he hadn't touched her more intimately than on her breasts. Flash images of him taking her in all the ways he described battered her mind. Her body swelled and quivered. Oh God, it was coming, and there wasn't a damn thing she could do about it.

As she fought the inevitable, suddenly Damon was over her,

spreading her legs with urgent hands. He rammed into her, and her gasp of surprise quickly became a shrill cry of release. As soon as his cock reached its depths within her, her orgasm exploded with vicious ferocity.

Her vision blurred as he humped over her body, his hips pummeling hers with speed and strength. Her body wasn't her own. It had broken into tiny little pieces, sharp and jagged. Pleasure foamed in her groin, swelling and splintering outward, and still he thrust. Deeper. Harder. Unmerciful.

Her pussy, tender and hypersensitive as it came down from her orgasm, protested as Damon's cock dragged back and forth over the swollen tissues.

She moaned low in her throat, unsure of whether it was pain or pleasure that stabbed at her.

"Please," she said hoarsely, but she wasn't sure whether she was begging him to stop or not to stop.

"Your body is mine," he said. "I take what is mine."

"Yes, yours," she murmured.

Faster he rocked against her hips, forcing her body up the bed until her bound hands slapped at the headboard with each thrust.

He reached underneath her and cupped her buttocks, tilting her upward as he plunged forward again. She gasped as he came to rest deeply within her.

Liquid heat filled her womb. His hips jerked spasmodically against her as he quivered with his release. For the longest time he remained locked within her as she sucked the last of his cum into her womb.

His body fell like a blanket over hers. He buried his face in her neck as he struggled for breath. There she lay, her hands above her head, her legs spread wide as the man who owned her lay between her thighs, her body full of his seed.

He was still hard within her, and he made no move to withdraw from her pussy.

"Sleep, Serena," he murmured against her neck as his teeth nipped affectionately at her skin. "Tonight I'll sleep buried inside you to remind you of my ownership. In the morning, after I've taken you again, I'll bathe you and wash my seed from your body."

CHAPTER 15

*D*uring the course of the night, Damon eased off her and rolled to the side. She registered it with hazy lethargy before falling back asleep.

When she next awoke, it was to urgent hands fumbling at her body, sliding over her breasts and down to her hips. Her eyes fluttered open as Damon moved over her even as he spread her legs wide and impatiently stabbed his cock at her opening.

In his impatience he bumped against her clit before repositioning himself. Then he found her entrance and slid deep, eliciting a gasp from her as she came fully awake. The remnants of last night's interlude were dried on the inside of her thighs, but what remained inside her pussy, warm and wet, eased his passage.

Her arms strained at her bonds, but he held tight, and she was helpless beneath him as he sought to avail himself of her body.

There was no finesse to his movements, no attempt to pleasure her equally, but oddly, she was very much turned on by the roughness and crudity of his motions. Even as he thrust deeper and harder, his eyes clenched shut and his jaw tight, her pussy bloomed with fire.

She watched the strain of his muscles as each movement rippled through him. His hands clenched desperately at her waist, her hips, and then again at her waist as he buried himself repeatedly in her body.

The vulnerability of her position, how helpless she felt, ignited fierce arousal. He was using her. There was no other word to describe his actions, and yet she felt oddly content. Powerful, even.

He pressed her deeper into the bed as his tanned buttocks rose and fell over her. Flesh against flesh, the only sound that echoed through the room was the harsh slap of his body meeting hers and the soft grunts that somehow escaped his tightly closed mouth.

He spread her wide as he arched over her one last time. She could no longer control her cry when he drove impossibly deep.

Instead of retreating, he held firmly against her as he emptied himself into her. She could feel him in every inch of her pussy. She was stretched so tight around his cock, and her body was already sensitive and sore from the previous night.

Her clit quivered and pulsed, and she ached for release, but she lay there quietly, her body a receptacle for his.

With a sound of regret, he finally slid from her in a rush of fluid. As he knelt between her legs, he pulled at her knees, spreading her pussy wide.

He gazed down at her, supreme satisfaction glinting in his dark eyes.

"You're so beautiful," he said. "Your pussy is so swollen and red and glistening with my cum."

He slid one finger inside her opening and then withdrew, holding his finger up so she could see. Then he leaned down and traced a line around her mouth, leaving a damp trail on her lips.

"Lick them," he whispered. "Lick my cum from your lips, Serena mine."

Slowly she obeyed and ran her tongue over first her bottom lip and then around the corner and over her top lip.

"You have pleased me," he said.

She smiled tremulously, too shaky, too edgy with need to speak.

"Would you like to come, Serena?" he asked in a low, silky voice.

"Please," she whispered.

He reached above her head to release her hands. He caught them in his and gently lowered them to her belly.

"Okay?" he asked.

She nodded even as she flexed her hands to return the feeling to her fingers.

He took her left hand and lowered it to her pussy. "Touch yourself," he said huskily. "Make yourself come while I watch."

He scooted down the bed until he got off and stood at the foot, his gaze never leaving her. A little nervously, she slid her hand between her legs and parted her labia.

Her flesh was slick with his cum, and her fingers moved easily through her folds.

It wasn't as though she was a stranger to masturbation, but she'd certainly never done it with an audience. Still, she wanted—needed—to come so badly that she didn't care who was watching.

She rolled her middle finger over her clitoris, moaning as

her entire body tightened. She found her sweet spot and rotated in a tight circle as her pussy pulsed and clenched in response.

Damon walked around to the side of the bed, his gaze fastened on her groin. When he reached her side, he lowered his dark head and latched on to her nipple with his teeth.

Her back arched off the bed, and her finger worked faster over her clit. He nipped sharply, sucking and biting with enough force that it caused delicious pain.

Her breathing rose sharply as her body wound like a rubber band. Tighter and tighter. She stroked faster and he sucked harder until she writhed uncontrollably. Up and down her hips rose and fell, as if she were actually being fucked.

Then his teeth sank sharply into her nipple, and she simply broke. In one sudden burst she catapulted over the edge and her orgasm flashed like a bomb around her.

For a moment her hand moved in a frenzy and then the sensation became too much. She slowed her movements and rubbed more leisurely as she worked down from her orgasm. Damon raised his mouth from her breast and then simply laid his head over her chest.

With her free hand, she tentatively touched his brow, smoothing her fingers over his skin and into his hair. When she traced a line to his temple, and down his jaw to his mouth, he kissed her fingertips when she brushed over his lips.

"Ah, you please me, Serena mine," he murmured against her breast.

She smiled faintly, too boneless to do more. "You please me too, Damon."

He raised his head with obvious reluctance. "Come and I'll bathe you. Then we'll go down for breakfast."

CHAPTER 16

*A*fter a leisurely shower in which Damon once again took charge and washed every inch of her body, he dried her and then positioned her between his legs on the bed while he brushed her hair.

It crackled and shone by the time he put the brush down, and he ran his hands through the tresses.

"Your hair is beautiful. I don't think I've ever seen hair so black and shiny."

She smiled in pleasure as he continued to stroke her hair with light touches.

He got up from the bed and held his hand out to her. He pulled her to her feet and stepped away to examine her. Her nudity didn't bother her as much as it had the night before. That is until they started for the kitchen, and she remembered that he employed a full staff.

When Sam passed them in the living room, she quickly ducked behind Damon and huddled against his back. Sam merely nodded as Damon said good morning and continued on toward the front door.

When he was gone, Damon turned and gently pried her hand away from his back.

"I realize this is new to you, and that is why I'll be patient, but you aren't to ever hide your body."

"But you said that you were the only one who would enjoy, who would see . . ."

He held up a finger to her lips. "Only I will touch you, Serena. Only I will hold you. Only I will possess you. The people in my employ are discreet and they will not stare. In time, it won't bother you to be nude in front of them."

She opened her mouth to protest again, but he effectively hushed her. "These are my wishes. You will heed them."

The word *no* hovered precariously on her lips, but she remembered well that he'd said the moment she said no, it was over. He'd been honest with her. Told her he'd push her, that he was demanding and arrogant. But she could say no. And if she did, he would back down immediately. The downside would be that she would lose everything. Her fantasy. Her chance to satisfy her deepest desires and cravings.

"Yes," she whispered.

He smiled and took her hand in his as he leaned in to brush his lips across hers. He squeezed her hand when he kissed her, showing her with more than words that she'd pleased him with her response.

A giddy thrill fluttered in her chest. She did want to please him. Wanted it badly.

He gave her hand one last squeeze and then tugged her toward the kitchen. They passed a formal dining room on their way to the large gourmet kitchen. It was absolutely gorgeous and almost made her wish she cooked. Almost. That was one skill she'd never really mastered, and she wasn't too torn up about it either.

There was a smaller table in a cozy little alcove in front of a bay window that thankfully had shutters, closed shutters. Breakfast was already laid out for them, a selection of bagels, toast, grits, eggs and biscuits. And juice. Orange and grape.

Then she saw that there was only one chair. She frowned and glanced at the floor. Surely he wouldn't expect her to sit on the floor.

He sighed and ushered her forward. He pulled the chair out and sat before tugging her down onto his lap. He settled her crossways so her side rested against his chest.

"Will you always feed me?" she asked. It seemed okay at times, but every time? It would grate on her nerves after a while.

"I'll feed you when it pleases me to do so," he said simply. "And it pleases me this morning."

She had to smile. He could be infuriating if she let him get to her. He was a calm bastard. Calm and convinced. She just loved a confident man. Borderline arrogant was even better, but then nothing about him was borderline. He was absolutely arrogant, all male, sexy as freaking hell and he fucked like a dream.

She made a little contented noise and burrowed deeper into his chest.

"Do you prefer grape or orange juice?" he asked.

"I'd love grape."

He poured the juice in a small glass and then brought it to her lips, tilting it just enough that she could sip the fluid without spilling it. After several long swallows, he pulled it away.

"Get enough?"

She nodded and licked the juice from her lips.

He alternated giving her bites of the eggs and then the grits. Then he'd break off a piece of biscuit and hold it to her lips. Often he'd gently wipe his finger on her tongue, and even that became an exercise in the sensual. Who knew that the act of being fed could be so intimate?

She noticed that he hadn't eaten much yet, and she was nearly full, which gave her an idea. She was, after all, supposed to be his slave, but so far he'd treated her like he was the slave and she was royalty or something.

When he next offered her a bite of the biscuit, she put out her hand to stay his. Surprise rippled across his face when she took the bread from his fingers and slowly pressed it to his lips.

He opened his mouth, and she slid her fingers in, letting the bread crumble on his tongue and the tips of her finger brush his warmth. As she withdrew, he closed his mouth around her finger and sucked lightly.

Damn, but now she knew why he liked feeding her so much. Encouraged by his response and the fact that he hadn't indicated she'd overstepped her boundaries, she reached for the fork and speared a piece of egg.

She guided the fork to his mouth and gently fed him the morsel.

"Your fingers," he said as she pulled the fork away. "Use your fingers."

With a smile, she reached down and swiped her finger through the grits and quickly raised it to his mouth. Some dribbled onto his chin when she wasn't fast enough, and after he'd sucked her finger clean, she leaned up and licked away the spot on his skin.

He sucked in his breath and tensed against her. Oh yeah, she liked this feeding thing.

When she reached for the juice to hold it to his mouth, he put a hand on her wrist. "What are you doing?" he asked. There was no reprimand in his voice, just mild curiosity.

"I'm your slave," she said. "Am I not supposed to care for you? See to your needs?"

Something flashed in his eyes. Primitive and dark. His pupils flared and dilated for a brief moment before returning to their normal size.

As she moved the glass closer, he parted his lips for her to let him drink. His gaze never left her as he sipped at the juice. When she pulled it away, she reached up and gently wiped at a small droplet at the corner of his mouth.

He caught her hand and pressed a kiss to her palm.

"You like being fed," she said.

One corner of his mouth quirked upward in a smile. "No one has ever offered to take care of me before. I find I rather like it."

She touched his cheek and stroked lightly over his strong jawline. "Then I hope we can make this a two-way street. I very much want to please you, not only by ceding to your wishes but by taking care of you and seeing to your needs as you see to mine."

He looked stunned by her declaration. Confusion swirled for a moment before he blinked and it cleared away. It appeared that she'd struck him speechless, but he also seemed inordinately pleased by her request.

"I'd like that very much," he said in a low voice.

She couldn't hide her smile. He reached out and brushed his fingers across her lips.

"You have such a beautiful, open smile," he said. "It lights up your entire face and makes your eyes turn the most spectacular shade of blue."

For the longest time they simply stared at one another, their gazes locked as if each was searching deep into the other's soul.

Finally, he touched her cheek and dipped his head, moving first one way and, when she moved, adjusting again so that their lips were in line. When he had her just where he wanted, he put both hands to her face and held her as he lowered his lips to hers.

It was so much more than she'd anticipated. The first touch of his lips was like an electric shock to her very depths. It was the lightest of touches. So exquisitely gentle that she sighed into his mouth.

He treated her like a piece of finely blown glass. His tongue, tentative at first, licked at her lips, coaxing her to open to his advances. She readily complied, parting her lips to allow him entry.

The sweet taste of grape juice filled her mouth as their tongues dueled. This was no passionate, urgent kiss, no mauling of mouths. Rather, it was warm and slow, lazy like a hot summer day.

Comfort. If there was a word to describe the feeling that flooded her heart, it would be comfort. Companionship. Trust. How odd that these were the things that sprang to mind as she gave herself over to the delicious sensations that his lips plied her with.

They both gasped for breath but neither pulled away. Her arms twined around his neck as his hands framed her face to pull her closer still. Light smooching sounds echoed, the soft click of lips on lips, tongues against tongues.

This was more than master and slave, hot sex, rip-roaring fantasies. There was a tangible connection being forged in this moment—one she didn't want to break. There was so much feeling behind this kiss that she wanted it to go on forever.

Starved for air, she broke away long enough to gulp in a breath before he reclaimed her mouth. His lips glanced off hers and landed at the corner of her mouth. He peppered a line of kisses down her jaw and to the tender skin below her ear and lower to her neck.

She closed her eyes and tilted her head up to give him better access as he worked to the front of her throat. Slowly, he slid his tongue and lips upward again until he nibbled at her chin and then finally came back to her mouth where he kissed her harder this time, with more savagery.

This was a kiss, like none she'd ever received. No quick peck. No messy, sloppy mesh of tongues. No clumsy slapping of lips together. The man could seriously kiss.

"I could do this all morning," he murmured as he pulled slightly away. His breath came heavy, and she could see he was affected as she was.

"Mmmm, me too," she said as she cuddled back into his arms.

"Did you get enough to eat?"

She nodded against him. "You?"

He stroked his hand down her arm. "Yes, thanks to you. I think I could get used to being a kept man."

She grinned. "You're too much of a control freak to ever be a kept man."

"You doubt your abilities, Serena mine. A man would have to be crazy to object to a woman such as you taking care of him. I find myself looking forward more than ever to the month ahead."

Her cheeks warmed as she basked in his words. She'd had her share of relationships. Flings and all things in between, but she'd never felt as appreciated as she did in the short time she'd been with Damon. It made absolutely no sense to her that they could have this sort of connection so fast, but she couldn't doubt its legitimacy.

He made her want to go that extra mile to make him happy. She wanted his approval, wanted to see his eyes flash in satisfaction.

"I need to get you dressed," he announced.

She leaned back and raised one eyebrow. "What happened to keeping me naked at all times?"

He laughed. "As appealing a prospect as that is, I can't take you out in public wearing only the jewelry I gave you." His hand slid playfully to her rump, and he gave her a light squeeze. "I'm taking you shopping for appropriate clothing for the next month."

"Hmm, a man who likes to shop. What on earth is this world coming to?"

"Not only do I like to shop, but I like to spend money on my woman," he said with a wink.

"For that I'll gladly get dressed," she said as she grinned broadly at him.

As he started to move her from his lap, she suddenly remembered that she was supposed to call Julie. And knowing Julie, she would indeed have the cops beating on Damon's door if Serena didn't check in.

"Crap," she muttered. "Damon, I need to use the phone. My friend Julie. You met her at Cattleman's. She was sorta worried that you were going to kill me last night so unless I call her, she's going to call the police and have them knock on your door."

Damon threw back his head and laughed. "By all means, call your friend. She sounds like quite the tigress."

Serena smiled. "She means well, and she has a big heart, even if her mouth is bigger."

"I'll leave you to your phone call then. I'll go up and get your change of clothes from your bag."

He moved her from his lap and stood. "I'll take you into my office so you have privacy."

This time she readily threaded her fingers into his as he walked her out of the kitchen and across the living room. He showed her into a smaller room off the living room and gestured toward his desk.

"Take as much time as you need. I'll be in the living room, so just come out when you're done."

He dropped a kiss on her forehead and then turned and strode out of the room, shutting the door behind him.

CHAPTER 17

*S*atisfied that her friend was still alive and kicking, Julie hung up the phone. Serena wasn't giving any details, but she sounded pretty darn cheerful for someone who'd just spent her first night in slavery. Not for the first time, Julie wondered if she'd given the whole submission thing a bum rap.

Nah.

She shook her head and eyed the phone with trepidation. Serena had asked if Julie had called Nathan yet, and of course Julie had lied and said yes. She couldn't have Serena thinking she was a chicken even if she was growing feathers and developing a cluck.

When had she become such a coward?

She grabbed her cell phone and punched in the number that Nathan had left as his personal contact when he filled out his card at the salon. She had no idea where the hell she was calling. She only hoped it was private.

Cursing her nervousness, she put the phone to her ear and

listened to it ring. After the third ring, the call connected, and she sucked in her breath.

"Nathan Tucker."

"Nathan. Uh, hi, this is Julie Stanford from, um, the salon . . . the massage place."

God, could she sound like a bigger moron? To make matters worse, there was a long pause on the line like he was trying to place her.

"Julie, hi. Hey, I'm sorry I haven't called to reschedule. I just got busy."

"No," she said quickly. "I mean that's not why I'm calling. I, um . . . I wanted to thank you for driving me home the other night."

"Not a problem. I was glad to do it," he said with easy charm.

"There's one other thing," she hedged.

"I'm listening."

She closed her eyes and shook her head. "Did anything happen that night? I mean did I act inappropriately?"

Jesus, Mary and Joseph, she sounded like some sleazy politician apologizing for being caught out with a hooker.

"I don't understand," Nathan said. She could hear the genuine confusion in his voice.

"Did I jump you? Rape you? Did we have sex?" she asked impatiently.

"Good lord, no."

Well, he needn't sound so appalled.

"Then how . . . why did I end up naked in my bed?" she asked quietly.

"Goddamn it!" Nathan roared.

Julie jumped and held the phone away from her ear.

More muttered cursing ensued, muffled, as he no doubt was

holding the phone to his shirt. Then more rattling and he came back on.

"Sorry, not you." Then he broke away and shouted again. "Micah, you motherfucker, I'm going to kick your ass this time."

"Look, I've obviously caught you at a bad time," Julie said loudly, hoping he'd hear.

"No, I'm sorry. Micah and his friggin' practical jokes. About the other night . . . Nothing happened, Julie. If I had any idea you'd be worried, I would have called you. You were sort of out of it so I put you to bed. Someone spilt beer on your shirt and so I stripped you down. I didn't even look at you, I swear."

"Well, why the hell not?" she asked in exasperation. "Am I that ugly?"

"*What?* No. Hell, what the hell?" he sputtered.

It was obvious he didn't have a clue whether to shit or go blind.

"I'll let you go," she muttered.

"Wait, Julie, don't go yet."

She pulled the phone away from her ear and punched the End button. Then, as mortification boiled over her, she powered the phone off, just in case he had any ideas about calling back.

Laying the phone aside, she closed her eyes and shook her head. Where was a giant hole in the earth when she needed one?

Serena sat in the backseat of Damon's car, nestled close to his side as they drove toward the Galleria. She looked—and felt—beautiful.

Damon had chosen a simple knee-length sleeveless dress and a pair of sandals out of the two outfits she'd brought with her. She'd worn it before, but the dress had never made her feel so utterly feminine.

The cuffs she wore on her arm and above her ankle looked gorgeous. She felt exotic and vibrant with the gold jewelry decorating her skin. That they were the symbol of a man's ownership added even more of a secret thrill.

It didn't take her long to figure out the type of clothing Damon preferred. And she had to hand it to him, he had an excellent eye for what complemented her figure and coloring.

He chose silk skirts, casual, almost like a beach cover-up. Simple camisole-type tops. Several dressier gowns and one formal black sheath.

After choosing appropriate shoes, he took her to a spa where he directed the attendant to give her a complete body pampering package. Even her toenails were painted a feminine pink.

By the time she was finished, there wasn't a tense muscle in her entire body. She was limp and loose, and what she wanted most was to curl into Damon's arms and nap.

He carried the bags with her things in them with his left hand and tucked his right arm around her waist as they left the spa. She leaned into him and marveled at how comfortable they looked and felt together.

"You realize Julie is going to kill you for taking me somewhere else for my pampering," Serena said with a smile in Damon's direction.

Damon grinned. "It was for you that I didn't bring you there. I figured she would interrogate you mercilessly and possibly even kidnap you for your own good."

Serena burst out laughing. "Oh my God, you're probably right. She's completely overbearing, but her heart is certainly in the right place."

"I would say so," he agreed. "She's looking out for your best interests, so I can't fault her for that."

"So what now?" she asked as he ushered her toward his car.

He settled in beside her and gave Sam the order to take them home. Then he turned to look at her. "Now, I take you home and take those clothes off your body. I have a little work to do, but I look forward to having your company while I take care of a few things."

"Are you sure you can concentrate on work when I'm naked?" she asked innocently.

Amusement glittered brightly in his eyes. "If I must work at all, I'd much prefer you to sit at my feet naked rather than fully clothed."

She rolled her eyes. "You're such a caveman beneath all that polish and sophistication."

"And you are my cave girl? Bound to submit to my every desire?"

"Yes, I suppose I am," she murmured.

"That's good to know," he said. "Undo my pants."

She blinked in surprise and cast her gaze down at the bulge in his crotch.

"Get on your knees in front of me and use your mouth to pleasure me," he ordered.

Bubbles of excitement swelled and burst in her pelvis. Her clit was doing a little spasm dance between her legs, pulsing with unquenched need.

"Shall I be crude?" he murmured. "Suck me, Serena mine. See to my pleasure, and when you are through, lick every bit of cum from my dick."

Slowly she crawled over his knees and wedged herself between the seats. Her knees scraped the floorboard as he spread his legs to give her easier access. Nervously, she glanced over her shoulder to look at Sam, but the driver's gaze was focused out the windshield.

"He heard me, you know," Damon said with a slight smile. "He knows precisely what you're going to do."

She frowned up at him. "Why taunt me? You know I'm not comfortable having another person see or hear us."

He cupped her chin. "I'm not taunting you, Serena. I'm acclimating you. I'm teaching you that the only person you need to concern yourself with is me. It doesn't matter what Sam sees or hears. It's my needs you'll see to and me you'll concentrate on. You must learn to block out everything else. Now, unfasten my pants and pleasure me."

She blinked at the power in his voice, at the thread of authority woven into his every word. With shaking hands, she reached for his fly and undid his pants.

His cock shoved impatiently at his boxers, and she pulled down the band. His erection sprang free, bobbing and straining upward toward his tight belly. Her fingers trailed through the crisp hairs surrounding the base as she circled the shaft with her fingers.

Her hair fell forward as she leaned down to take him in her mouth. His fingers tangled at her scalp as he shoved the heavy strands away from her face. Knowing he wanted to watch, she angled her head so that he could see his cock disappearing into her mouth.

She loved his taste. She wasn't new to going down on a guy, but admittedly, it had never been a favorite sexual favor of hers. To be honest, she'd done it out of a sense of obligation, a reciprocal deal, when she'd received oral sex from one of her lovers.

But with Damon she enjoyed it, savored it and even looked

forward to it. Swallowing? Um, never. Not with any of her previous lovers. Somehow, with Damon, it seemed a rejection she wasn't prepared to hand him. Even if he hadn't asked it of her, she would have willingly taken all he had to give.

She wet her lips again as she slid her mouth down his length. Inhaling through her nose, she stifled her urge to gag and held him in the back of her throat before finally releasing him and raising her head until just the tip of his penis rested on her tongue.

His sac lay heavy and swollen at the juncture of his legs. Dotted with short, dark hairs, it posed a contrast to the smooth length of his erection. She caressed his balls, loving the slight roughness, and then gripped the velvety sheath covering his penis.

Up and down she worked her hand, moving in conjunction with her mouth. She followed the motion of her fingers with her lips, chasing them downward and then sliding back up.

Both of his hands now gripped her head. He fisted handfuls of her hair, holding her tight as she sucked and lavished attention on his cock.

His back bowed off the seat, his thighs digging into her waist. His sac bulged and tightened, and his penis hardened until it was a rigid piece of steel in her hand.

As she pulled her mouth away, a drop of pre-cum glistened from the slit on the top of the head. It grew larger and then slowly dribbled over the crown and collided with her hand.

She darted forward and licked it away. He groaned and urged her head back down, raising his hips to meet her halfway.

"Make me come, Serena mine," he said hoarsely.

She took him hard. As ruthlessly as he'd taken her pussy that morning. She tightened her grip on his cock and jerked up and down as her mouth surrounded and swallowed him. Her eyes closed and she surrendered to the pleasure she gave as well as took.

His finger curled into her scalp and suddenly he yanked her down, thrusting hard and deep into her mouth. Hot cum splashed into her mouth, covering her tongue. She swallowed and still more shot down her throat.

As he quivered and twitched beneath her, she eased up and gentled her movements. Lovingly she sucked and soothed with her tongue, lapping every drop of moisture from his cock.

Still holding his pulsing cock in her hand, she let go with her mouth and lowered her head to swipe her tongue over the puckered skin of his sac. His balls rolled beneath her mouth as she captured a stray drop of semen that had spilled onto his skin.

He groaned and stroked his hands through her hair, over her scalp and then over her face. He touched and petted as though he couldn't get enough. Approval was there in each caress, and when she finally looked up, his eyes glowed with contentment.

"How much longer, Sam?" Damon called to the front.

Serena flinched but controlled her embarrassment. She knew why Damon had once again drawn attention to the driver. As he stated, he wanted her to get used to being used whenever and wherever the mood struck him. A curious curl, a tingle almost, did a slow roll through her belly at the idea that Sam could hear but not see everything that went on in the backseat.

"Fifteen minutes, sir."

"Plenty of time," Damon murmured.

She lifted her eyebrow in question as she reconnected with his gaze. "Plenty of time for what?"

"Take off your panties, Serena," he said, ignoring her question. "Do it quickly."

Flushing, she reached down, fumbling with her dress as she

reached for her underwear. Holding on to his leg with one hand, she worked the panties down with her other. It was difficult, wedged between the seats as she was, but she finally wrested her legs free of the material and dropped the underwear on the seat.

Damon smiled. "Now, suck me hard again. You have five minutes. When I'm ready, I want you to climb onto my lap, pull up your dress and sheathe yourself on my dick."

CHAPTER 18

Damon's cock lay at an angle, the tip resting on his abdomen. Carefully, she curled her fingers around it, bringing it upright and to her mouth.

It was warm and softer in her mouth than just a moment ago, but at the first touch of her tongue, it twitched and spasmed. Lovingly, she stroked and sucked, feeling as he gradually hardened again. It took him longer this time, but she coaxed and licked until he was stiff and erect.

Still, she waited for his command.

"Are you ready for me, Serena?"

She nodded, never taking her mouth from his cock.

"Are you wet?"

Again she nodded.

"Show me. Take your hand. Slide it between your legs. Touch yourself and then show me your fingers."

She released his cock and reached down, fumbling with her dress. She was definitely wet. Very wet, and her pussy ached for release. When her fingers slid over her clit, her shoulders shook. Lower, to where her moist center pulsed, she inched her finger until it was adequately coated. She retracted her hand and held it out to Damon.

He captured her wrist in one hand and gently pulled her fingers to his mouth. He put one in his mouth and sucked it inside.

"Come to me," he said in a voice that was deep and honeyed. It mesmerized her.

Clutching at his leg with her free hand, she rose from her perch on the floorboard. He reached for the ends of her dress, lifting as she moved to straddle him. He dropped her wrist and gripped the tops of her thighs, spreading her as he positioned her on his lap.

"Put your hands on the top of the seat," he ordered. "Lean up so I can penetrate you."

She did as he said and lifted herself slightly as he reached underneath her to position his cock.

"Now take me, Serena."

She eased back down, and the head of his dick bumped against her core before finally rimming her entrance and sliding within. His hand gripped her waist, and he pulled her down to meet his upward thrust.

The first shock of his possession nearly sent her orgasm crashing around her, but he cupped her chin and yanked downward until she met his gaze.

"You will come only when I tell you that you may. For now, you'll see to my pleasure."

She sucked in her breath and nodded even as she wondered if she'd be able to prevent something as inevitable as her release.

"Ride me," he said.

Gripping the top of the seat behind his shoulders, she rose

and fell, taking him deep with each downward plunge. He was thick, and she was so tight around him. Her pussy stretched to accommodate him, and she could feel him in every nerve ending.

He released his grip on her waist and slid both his hands up her belly to her breasts. Through the material of her dress, he plucked and tweaked at her nipples until they thrust forward, hard and erect.

"Harder," he urged. "You're running out of time. We'll be home soon and fucking in my driveway as Sam waits for us to get out."

Instead of dousing her ardor, the image he evoked sent a decadent thrill through her system. A warm flush surged through her veins, and for a moment, she was tempted to delay his orgasm until they were, indeed, fucking in the driveway of his home.

"It excites you," he murmured, and as she opened her eyes, she could see he looked pleased.

He ceased toying with her nipples and cupped her shoulders, grinding her down over his cock. After a few moments, he ran his palms down her back until he reached the rumpled hem of her dress resting against his legs.

He tugged until the material came free, and then he reached underneath to cup her ass. His hands weren't gentle as he gripped the globes. His thumbs dug into her sides as he lifted and then pulled her down. His cock hammered at her pussy, stretching her entrance with each thrust.

The car slowed, and she caught her breath as she frantically looked out the window to see that they had pulled up to Damon's house.

"Do not stop," Damon warned. "You will finish this before we get out."

The car stopped and Sam got out. The car shook slightly when he closed his door, but he didn't open the backseat. She could see that he stood with his back to their window, simply waiting for them to finish.

"Fuck me, Serena. Fuck me hard."

She rode him, faster and harder as she stared out the back window of his car.

"Use your hand," he said. "Touch yourself while you fuck me. I want to feel you come around my cock before I empty myself into your womb."

Only too glad to accommodate him, she reached down and yanked impatiently at her dress to move it out of the way. Her fingers found her clit and she immediately began stroking the swollen nub.

His hands tightened around her ass, and his hips bucked upward, fucking her with savage intensity. For all his calm and control, when it came to sex, he was an animal.

"Come," he gasped. "Orgasm for me, Serena. Let me feel you go wet around me."

She moaned. Her mouth went dry and she swallowed rapidly as her hand moved faster, and he pumped harder.

"Yes," she whimpered. "Please don't stop, Damon."

She went crazy in his arms, writhing and bucking as her fire raged stronger. Unbearable pressure built within her, straining to its breaking point.

And then she burst. Scattered like leaves in the wind. She went in a hundred different directions.

Vaguely she registered him holding her, soothing her with gentle hands as he whispered in her ear. Every part of her trembled and shook, almost violent and out of her control.

As she sank onto his chest, he rammed upward one last

time, shaking her body with his strength. And then he stilled. His arms wrapped around her, and he held her tightly to him, both of them spent and shaking.

For the longest time, he merely held her, their bodies still connected. She couldn't move. Could barely process what had just happened.

Then he lifted her slightly and slid out of her pussy. He rolled her to the side so that she sat in the seat with her legs over his lap. He arranged her dress so that it covered her bare flesh, and then moved her legs so that he could fasten himself back up.

He reached over and tapped at the window, and Sam immediately turned to open the door. Damon got out first and then he reached his hand to help Serena out.

Her bare feet hit the hot pavement, and she stood up on shaky legs. But Damon didn't give her time to regain her footing before he simply swept her into his arms and strode toward the house.

She could only imagine what she looked like, and thank God Damon shielded her so well. Her face was buried in his neck, and he held her up and turned into him so that she was afforded as much modesty as possible under the circumstances.

She didn't see who opened the door, only that it was wide when Damon got there. He swept in and carried her toward the bedroom. When he set her down on the bed, she just lay there like a limp noodle, tired and sated.

Warm lips nuzzled her temple as gentle hands smoothed the hair away from her face. He tugged her dress from her body, leaving her naked on the bed. Then he was gone. Given no instructions, she opted to remain where she was, not that she could have moved anyway.

In a moment, Damon returned with a damp cloth. Tenderly, he bathed her thighs and cleaned his seed from between her legs.

"Roll over onto your belly," he said softly.

With his help, she managed to roll until her face was buried in the sheets, her arms splayed wide over the bed. He chuckled.

"Have I worn you out, Serena mine?"

"Mmmm." It was all she could muster.

"Soon you will rest," he murmured.

Soon? That meant he had something in mind. She only hoped it didn't require her to move.

He began to caress her back, his hands rolling and kneading. She moaned in pleasure, the sounds slipping past tired lips.

Up and down her body, from her neck and shoulders to the globes of her ass, he touched, petted and massaged. Then he pulled his hands away and she heard a top being uncapped. Plastic. Warm liquid dribbled down her spine and then his hands returned, rubbing the oil into her skin.

The bed dipped as he crawled onto it beside her. There wasn't an inch of her skin he didn't mark in some way. His touch branded into her flesh, hot and sensual.

Chill bumps beaded and popped down her arms even as exquisite pleasure bathed her body. Julie's massages had nothing on the magic Damon performed.

His palms cupped her bottom, squeezing and plumping, his fingers working ever closer to the cleft between. She inhaled sharply when his finger rimmed her anal entry, feather soft and seeking.

Again she heard the cap being opened. Two fingers spread her ass cheeks, baring her opening. Oil dropped into the cleft, sliding over her skin. His fingers wiped at the lubricant, spreading it and then pressing at her anus.

Her hands gathered the sheets in a ball and she squeezed her eyes shut. Did he mean to fuck her ass now, when she didn't have the strength to possibly formulate any kind of protest? She knew he wouldn't hurt her, but this was something alien to her. She'd never had anal sex before. It hadn't even crossed her radar.

"Relax," he said gently as he probed delicately with his finger.

His finger slid in, and she gasped aloud. Back and forth he slowly worked his finger. It didn't hurt. It felt . . . She wasn't sure what it felt like. It was new. Forbidden and exciting.

As his finger continued to stroke inside, he dribbled more lubricant into her opening until it was slick. Then he added another finger.

She moaned through clenched teeth as he stretched and manipulated her. Was it supposed to feel good? Heat bloomed in her ass and radiated to her pussy until, despite her fatigue, her loins tightened, her clit swelled and the ache of a new orgasm lurked on the horizon.

When he pulled his hand away, she damn near cried out her protest. Before she could turn her head to see if he was leaving her, something else replaced his fingers. It lacked his warmth and was much harder. It felt . . . plastic.

Her eyes flew open as it breached her opening, slick with lubricant but hard and unyielding. Back and forth, barely rimming her entrance, Damon patiently worked the object.

Then her opening widened, stretched tighter around the plastic as he pushed it further inside. It was smaller at the tip but larger as it gained depth.

No longer able to contain her curiosity, she tilted her head up and asked, "What is it?"

Damon's free hand settled on the small of her back. "It's okay, Serena. Trust me. I won't hurt you. I'm inserting a plug. I don't want taking me to be painful for you so you'll wear this for a while."

With that he gave another little push and her opening stretched even further.

"Oh," she gasped.

"Just relax and don't fight it," he murmured. "Trust me not to hurt you. Enjoy it."

For several more seconds he continued the in-and-out motion, each time pressing just a little harder. And then with one firm shove, he lodged it into her anus.

Her head reared off the bed, and she cried out in surprise. Her ass throbbed and burned around the seemingly mammoth plug. Her legs spasmed and seemed to act of their own accord as she fought the intrusion.

Damon's lips pressed to the small of her back as he kissed and murmured soothing words to her.

"It will be all right. Breathe, Serena. It will get better."

"Yeah?" she muttered as she sucked in deep breaths. "Have you ever had one of these up your ass?"

He laughed. "No, I haven't."

"Then don't tell me how it feels," she ground out.

He rolled her until she was lying on her side, facing him. He wore an amused smile as he gazed down at her.

"All right, then you tell me how it feels."

She swallowed as some of the hot buzz abated in her ass. Replacing it was a warm . . . hum. Low and thready, simmering in her veins, like coffee just before it boiled. As worn out as she was, she could totally go for another orgasm about now.

"It feels . . . edgy. Sharp but not unpleasantly so. I feel full.

There is pressure there that makes my skin crawl and feel itchy, like I want something, but I'm not sure what. Does that make sense?"

His hand settled over her hip. "It makes perfect sense. Do you like it? Can you imagine my cock inside your ass?"

Her entire body trembled at the image of Damon riding her, plunging deep into her bowels.

"It feels so big," she said.

He grinned. "I'm bigger."

She closed her eyes and groaned. "How the hell do you think you're going to get your cock in there if you're bigger than that damn plug?"

"Oh, I'll get there," he said, his voice deep and husky. "And you'll love every minute of it, I promise."

"I didn't expect the pleasure," she said as she wrinkled her forehead in confusion.

"Is it pleasurable then?" he asked.

"I honestly don't know if the act itself is pleasurable or if it's because of who is doing it, but yes, it feels . . . good. It's exciting and I feel restless and aching, like I have a need that's unfulfilled."

He moved over her then, pushing her until she lay flat on her back. The pressure in her behind intensified as some of her weight fell on the plug. He positioned her to his liking underneath him, and then he slowly moved down her body until his head was just above her mound.

He spread her legs wide, bending them until her knees hit the mattress. Her pussy was wide open to him, and suddenly she felt small and vulnerable.

He ran a finger through her folds, teasing and light until he came to her pussy entrance. He slid one long finger inside, pressing down until she could feel him touching the plug through the thin barrier of flesh that separated her vagina from her anal entry.

"As much as I want to bury my dick in your sweet pussy, I won't do so now. You're tired and probably sore and if I take you now, it will feel tight because of the plug in your ass. I don't want to cause you any discomfort. But later . . . later I'll show you what it feels like to take two cocks at the same time."

She trembled and shook underneath his questing fingers. How could she be so close to orgasm again?

As he withdrew his finger, he lowered his mouth, nuzzling between her folds until his tongue slid over her clit. Her hips bolted upward as lightning seized her groin.

He parted her further until she lay helpless and open to his mouth. Tiny air currents blew over her most intimate flesh, coupled with the warmer puffs of his breath. His tongue slid erotically from her entrance to the hood protecting her sensitive nub. He licked lightly at her clit, drawing it to a taut peak. Then he sucked it into his mouth, and wave upon wave of electric sensation exploded through her groin.

She arched into him, each movement rocking the plug deep within her ass. Each sensation, like an ocean wave, rolled inward, broke and then fanned out, surging like liquid through her muscles.

Hungrily, he licked and sucked at her pussy like he was starved for sweetness. He circled her entrance once and then again before sliding his tongue inward.

She shuddered and convulsed, but he gripped her hips and held her tightly in place as he gave her pleasure.

In and out, he fucked her with his tongue. Slow and sensuous, as though he were tasting the finest of wines and savoring each sip.

Her orgasm began as a slow curl, a heated wisp rotating deep within her core then fanning out as it grew and billowed, a storm gaining power.

Swelling like a symphony on the cusp of its crescendo, her release built until she could bear it no longer.

"Please," she begged. What she pleaded for she wasn't sure. Mercy? Satisfaction? Relief from the unbearable tension pulling at her body?

And then he whispered, soft and gentle against her moist flesh. "Come, Serena mine. Come for me."

Sweet agony flashed and sped through her pelvis. Her movements were no longer her own. She cried out as her body slammed back against the bed, her legs suddenly wrapped around his shoulders.

Tears slid down her cheeks, and she puzzled over how they got there. She hovered on the brink of consciousness, fighting for the briefest of seconds to remain aware, to not let go of the piercing fragments of her orgasm.

But as the frantic pleasure slowly faded away, replaced by a more lazy sweetness, she let go, no longer able to keep her eyes open.

A thumb brushed across her cheek, wiping away the wetness of her tears, and then she heard his gentle command.

"Sleep, Serena mine. I'll take care of you."

Comforted by that quiet vow, she allowed herself to slip away into the welcoming oblivion that sleep offered.

CHAPTER 19

$\mathcal{D}$amon watched as her eyes fluttered shut, and almost immediately, her breathing became soft and even. She was exhausted.

He smiled and carefully slid his arms underneath her. As he picked her up off the bed, she moaned in protest.

"Shhh," he soothed. "I want you with me, Serena mine. You can rest as soon as I've made you comfortable."

And he did want her with him. The ferocity of his desire to have her near him startled him. But like her, he was indulging in a fantasy. It wasn't real, no matter that he might wish differently.

He carried her from the bedroom and toward the spacious living room where a fire burned in the hearth. Her plush pallet had already been arranged at the foot of his armchair and was several feet from the fire.

Kneeling, he set her naked body on the down-filled, body-sized cushion. She murmured sleepily, but curled into a ball and fell back into a deep sleep. He stroked a hand through her hair, pulling it away from her face. Then he let his fingers glide down her lean body to her hip and finally to her pale buttocks.

The flesh-colored plug split the cheeks of her behind, and he hardened slightly at the idea of thrusting his dick where the plug currently resided.

Rising to his feet, he collected his laptop from the coffee table and settled into the armchair. He kicked off his shoes and sent them sliding across the floor and away from where Serena lay.

He stretched his legs until his feet touched her slender back. Absently, he rubbed his toes up her spine and into the silkiness of her hair. He liked touching her, having any contact with her he could.

He opened his laptop and left his feet lightly resting on her side. As he worked through his e-mails, he occasionally glanced up, his gaze seeking Serena out. Every once in a while, she sighed and her body rose and fell harder before a sleepy, contented sound whispered past her lips and she settled back down again.

When he was down to his last e-mail, his cell phone rang. Frowning, he yanked it up without looking at the LCD and punched the on button so the ring wouldn't disturb Serena.

"Damon," he said shortly.

"Damon, hi, this is Faith."

His expression eased and he relaxed in his chair. "Faith, it's a pleasure to hear from you. How are you? How is Gray?"

"We're both fine."

He could hear the smile in her voice, could envision her sweet features.

"How is Serena?" Faith asked.

There was slight hesitation behind the question as though she wasn't certain how to voice her concern. He smiled and glanced down at Serena even as he rubbed his foot lightly over her hip.

"She's asleep at my feet," he replied.

"Your feet? Good grief, Damon, you really do take this slave thing a bit far. I thought you went for collaring and tying them to your bed?"

He chuckled. "Only at night."

He heard her mutter something under her breath.

"Serena is fine, Faith. Surely you didn't think I'd mistreat her."

"No, of course not!" She quickly defended herself. "I hope that isn't what you think. I can't imagine you ever hurting a woman. Not intentionally, anyway."

Damon's brow rose. "I'm not even going to ask."

Faith paused for a long moment. And when she finally spoke, there was a glint of steel in her tone. A direct contradiction to her usually sweet manner.

"Look, Damon, you're my friend. I count you among my dearest friends."

He smiled. He considered her a dear friend as well.

"But so is Serena," she continued. "And I'm a little worried. About you both."

"There's no need for you to concern yourself, Faith. Serena and I are consenting adults, and we're both very aware of what's at stake and what isn't."

Faith made a sound of impatience. "You hate games, Damon. You of all people like things ordered and to your liking. I daresay you're quite spoiled and used to having what you want when you want it. This whole fantasy thing . . . I just hope you aren't going to end up expecting something from it that Serena can't or won't give you."

"I do believe you're trying to protect my heart," Damon said in amusement. "I'm a big boy. I can take care of myself."

"I just don't want either of you hurt," she said softly. "Especially you, Damon."

A flood of warmth entered his chest and bathed his insides. Faith . . . she was like a ray of sunshine on a cold, gloomy day. There wasn't another way to describe her. She had a heart of gold and was tenaciously loyal to the people she loved. Even to her detriment, as Gray Montgomery would certainly attest.

"I appreciate your concern, Faith. Truly I do. But this is between me and Serena," he said gently. "We've both made our terms very clear. No one is entering this blind."

Faith gave a small laugh. "That was a tactful way of telling me to mind my own business."

"Yes, it was," he said with a smile.

"Okay, I can take a hint. I worry about you, Damon. That's all I wanted to say."

"Your worry is wasted on me."

He smiled as she told him again what a dear friend he was and then they rang off. He was still smiling as he put the phone down between his leg and the side of the chair.

Quietly, he closed his laptop and laid it aside on the end table next to his chair. For a long while, he stared into the flickering flames in the hearth and absorbed the sensation of being content in his home, a beautiful woman at his feet. He was . . . happy.

A few moments later, his housekeeper Carol entered the room, clearing her throat to draw his attention. He looked up to see her standing in the doorway, her eyes cast discreetly away from Serena.

"Is there anything you need, Damon?" she asked.

"I'd like a glass of wine for now," he said after a moment's consideration. "In an hour's time, I'd like dinner served here in the living room."

Serena would be hungry, and he easily pictured her comfortably settled between his knees, her head on his lap as he fed her with his fingers. Then he'd stroke her hair and they'd talk while they relaxed and enjoyed the evening. Later . . . He wouldn't get into later just yet. Sitting with a hard-on and nothing to ease it wasn't exactly fun.

After Carol retreated, Damon reached for the novel he was halfway through and opened it to read, after another glance at Serena.

He was pleased by the trust she'd granted him thus far. She had reservations, as he'd expected, but she'd handled them bravely and with grace. She wasn't a coward, nor was she a quitter.

And she pleased him. How she pleased him. He'd told her often enough, for he wanted her to be secure in his approval, but there was no explanation for the surge of pleasure her presence brought him. He wasn't sure he wanted her to know the extent of his somewhat muddled feelings. Hell, he wasn't even going to try and sort through them.

He frowned as he remembered Faith's concerns. Her worry hadn't been for Serena. It had been for him. Was he so transparent? Had he no strength to enjoy a brief affair with no emotional involvement?

His frown eased, and he became more pensive than irritated. His emotions were already involved. He'd never viewed sex as a stark, mechanical process that two mating bodies participated in, absent everything else. Even when he knew there was no future for him and the woman he took to his bed, he still treated her with respect, and he kept a small part of his heart reserved for each one. He knew all their names, what

they looked like, what they enjoyed, what their dreams and aspi-
rations were. Even when those dreams took them beyond him.

Each time, he steeled himself going in, knowing that what
he enjoyed with his partners couldn't last, and at the end of the
affair, he'd viewed their parting with only a small amount of
regret and sadness.

He stared down at Serena over the top of the book that he
still hadn't read a word of today. The idea of her moving on did
odd things to him. Inspired a sort of panic deep in his soul. A
stirring, a protest, a cry of a man for his mate.

He shook his head to rid him of such absurdities. This was
sex. Sex with emotion but still just sex and fantasy. It wasn't
real. None of it was real.

Letting go of Serena would be hard, but he would do it.
Keeping a woman tied to him when she had no wish to be there
wasn't something he wanted any more than he wanted to con-
template the idea that he'd never find a woman who could love
and accept him even knowing what he'd demand from her.

Carol returned with his glass of wine, and he sat sipping as
he stared into the fire. His book, now forgotten, was laid care-
lessly over his lap, marking a place he had no intention of returning to.

Feeling the need to touch Serena, he slid the balls of his feet
over her satiny skin, tracing the line of her spine and then the
curve of her hip and her small waist. Her hair spread out behind her, a splash of midnight, inky and smooth, like liquid
silk.

He would definitely see to her hair every day. It was a joy he
had no intention of denying himself. He would be the one to
wash it when she bathed, and he would dry it and comb through
every single strand.

The fire had died down to a bed of glowing coals, but he couldn't make himself get up to go add more logs. He was content where he sat, his woman across his feet where he could feel every breath she took, every little sigh and twitch.

Shadows crossed the room as dusk fell, sweeping softly over fading daylight. A single lamp illuminated the room, casting a glow over Serena's sleeping form. As if wakened by the warm fingers of light, she stirred beneath his feet.

He watched her shake off the web of sleep and slowly raise her head. She turned immediately as though in search of him. Their gazes connected and satisfaction coiled deep in his chest that her first waking thought had been of him.

"Come to me," he whispered, holding out his hand to her.

She blinked away the last vestiges of fatigue, and her eyes brightened and glowed in the soft light. She got to her knees and slid her hand into his.

For a moment he merely enjoyed that first touch, the tingle that slithered up his arm, bathing his skin in prickles of awareness. Then he pulled her upward and coaxed her onto his lap.

She settled into his chest, snuggling like a kitten seeking warmth. He wrapped both arms around her, holding her close. To his surprise, her lips nuzzled against his neck, pressing tiny kisses to his skin.

"Are you hungry?" he murmured.

"Starved."

"Carol will be bringing our food any time now."

He slid one hand over the curve of her hip and to the softness of her buttocks. His fingers glanced off the plug, and she tightened against him.

"Does it hurt you?" he asked as he traced the edge of the plastic.

She shook her head against him.

"I'll remove it when we go to bed," he said.

Unable to resist, he brushed his lips across her forehead. In response, she tilted her face up, a clear invitation for him to taste her lips.

Sweet, like licking a drop of syrup from a spoon. Her taste was familiar to him yet each time was like the first. Exciting and electrifying.

Her fingers fluttered to his jaw, stroking and touching him as he deepened the kiss. When she started to withdraw, he put his hand to cover hers, pushing her back to his face. He enjoyed her touch. Needed it.

A part of him long buried beneath ice thawed whenever her warmth enveloped him. The aching part of his soul eased. She was his comfort when he'd long decided he would have none.

A sound behind them caused him to pull away. He glanced behind him to see Carol standing in the doorway with a dinner cart.

He motioned her forward then arranged Serena in a position that afforded her the most modesty, despite his earlier assertion that she would grow to ignore the presence of others.

Carol poured wine into the glasses, uncovered the plates and then briskly walked back out of the living room.

The enticing aroma of the food wafted through his nostrils. Next to him, Serena shifted and sighed in contentment as she too caught the smell.

He reached out to pull the cart a little closer to the chair. As he'd requested, Carol had prepared an array of finger foods. Shrimp. Decadent pieces of scallop and lobster drenched in butter. Crabcakes and grilled salmon.

"Mmm, I love seafood," Serena said.

He took a piece of the lobster and held it to her mouth. He coaxed her lips open and left the morsel on her tongue. Before he could take another piece of the food, she sat up and reached for the plate to choose an offering.

She picked a shrimp and held it to his mouth. He opened and allowed her to feed it to him, her fingers brushing like fire across his tongue.

They fed each other in silence, taking turns offering food from their fingers. Their gazes never left each other for long, only to take the next bite and return with a smoldering blaze.

When at last the food was gone, Serena laid her head on his shoulder with a contented sigh.

"Full?" he asked as he stroked her hair.

"Mmm-hmm."

"You sound . . . content."

She raised her head just so she could see him. His hand stayed tangled in her hair and continued its downward trek.

"I am."

Her husky sweet voice stirred a longing inside him that had nothing to do with sex or the urge to bury himself deep inside her. It was more. Something just out of his reach that he was at a loss to explain.

"I'm glad."

He pulled her back to him, letting her softness mold to his body. Against his neck, she yawned and snuggled sleepily into his arms.

"Why don't I take you to the bedroom and remove the plug? You can have a long soaking bath, I'll wash your hair and we can have an early night."

She stilled against him and then once again, she pulled away to stare at him with confused eyes.

"You're asking?"

He smiled. "Not everything is a dictate, Serena mine. I'm a reasonable man when it suits me."

She answered his smile with one of her own. "Then yes, I'd love a long, hot bath."

CHAPTER 20

$\mathcal{D}$amon glanced over at Serena sleeping beside him in the bed. Only the lamp to his side illuminated the room and even then he tilted the shade away so the light didn't shine directly on her and disturb her sleep.

He'd removed the plug and then drawn her a hot bath. She'd soaked for half an hour before he'd helped her out, dried her and then saw to her hair. He could see the surprise in her eyes when he simply put her to bed without any sexual overtures.

He glanced up at her bound wrists and felt himself grow hard. Waiting until morning to take her would make for a long night, but she was clearly exhausted and he had no desire to take too much from her too soon.

He turned back to his computer that was open on his lap. It wasn't work that occupied his thoughts tonight. It was her fantasies.

As he scanned back over the e-mail she'd sent him detailing not only the auction fantasy but several others as well, he frowned. It was as though she'd paraded out a laundry list of all the things she thought a master would do to a slave. Take out any slave/master manual and create a checklist.

He shook his head. She even had a fantasy of being tied up and whipped by another man while Damon watched. As if he'd allow another man to have such mastery over her. Any punishment, any pain, any pleasure, would come at his hands or his supervision. No passive bystander would he be when it came to her.

There was no mention of a threesome or more, but he couldn't rule it out of her thoughts, much to his chagrin. He didn't share. Ever. If another man touched her, it was because Damon allowed it, but it would never go beyond preparation. Only Damon would enjoy the full extent off her body, of her sweetness.

Still, there were many instances listed that were textbook clichés for the whole dominant male, submissive female spiel. As much as he wanted to make her fantasies come true, if only for a short period of time, he couldn't bring himself to make it all an act.

So what to do about Serena's fantasy sexual situations?

There were a few of her scenarios that definitely appealed to him, and he looked forward to those. They weren't anything he wouldn't have come up with himself, but it gave him satisfaction that she was open and accepting of his desires, even if she didn't know they shared them.

He put away his laptop and turned off the lamp. When he got comfortable in bed and moved close to Serena, she stirred and nestled her body against his, seeking him even in sleep.

He smiled in the darkness. Today had been about easing her into the fantasy. Not moving too fast. But tomorrow, he'd step it up a notch and push her further. He had a feeling she'd not only take it but beg for more. And that excited him a whole hell of a lot.

Serena awoke to lips moving heatedly against her neck. Impatient hands framed her hips, spreading her as Damon settled between her thighs.

"Good morning," he murmured as he slid deep inside her.

She moaned at the sense of fullness. A low throb began in her groin, heated and aching. He didn't wait for her to adjust. He withdrew and thrust forward again, moaning his satisfaction in her ear.

His movements were quick and urgent. He looped his arms underneath her legs and pushed higher until her ankles rested on his shoulders.

The position left her bare and vulnerable, her pussy wide-open to his thrusts. Each movement forward pressed his warm flesh to hers. His hips slapped against the underside of her thighs and her buttocks as he drove deep and hard.

Still trapped in the fog of sleep, she closed her eyes and gave herself over to his care. Her pleasure wrapped, warm and fluid around her, carrying her on a lazy stream. She was too lethargic to participate, so she let him take her, do as he wanted.

And then he slipped from the clasp of her pussy, and his swollen cock bumped against her stomach. Warm fluid surged onto her belly as he continued to rock against her.

With fumbling fingers, he guided his cock back to her pussy and slid back in, warm and pulsing. He thrust more slowly into her body as the last vestiges of his release were wrung from him.

Her eyes slowly opened, and she stared up at him as he held himself inside her. His brown hair was mussed, sticking up on top, and the shadow of a beard dotted his jaw. His dark eyes glittered with deep satisfaction, and that was what she looked for. She'd pleased him.

She smiled up at him but said nothing. He smiled back then leaned over to kiss her as he slid from her body.

He checked her bonds and then got up and strode naked toward the bathroom. He had a nice ass. Firm and well muscled. Like the rest of him.

Not overly muscled. No Neanderthal type wearing a tank shirt who flexed a muscle every time he moved. He was more whipcord lean, slim but hard.

She relaxed into the plush mattress and stared up at the ceiling as she waited for Damon to free her. There was an odd patience to her mood that didn't fit her personality. She was extremely impatient. She didn't like to wait for anything. And yet, she waited for him with a contentment she wouldn't have thought she'd feel.

Several minutes later, Damon walked out of the bathroom, his hair damp from a shower. She turned her head to the side and watched as he went to his closet and dressed. In a moment, he walked to the side of the bed and reached for the cuffs binding her wrists.

He gently pulled her arms down to her belly, and he massaged her wrists, his fingers light and caressing. Then he pulled first one and then the other to his lips for a tender kiss.

He produced a damp washcloth and carefully cleaned his seed from her skin, his movements slow and gentle.

"Roll over onto your belly," he said as he gave her a little push.

She complied and burrowed a little deeper into the sheets. Her eyes closed involuntarily, and he chuckled above her.

"Sleepy this morning," he said as he stroked his palm down her spine and then over the curve of her buttocks.

Then he left her for a moment, and she heard a noise across the room. A drawer opening and then shutting and his footsteps as he walked back. The bed dipped underneath her as he settled onto the bed at her knees.

His palm cupped her bottom lovingly, squeezing and fondling the plump cheek. His fingertip feathered over the cleft and burrowed deeper until he brushed across the tight seam of her ass.

She stiffened and his coaxing words spilled over her.

"Relax, Serena," he crooned. "I'm going to put the plug back in."

She forced herself to go limp, lulled by the pleasure of his touch. He was patient, stroking and petting her. Each brush of his fingers across her entrance added more lubricant until her body was awash with fiery need.

A single finger breeched the tight opening, and she moaned softly. There was no pain, just an edgy need that left her quivering against his hand.

"Get to your knees," he directed. "Head down on the bed, legs apart."

Slowly she did as he asked, positioning herself so that her ass was high in the air and her face pressed into the mattress.

More lubricant eased over her entrance, inside, outside, stroking and gentle. And then the firm pressure of the plug, pressing with unrelenting force. Her body stretched and protested, held firm.

She closed her eyes and pressed her lips together to keep out the soft moan of protest as her opening stretched to accommodate the thickness of the plug.

Back and forth, he eased, each time gaining more ground

until finally, with one firm push, he seated it deep into her rectum.

Her head came off the bed as her body spasmed and clenched. She sucked air through her nose as she tried to steady her reaction. Her hands curled into tight balls, the sheet rumpled in her palm.

Damon pressed a gentle kiss to her bottom and then got up from his seat on the bed.

"Take your shower then come downstairs. Bring a brush so I can see to your hair. I'll be in the dining room eating."

She nodded, her eyes still closed.

Gingerly, she climbed from the bed, the unfamiliar sensation of the plug stretching her behind making her cautious. She gave a little sigh as she walked toward the bathroom. What she could really use was another long, hot bath, but she wouldn't keep Damon waiting.

She showered quickly and stepped out to dry herself. The gold band on her arm gleamed in the mirror, and she paused to examine the intricate design. Wearing the band that marked his claim made her feel like one of the slave girls from Egyptian times.

A delicate shiver paraded up her skin as she glanced down at the matching band around her ankle. He'd claimed her publicly. Branded her his own. He'd done everything she'd fantasized about and more.

As fantasies went, this was certainly one of her more successful jobs. Everything had come together as planned and had gone off without a hitch. If only all her clients could be so well satisfied.

The reminder that this was purely business put a damper on the decadent thrill that had washed through her just moments ago. Damon had a way of making her believe it. Even when everything had been orchestrated, down to the most finite detail. He made her believe it was real.

She toweled her hair as dry as she could and arranged it so it was out of her face. The towel she'd dried off with was a temptation. She wanted to wrap it around herself to go downstairs in, but she sensed that him leaving her to shower and come down alone was a test. He'd specified that she not dress unless he instructed her to, and as awkward as she felt going naked, with a plug in her ass, she'd do it.

A blush staining her skin, she walked out of the bedroom, dreading the thought of running into Sam or Damon's housekeeper en route to the dining room.

She picked up her pace when she didn't immediately see anyone and hurried down the hallway toward where Damon waited. At the doorway, she stopped abruptly and would have turned and walked away but Damon looked up and saw her.

There were two men seated at the table with Damon. They were all in conversation and it sounded businesslike in tone. Had she messed up by coming down naked? Or had Damon not known of his visitors before he asked her to come down with the plug embedded in her ass?

Damon watched her silently then held out his hand. God, he wanted her to come to him. The other men, seeing Damon's gesture, turned and saw her in the doorway. There was no surprise in their expressions, just the bright flare of lust.

When she didn't immediately move, Damon raised one brow and continued to hold his hand out to her. Hell. He did mean for her to join them.

She started forward, feeling the men's gazes on her bare flesh. As she drew closer, some of her embarrassment faded under the stark approval in Damon's eyes. He captured her hand and drew her close against him.

"Serena, I'd like you to meet Mr. Phillips and Mr. Granger, two business associates of mine. Gentlemen, this is Serena. She belongs to me."

His words echoed in her mind, sharp, reminding her of the e-mail she'd written when her fantasies had been alive and fluid in her mind. She gasped as she realized that this, like the auction, was an incarnation of one of those fantasies.

Her knees trembled, and nervousness skittered up her spine like a splintered piece of wood catching on silk.

Damon pulled at her hand and guided her down to the floor between his legs. There was plenty of space between his chair and the table, and she settled gingerly on her heels, careful of the plug stretching her ass as she moved.

He cradled her head in his lap as he continued his conversation with the two men. She didn't even try to make sense of it all. Her nerves were jumping like frogs on speed.

The entire time he talked with the other men, his hand caressed and fondled her face, positioning her closer to his crotch. When her cheek was pressed to the inside of his thigh, he casually loosened his trousers and tugged his cock from the fly.

Never missing a beat in conversation, he cupped her head with one hand and grasped his cock with the other and guided himself into her mouth.

He was hard and turgid, filling her mouth and thrusting to her throat. She barely had time to catch her breath before his hands buried in her hair and held her tightly against him.

He never spoke to her, never gave her instruction, but his demand was clear. Pleasure him. There as he conversed with his colleagues, she was to perform as the slave she wanted to be.

Long, hard strokes. Breathless. His taste filled her. And then as she tasted his pre-cum, he pulled sharply at her hair and held her head away from his cock. Her head was tilted back so that her neck was exposed and she stared up at him, helpless in his grasp.

And then she heard it. The line from her fantasy as one of the other men calmly asked if Damon would loan out the services of his slave so that he too might be pleasured.

Her heart thumped wildly. She remembered this, had almost been ashamed to put it down on paper. In her fantasy, Damon had commanded her to kneel between the knees of the other two men in turn and pleasure them with her mouth while he watched.

"I don't share what is mine, gentlemen," Damon said in a terse voice.

She blinked in surprise. Though the words had been directed at the two men, Damon stared down at her the entire time as though his statement had been directed solely at her.

"You are, however, free to observe as my slave pleasures *me*," he finished softly.

CHAPTER 21

$\mathcal{S}$erena sucked in her breath but it only made her chest tighter. Damon's cock was hard and distended, reaching upward toward his waist as it lay flat against his open pants.

"Stand up," he ordered quietly as his grip tightened in her hair.

She placed her hands on his knees and pushed herself up. His hand fell from her hair as she came to her feet in front of him, her back to the two men sitting at the table.

He grasped his cock and stroked, maintaining his erection while his gaze raked over her body.

"Turn around."

Her eyes cast downward, she turned until she faced the table. Behind her, Damon stood, his hands skimming over her back. His hands cupped her shoulders and he pushed her down until her upper body lay on the table with her ass in the air and her legs dangling from the vulnerable position he'd placed her in.

Her breasts pressed into the polished wood, the surface cool against her skin. Her cheek lay against the table, her gaze now focused on the two men who'd risen from their chairs.

They were attractive men, one about Damon's age and one older. The bulges at the juncture of their legs told Serena they wanted her, wanted the pleasure of her mouth and her body, only Damon had been adamant in his denial.

And then, to her surprise, one of the men reached for her arm and pulled it upward until her palm rested against the table and his fingers formed a tight restraint around her wrist. She lost sight of the other man, but then her other wrist was captured against the table. Her breath caught, and nervous apprehension raced through her veins. She was captive and helpless, trapped against the table at her most vulnerable.

Damon's fingers gripped the plug, and before she could draw in a breath, the still-lubricated device slid easily from her body. Her anus quivered in reaction, still stretched from the plug.

Before her body could relax and take back its shape, the blunt head of Damon's cock pressed firmly against her sphincter. The two men held her tighter as if expecting her to resist. She could hear the rapid intake of their breaths. She could feel the tangible spark of their arousal as they watched Damon master her.

In one thrust, Damon pinned her to the table, his cock sliding deep into her ass. The sensation of him rasping across the delicate tissues of her anus was almost more than she could bear. She cried out, rearing her head from the table, but one of the men pushed her down again, his palm resting firmly against her cheek. The force and dominance sent a myriad of arousal tumbling through her shaking body.

He stretched her impossibly, his balls pressed against her pussy as he strained forward. She was full, so full, the bite of pain making her head swim even as the fringes of ecstasy called to her, inviting her on a decadent ride.

His hand snaked up her spine to tangle in her hair, hair that he had yet to brush as he'd promised. The other man moved his palm from her face, and Damon's fingers caught in the still-damp snarls and pulled, forcing her head up.

She knew what he wanted, knew that he wanted her to look at the men holding her down, to understand that while they could look, and touch, they could never have her.

His body was over hers, mounting her possessively, a show of his ownership. For a long moment, he remained seated in her, pinning her to the table as the two men watched with glittering eyes, their fingers digging into her wrists.

Then he began to move. Gently at first, he withdrew, sliding across the distended hole, opening her wider to him. Then, when the crown of his dick rimmed her opening, he surged forward again, slamming his hips against her ass.

She tried to process the barrage of sensations. Tried to put a name to the delicious thrill of having a man deep in her ass. Never before had she felt anything to rival the bite of pain and the kiss of pleasure that melded together so beautifully, so seamlessly that where one began and the other ended she wasn't certain.

The relief when he withdrew, when the overwhelming fullness abated, was intensely pleasurable. But when he thrust forward again, reopening her to his advances, the dark swirl of pain nipped and took hold until she gasped for breath. For mercy.

His hands left her hair, and his fingers gripped the globes of her ass, spreading her as his thick cock worked in and out of her tiny entrance.

She lay there, helpless against his passion, her vision glazed and the two men on either side of her as dim as her other surroundings. There was only Damon and the pleasure he gave her. The pleasure he forced her to take.

He withdrew, pulling all of the way out of her, letting the head of his cock rest between her cheeks.

"Tell me you want it," he said in a guttural voice, raspy and hoarse with need. "Tell me you want my cock in your ass."

"Please," she whispered.

"I can't hear you," he said harshly.

"Please!"

"Tell me what you want, Serena."

"Your cock. In my ass. Please," she pleaded.

He tucked the crown against her puckered entrance and thrust forward, reopening her ruthlessly. And then he withdrew. Completely. Her aching ass pulsed and throbbed.

The hands at her wrists released her. Damon gripped her hips and flipped her over so that her back was now pressed to the table. For the first time, she stared into his eyes, and what she saw took her breath away. There was a feral light. Ruthless intensity as if the calm, cultured man had been replaced by a snarling beast bent on dominating his captive.

He spread her legs as the two men took her arms and pinned them above her head. The position forced her breasts upward, and Damon leaned down, his hungry lips devouring the rigid peaks. His mouth was rough, ravenous, his teeth scraping her nipples as he bit sharply. She stirred restlessly, wanting to touch him, but her captors held her tight against the table.

As Damon pulled away, he roughly pushed her legs up and the two men each grabbed an ankle and pulled up and outward so that her ass and pussy were helplessly bared to Damon. He cupped her buttocks, kneading the globes forcefully even as he spread them.

The men spread her impossibly wide as Damon tucked the fat head of his cock against her now-closed rectum. Oh God. He wasn't gentle. He reopened her with ruthless precision, and the new position made his angle something she wasn't prepared for. She cried out and bucked upward but even as the bite unsteadied her, it gave way to a dark, edgy pleasure wrapped in pain's embrace.

His gaze bore into her as he flexed his hips and drove deeper into her sensitive nether regions. He pushed until she was completely and utterly open to him.

She closed her eyes and opened her mouth in a silent scream of agony. Of pleasure. Of the sweetest, darkest ecstasy she'd ever known. It overwhelmed her. Boiled up and over, sending her spiraling down, down until she couldn't think. She could only feel.

He owned her in that moment. Not only did he take possession of her body in the most primitive of manners, but he possessed her soul. His. Taken. Possessed.

The other men were forgotten, and they were no longer her fantasy. They meant nothing, had no hold on her desires. There was only Damon and the way he made her feel. Cherished. Protected. She belonged.

He leaned over her body and swept his tongue over the nipples he'd ravaged just moments before. Heated lips nuzzled her, licking and kissing as he murmured sweet words against her skin.

His muscles bunched and tightened above her as a shudder rolled through his body. His hands slid up her waist even as the men's grips tightened and pulled harder at her arms and legs.

Holding her tightly in place, he pumped against her ass,

straining wildly against her as if he were trying to insert himself into every recess of her soul.

She opened to him. She let go and embraced him, allowing him in, allowing him to see her at her most vulnerable, her hopes and fears, her most secret desires.

"I'm going to come, Serena," he whispered as he raised his head from her breast. "I'm going to come so deeply inside you that you'll know I belong there. A part of you."

She closed her eyes and inhaled, allowing those sweet words to flow like honey over her body. He was moving faster and harder, his hips powering against her ass, the sound of flesh meeting flesh sharp in the air.

And then he stilled. Huge and swollen within her, he pulsed as his cock split her ass wide and he poured hot liquid inside her.

The two men at her sides let her go abruptly as Damon stood there, his shaft thick and hard inside her. She heard them fumbling and soft, impatient curses filled her ears.

"Look at me, Serena," Damon said firmly as he stood between her limp legs, wedged so tightly inside her. "Never take your eyes off of me."

She nodded slowly, her lethargy making her slow and hazy.

She heard soft groans, and saw the two men from her periphery. She was tempted to look, but Damon surged against her, sending a ripple across the raw flesh of her anal entry stretched so tight around him.

"Me, Serena. Only at me."

Hot liquid spattered her chest and she emitted a gasp of surprise as she realized the two men were coming on her skin. It splashed onto her breasts, coating her nipples and sliding into the valley between the soft mounds. A spurt landed on her cheek and then one on her lips. The warm shower coated her upper body even as her bowels squeezed the last of Damon's semen from his cock.

The difference wasn't lost on her. Damon had come inside her. The men had only been allowed to come on her skin, and they hadn't been allowed to enter her.

Finally, their soft moans dissipated and the hot liquid that coated her face and breasts ceased to fall.

Even when the last of Damon's cum was spent, he leaned heavily into her, his breaths coming in ragged spurts. Still embedded in her ass, his cock twitched and finally softened to a semierect state.

He raised himself off her, which sent his cock seeking deeper. She moaned softly as her stretched and well-used entrance protested the movement.

Gently, he withdrew in a warm rush of semen. He helped her from the table to stand in front of him on wobbly legs. Fluid trickled down the back of her legs, but still she stood, waiting his command.

He looked down at her body in satisfaction, and she wondered how she looked to him, covered with other men's fluids and Damon's own trickling down the backs of her legs.

"Go get cleaned up," he said softly. "And then return to me."

When Serena returned a half hour later, the men were gone and Damon sat in the living room in his chair, the pallet she'd slept on the day before positioned at his feet.

She walked over without a word and knelt on the soft pillow.

Damon's hands found her head and guided it to his lap. She closed her eyes and nuzzled her cheek against his leg as he gently stroked his hand through her hair.

"Turn around so I can brush your hair," he said after several minutes of silence.

She complied and settled between his legs as he ran the brush through her long locks. A contented sigh escaped her as she let the pleasure of his attention settle like a warm haze.

For a long while she let the silence lay, reluctant to break it with her questions. When he tugged through her hair one last time and laid the brush aside, she turned to look at him.

She cocked her head to the side, unsure of how to voice her curiosity.

He touched her cheek, drawing a line from her temple to her jaw with his finger. "Ask your question, Serena mine. I can see it about to burst from your impatient lips."

She smiled and leaned into this touch. "Why did you deviate from the fantasy?"

He paused, his finger stopping at the corner of her mouth. "Did it bother you that I didn't want your mouth on their cocks or their cocks inside you?"

"No," she admitted. "I don't think I would have liked the fantasy as I envisioned it. I mean, in theory it seemed sexy; daring even. In reality, the idea of . . ." She couldn't bring herself to say that sucking the men's cocks wasn't as appealing in reality as it had seemed in the privacy of her fantasies.

"I am glad," he said simply. "I tried to remain as true to your fantasy as I could, but you should know that I don't share what I consider mine."

She rubbed her cheek over his hand. "I'm glad," she said honestly. "I thought . . . I thought I did, that it would be exciting." She sighed as Damon cradled her face in his palm as he listened intently to her. "It sounded . . . I don't know, like it could be arousing when Faith talked about it. Having more than one man focused on me or being forced to service the needs of more than one man."

She took Damon's hand between her own, brought it to her lips, her only need to have him close. "When it came down to it . . . this morning when I thought you'd command me to pleasure those men because it was something I had said I wanted . . . I was frightened. I didn't want it. I only wanted you."

Damon pulled his hands from her grip and urged her onto his lap. He cradled her close and tilted her chin up with one finger. "If there is something that ever frightens you, then you tell me at once. I won't be a party to anything that scares you. As for other men, I'm glad that you have no desire for their attentions, because it's something I won't tolerate."

She smiled. "You sound so possessive. I like it."

He returned her smile, but his expression was serious. It sent a delighted shiver over her skin and made her heart twinge. No man had ever wanted her so fiercely.

The truth hit her with sudden wrenching force.

This wasn't real.

It was an elaborate charade. They were actors in a play. A script written by her. He played the part she asked him to. His lust might be real, but it was just sex.

"Why did the light just die in your eyes?" he murmured as he rubbed his thumb over her lips. "And why did your smile disappear?"

"Because I just remembered that none of this is real," she said in a low voice.

Not a flicker betrayed his reaction to her statement. He continued to stare levelly at her, his eyes probing and assessing.

"Do you want it to be real, Serena?"

He left the question dangling in the air, much like a carrot in front of the proverbial donkey. Did she want it to be real? She swallowed, unsure of how to answer. How could she when she didn't know the answer?

Yes, there was some regret that it was just an act because she liked the idea of being cherished by a man like Damon. But she didn't want to be someone's slave forever. The benefits, while alluring and arousing, would become tedious after a while, right?

"I don't know," she finally said when it became clear he was still waiting for her answer. "I can't answer that."

"And yet you have regret because this isn't real," he said.

She nodded.

"It's as real as we make it, Serena mine. There is no one to judge but us."

"I like that." She leaned closer to him, her gaze seeking his. "Damon?"

He kissed her lips, one soft smooch. "Yes?"

"Can we forget about my fantasies? Could we instead play it by ear? I don't want everything to be so . . . practiced. I want to know how it feels to truly belong to you for the time we have remaining."

He kissed her again, his lips exploring hers with a gentleness that made her ache. He could be so demanding and yet so exquisitely tender in turns. She loved both parts.

"I think that's an excellent idea, Serena mine. I have no desire to share you with another man. There are parts of your fantasies that excite me, boundaries that I'd like to push. You please me in ways I can't even begin to describe. If you trust me to make your experience the best it can be, then we'll go forward, you as my slave and I as your keeper."

Unconsciously her hand went to the band on her arm, feeling its reassuring weight. His hand went to it as well, his finger tracing the outline of the jewelry.

"Do you like the mark of my ownership?"

She watched his fingers smooth over her arm and enjoyed the contrast between her pale skin and the glistening gold of the band. "I do. It's less harsh than a collar. It's feminine and yet there is power behind the symbol. I like looking at it and knowing it came from you. A collar just seems so . . . demeaning."

"And the last thing I want is for you to feel shame," he said.

"I'm hungry," she said with a smile.

He blinked at the change in subject and then laughed softly. "So you must be. My demands have been great this morning and I've yet to feed you. I'm not proving to be a very good keeper, am I?"

She framed his face in her hands and lowered her head to his. Their lips met and melted together. It was she who controlled the kiss, and he let her have her way. When she pulled away, they were both breathing heavily, and his eyes shone with a heavy glaze.

"You're the best," she said simply. "I know I'll never want for anything when I'm with you."

He squeezed her to him and kissed the tip of her nose. "No, Serena mine. You'll never lack for anything I can provide."

CHAPTER 22

$\mathcal{D}$amon hadn't told her where they were going, only that they were going out after a quiet dinner at home. He'd chosen her outfit, a filmy skirt and sleeveless silk top, and instructed her not to wear a bra or panties. Then he'd ushered her into his silver BMW and driven away from his house.

A half hour later when they pulled through the gate of The House, adrenaline slammed through her veins. She glanced over at Damon, but his expression was unreadable.

As if sensing her excitement and her nervousness, he reached over and captured her hand in his. He gave it a gentle squeeze as he pulled the car to a stop next to the other parked cars.

"You will stay by my side at all times. Men will seek your attention. They'll speak to you and flirt. You're to speak only to me and to anyone else only with my permission."

Her eyes narrowed as she stared back at him. The order rankled, and she suddenly felt like a child being disciplined rather than an adult woman.

He waited as if expecting her to say no, but she snapped her lips together and averted her gaze. This was what she'd asked for. He was only giving her what she wanted.

Damon stepped out of the car and walked around to open her door. She put her hand in his and stepped gracefully from her seat.

"Have I told you how beautiful you look tonight?" he murmured as they started for the door.

She smiled, her earlier irritation forgotten. "No, but it's nice to hear."

"I'll be the envy of every man here. Your hair shines like a veil of black silk."

"You're no stranger to pretty words," she teased.

"The words are only pretty when applied to a beautiful woman. With no point of reference, they're merely words."

"I find myself unable to argue with your logic," she said with a wide smile.

He ushered her inside where they were greeted by the butler. Damon directed her into a small dressing room just off the main entrance.

"Remove your clothing. The only things I want adorning you are my marks of possession."

She inhaled in surprise but brought shaking fingers to the waistband of her skirt. Yes, she'd gone nude the night of the auction, but somehow this was different. She was well-versed in what would happen that night; after all, she'd created that fantasy. Tonight, though, she was working from a blank script, learning as she went. It was disconcerting.

"Would you like me to undress you?" Damon asked. "You're shaking."

She shook her head mutely.

His gaze sharpened. "Serena, are you frightened? We can go home. Just say the word."

No.

It hovered like a black cloud. She'd grown to fear that word and what it meant. It went deeper than denial for it was an end to a fantasy she was desperate to live. Not just any fantasy. *This* fantasy. With Damon.

She shoved the skirt over her hips, letting it fall in a pool at her feet. With quick, jerky movements, she pulled the shirt over her head and tossed it aside. A cool draft from the air-conditioning vent above blew lightly over her bare skin, and she shivered.

Damon fingered a lock of her hair, pulling it over her shoulder to let it fall over her breast. Her nipple, hard and puckered, peeked erotically from the strands.

He touched the nipple, lightly, with just his fingertip. A silken brush across the tip, but she jumped as though she'd been shocked.

"Remember your instructions," he murmured and then turned to leave the room.

She followed him out and down the hall. They passed several smaller rooms where people mingled and enjoyed cocktails and conversation. She walked quickly so they didn't have a chance to look up and see her.

Damon continued toward the stairs, and she remembered a similar walk just nights before when she'd followed her keeper to the large common room above.

Tonight that room looked nothing like it had the night of her auction. As they entered, she stared in surprise at the flurry of activity. Unlike the rooms downstairs where people were dressed modestly, the participants here were at various stages of dress, from elaborate erotic costumes to plain nudity and all shades in between.

Each section of the room hosted a different . . . fetish. It was the only word she could come up with, and she was sure she'd gotten it wrong.

Never before had she seen so much naked flesh and utter carnality outside of a porn movie. They probably wouldn't appreciate the comparison, but that was her limit of experience in such matters.

"Would you like a tour?" Damon asked in a low voice. "No one here minds being observed."

At least she wouldn't be expected to participate. Damon had made his view on others touching her exceedingly clear. Armed with that knowledge, she nodded. Looking never hurt anyone.

The bombardment of erotic images hit her from all angles. There was a multitude of sexual scenarios, from a simple one-on-one couple fucking like bunnies to an outright orgy with no less than eight people joined like LEGOs. It all looked rather . . . bizarre.

The kink factor was high and there certainly wasn't a shortage of shock value in the room, but it failed to fire Serena's senses. All she could do was look with dumb confusion at the gyrating bodies and listen to the moans and cries.

And then Damon touched her. All it took was the soft brush of his fingers across her skin and arousal flared low in her groin. Her breasts tingled, heavy and aching, straining outward, seeking his attention.

"I am extremely gratified that only my touch excites you," he said as he caressed one breast. Then he ran his palm over the other, plumping the supple flesh in his hand. The soft mound cupped in his hand, he brushed his thumb back and forth over the sensitive bud.

"Now come, my pleasure—and yours—awaits."

As she followed him toward the center of the room, she saw others stop and turn around to stare. The sounds of pleasure ceased, and an eerie silence fell over the room where just moments earlier, the slap of flesh, heated moan and cries of passion had swelled and echoed off the walls.

A metal frame stood in the center of the room, and already a crowd has assembled around it. It was simple, and for that reason, she couldn't discern its purpose.

It was unassuming, a rectangular piece of metal that stood upright, but as she drew closer, she could see that it pivoted, moving up and down so that the rectangle could lay horizontal instead of vertical and all angles in between.

A man in jeans and a tight T-shirt stood nonchalantly, his hand on the frame, moving it up and down as he watched Damon approach. His gaze swept appraisingly over Serena's naked form, but a sharp look of reproach from Damon pulled him up short.

He offered a smile and nodded in Damon's direction. "Your slave is up for games tonight?"

"My slave does what I tell her," Damon replied evenly.

"Lucky man. Do you need any help restraining and preparing her?"

Serena glanced sharply at the man standing next to the frame. Restrain? Prepare?

Damon glanced between Serena and the unnamed man and then nodded. "Serena, this is Cole. Do as he instructs."

Serena swallowed and stepped forward as Damon motioned for her.

"I'll return in just a moment. I need to choose my equipment."

Equipment. Restraint. She began to tremble, though she knew it wasn't from fear. Excitement coursed through her veins along with a heady dose of uncertainty.

When Cole reached for her arm, she instinctively shrank from his touch.

"I won't hurt you," he said soothingly.

She looked around but Damon had disappeared.

Cole touched her arm, tentative and seeking to reassure her. She truly wasn't afraid, but neither was she enthusiastic. Yet. Apprehensive best described the current that arced through her body like lightning.

She forced herself to relax and went willingly with Cole as he directed her toward the device. When he flipped it, she could see leather loops, one at the very top in the center and two at the bottom on either side.

"Step over," he said as he gripped her elbow to assist her.

She stepped over the base of the structure and stood inside the rectangle, waiting for what came next.

Cole backed her toward the bottom edge of the frame where the two loops were situated. Soft leather circled her right ankle and then tightened when Cole cinched the strap.

She gave a little gasp as she realized then what the the loops were for. Restraint. He smiled as he saw her realization.

"Spread your legs so the other reaches the second strap."

She nearly stumbled and had to grasp his arm to steady herself.

"I won't let you fall," he said.

The leather circled her ankle and tightened.

"Arms above your head," he directed as he stood back up.

She glanced up and saw the one tie and realized the vulnerability of what he proposed. She looked at him, but saw an expression that brooked no argument.

Slowly she raised her arms and put her wrists together, high above her head.

"Very good," he said, but his approval meant nothing to her. It was Damon she sought to please.

He secured her wrists, tightening until she was stretched on tiptoe. Vulnerable didn't even begin to cover how she felt.

And then her feet left the ground as he rotated the frame so that she lay suspended from the straps at a slight angle. She stared down at the floor, and her mouth went dry. She licked her lips to try and add moisture.

The room spun, and she found herself staring up at the ceiling as Cole flipped the frame until she was stretched on her back. He threaded a wide support belt underneath her back, wrapped it around her belly and attached it to the sides of the frame with hooks. It took some of the strain off her arms and legs and gave her some much-needed relief. She wouldn't go as far as to say she was comfortable, but it was a hell of a lot better than before.

She jerked in surprise when Cole cupped her breast. He rubbed his thumb over the rigid peak, his expression never changing. Then he bent his head, and to her shock, sucked the crown between his teeth and nipped sharply at it.

When he released it, he looked up and gave her a satisfied smile. "Much better."

She stared at him in confusion, but before she could voice the question, she felt a sharp pinch followed by a rush of pain and then a burning numbness settle over her nipple. She writhed and gasped in protest and then yanked her gaze down to the throbbing ache.

He'd secured a nipple clamp to her breast. It dug into the puckered flesh and guided the nipple outward. She twisted and pulled against her bonds but they held fast.

"Please," she whispered. "Take it off."

Cole ignored her plea and walked around to the other side. She whimpered softly because now she knew what was to come. He gave her other breast the same treatment, plumping softly with his hand before leaning over to suck the tip into his mouth.

She moaned at the hypersensitivity. Though it was the other nipple clamped, she felt each nip of his teeth as though they were the tiny jaws of metal.

After a final sharp bite, he laved his tongue soothingly over the hardened flesh and pulled away. He waited this time. The bastard. Every muscle in her body tensed as soon as his mouth withdrew. And still he waited, a patient smile on his face.

He let her see it coming, guiding his hand with the open clamp toward the burgeoning point. There was no gentle coaxing, no gradual slide onto the nipple. He clamped it hard and let go.

She grit her teeth to prevent the cry of surprise and pain. The hungry teeth bit into her flesh with greedy eagerness. At first it was more than she could bear, and she arched her back, bucking against her restraints.

Then the pain diminished to a hot burn and finally, blessed numbness.

She lay there panting, nearly overwhelmed by the barrage of sensations, first Cole's mouth on her breasts followed by the sharp teeth of the clamps. Her nipples tingled with the slightest of movements, pushing back the numb.

And suddenly she moved again with one firm push by Cole.

Her feet rotated beneath her as she came to an upright position. He pushed a little farther until she was at a forty-five-degree forward angle.

Her breasts bobbed, and the clamps dangling from her nipples exerted a dragging pressure that sent razor-sharp darts straight to her pussy.

She was wet. She could feel the creamy moisture gather between her legs, feel the way her clit pulsed and ached from the tension applied to her nipples.

Hands cupped her buttocks, kneading slightly before spreading the cheeks. Shock raced up her spine, stiffening her muscles as she formed a protest with her lips. Before she could speak, Cole gently applied lubricant to the opening. His fingers smoothed over the cleft, spreading a generous amount in their wake.

Her shoulders shook, and her body trembled. Tiny little shivers, alternating hot and cold. She danced a fine line between fear and desire. Confusion. Hot, edgy need. She didn't *want* to be aroused by a strange man's hands.

One thick finger slid inside her anus. Air rushed past her lips as she inhaled harshly. Back and forth his finger rasped across her delicate tissues, opening her wider as he spread more of the gel.

Another finger joined the first, stretching until she was open to him. His fingers were large, and at first, her passage was snug around his knuckles but he continued to stroke and caress, adding more lubricant to ease his way.

Her vision blurred and she closed her eyes to steady herself. She fought the waves of . . . She wouldn't say need. Or desire. She didn't want this man. She enjoyed his skilled fingers, liked the assault he waged on her senses, the wicked, sinful tune he played on her body. It was in part painful, and if she were honest, she feared her response to this pain. For she didn't find it distasteful. She wanted, craved, more.

And then as quickly as he'd come to her, he withdrew and left. Silence that she hadn't noticed before buzzed in her ears. There was no sound in the room, and as she lifted her head, she could see that, as on the night of the auction, every eye was on her.

A warm sizzle began in her belly, pooled in her groin and spread rapidly through her veins, humming low and sweet. Damon. She felt him, though she couldn't see behind her.

She sighed when his hands cupped her buttocks and kneaded, gentle and loving. There was a marked difference between his touch and Cole's. There was more regard, a respect and tenderness that lacked Cole's clinical, methodical approach to preparing her.

Something soft, yet firm with the coolness of plastic or maybe rubber, ran lightly down her spine, eliciting a shiver from coiled muscles. It trailed over her buttocks then back up her side and to her shoulder. Damon walked slowly around to her front and she could now see that he held a long crop in his hand. The tip touched her ear, traced a circle around her lobe before stroking softly over her cheek to her lips in a gentle kiss.

He stopped there, watching her with dark eyes, holding the crop to her parted lips.

"Lick it," he commanded, low and husky. "Pretend it's my cock. Show me how you'd suck it."

Her eyes flew upward so she could watch his reaction. She dipped her tongue over the edge of the crop, absorbing the taste and texture of the leather. Growing bolder, she swiped at the flat side with a long lick before catching the flap between her teeth and sucking it inside her mouth.

He coaxed it deeper with a quick slide of his hand, and she savored the supple give as it rolled over her tongue. When he pulled back, she balanced it delicately on her bottom lip before he finally let the crop fall away.

Adjusting his grip, he popped the tip on his leg as he walked behind her. She lost him in her vision, and her breath caught and bubbled in her throat as she entered the unknown.

"Pain can be many things," Damon said just to her left. "Or it can just be pain. What will it be for you, Serena mine?"

The crop whistled as it sliced through the air. Before she could tense, pain, bright and explosive, sheared like lightning over her skin. Her body jerked in response, and she cried out. Before she could say the first word that sprang to her lips, heat simmered over her buttocks where before fire had flashed.

A warm hum, heady and pleasurable, invaded her veins, making her heavy and sluggish. It was difficult to process this odd pain that turned so quickly to pleasure. She wanted more. Feared it, but craved it in equal measure.

Fire tore through her other ass cheek as the slap of leather met flesh. Before she could suck in her breath and wait for the aftermath, Damon sliced the crop across her buttocks again.

She flinched, and he struck again, not as hard this time and over the sensitive skin just below the curve of her ass. Ribbons of razorblades ran circles over her skin.

Astonishingly, as she opened her mouth to ask him to stop, she found herself begging him for more. *Please. More.* She heard the words trip precariously from her lips like they'd been dragged from a reluctant tongue.

The crop found untouched skin. The leather covered every inch of her ass until heat poured off her flesh like liquid fire.

Damon ceased and she gave a little moan, whether of relief

or regret, she wasn't sure. Not moving from behind her, he leaned against her back, reaching and finding her breast. He flicked lightly at the tortured nipple, and her reaction was instantaneous. Feeling poured in, white hot, leaving her gasping and her eyes watering. But just as the blow to her ass bled into slow, sweet pleasure, so too did the fire die a quick death in her nipple and instead pleasure bloomed. Curled with desire and pushing upward as though seeking the sun.

He pulled away, giving one last tweak to the hypersensitive nipple.

"I wish you could see how beautiful you look," he murmured. "Stretched before me, open and giving. Your skin is radiant with my mark. It's like a warm blush, red in some places, pink in others."

She closed her eyes against the seduction in his voice. She felt beautiful when he spoke so. Cherished and treasured.

A loud pop echoed through the room, startling her first with the sound, and then the sizzle of red hot pain made her body surge forward, tearing and straining against the bonds that held her tight.

Tears stung her eyes, pricked at her eyelids and threatened to spill over. Again and again the crop rained down over her ass, her hips, the small of her back and up to her shoulders.

There was no pity, no mercy, no reprieve from the pain. And then, like a sunrise, the warm, hazy glow of indescribable pleasure rose and spread across her skin. A gossamer veil enveloping her in silk. Was she insane to want something so badly? To suffer for the ultimate ecstasy?

The room blurred, whether from the narcotic-like embrace of pleasure or from her tears, she wasn't sure. She floated, light and free. No longer was she restrained. She flew. Surrounded by a warm, comfortable glow. She smiled dreamily and let her chin drop to her chest.

Unbelievably, an orgasm stirred, awakened and spread like stretching at dawn. It gathered momentum and surged through her exhausted body, tightening each nerve receptor, making the pain of the crop rise until she couldn't tell the difference between a lash and the sweetest of kisses.

And then the pain went away, and she moaned in protest. Her orgasm lay suspended, waiting on edge, poised to hurl her over a jagged cliff.

Hands gripped her waist. A cock nudged at her ass. Her pussy clenched, feeling neglected. Damon shoved, impatiently, and lodged himself inside her ass in one forceful lunge.

Her ass, so sensitive from the crop, quivered each time he slid his hands over the raised welts. His grip tightened, and he began fucking her with brutal intensity.

The force of his thrusts shook her body, made her breasts jiggle, and each movement made the teeth of the clamps bite harder into her nipples.

She knew she was being observed, that men and women alike watched her with lust in their eyes. In that moment she didn't care. There was only her and Damon, fucking her, owning her, showing her that here she had no power except what he gave her.

She was beyond her limits. She had no control of the ragged pleas that tore from her mouth. Was she begging him to stop or begging for more? The only word she kept closely guarded, bound to her as tightly as she was bound to the frame was *no*. She wouldn't say it. Didn't want it to end.

"Release her," Damon said as he rammed against her ass again.

Hands cupped her breasts and suddenly the jaws of the clamps opened, freeing her nipples. Feeling, sharp and agonizing, returned to nipples that had been numb, tore through her and sent her spiraling into a yawning abyss.

Her eyes opened and widened, her lips formed a scream.

Damon's cock, thick and heavy, ripped into her ass, over and over. She was helplessly open to him, powerless and defenseless against his onslaught.

His hands circled her. His fingers found her nipples and rolled the points, pinching them slightly. It was too much.

As if he felt her orgasm breaking, he kept pounding furiously into her, her body shaking and swaying on the frame.

"Come, Serena," he commanded hoarsely. "Give me your pleasure."

He pinched sharply at her nipples, sending a fresh wave of agony through her chest. It matched the unbearable pressure in her ass as he buried himself as deep as he could go.

She needed, she needed just one more . . . push, pull, something to send her that extra inch. Her body couldn't take much more stress. Every muscle was tensed, her body straining and pulled in a dozen different directions.

And the hot fire ripped over her back. The crop landed just inches above where Damon was buried in her ass. His hands still covered her breasts, toying mercilessly with her aching nipples, so she knew it couldn't be him. Cole. It had to be Cole.

Like lava falling from the sky, the lashes fell. Damon pumped furiously against her buttocks. She closed her eyes, and the room went still around her. Silence, so sweet and blissful, settled like a soft rain. She simply let go, gave up control, quit fighting her needs and fears.

Her orgasm roared through her like an out-of-control freight train. It began in her groin, rolling, stampeding outward until her entire body shook uncontrollably. She screamed. Once. Twice. She lost count.

Pleasure, so much pleasure. It was too much and not enough. Even sated, completely and utterly exhausted, she wanted more. Like an addict desperate for a fix. She arched her body upward, seeking the crop that was no longer there.

Gentle hands soothed her ravaged back. Sweet words floated down over her, coating her like warm caramel. Lips touched the center of her back. Strong arms surrounded her, holding her up as someone else freed her arms and legs.

Then she sagged, her strength gone, into Damon's waiting arms. He gathered her close, wrapping his shirt around her quivering body. He swiped gently at her cheeks, and she realized they were wet with tears.

As he carried her from the room her arms curled around his neck, and she held him as tightly as he held her. More tears seeped from her eyelids, trickling down her cheeks.

She was barely aware of him getting into a car and directing Sam to take them home. All she heard were the murmured words of approval Damon whispered into her hair as he kissed and petted her.

"Go to sleep, Serena mine. I'll take care of you."

CHAPTER 23

$\mathcal{S}$erena awoke to the dim light of first dawn. The room was bathed in pale lavender as the sun stretched and made its way over the horizon.

She lay there for a moment, processing her surroundings, content to savor these first few moments of comfortable bliss.

The first thing she registered was that her arms weren't bound as usual. They were in fact folded over Damon's arm, which encircled her waist. A glance down picked up on the fact that Damon's leg was over hers, and her body was tucked securely in the shelter of his.

Unable to resist the freedom to move as she wished and to touch Damon, she rolled and wiggled until she faced him. He opened his eyes and regarded her with warm affection.

She snuggled into his chest and slid her arm around his waist. The steady rhythm of his heartbeat faintly against her temple, and she inhaled his scent, savoring and holding it before finally exhaling.

She kissed his chest and then scooted her body upward, tilting her head so that she was level with his lips. She pulled her arm from around his waist and reached up to touch his cheek, rough from overnight stubble.

He lay there watching her, making no move to stop her or to direct her in any way. She moved closer until she could feel his breath on her lips. Slowly, with great deliberation, she touched her mouth to his.

She sighed into his mouth, unable to call back the deep contentment over the simple kiss. She loved touching him, and so far had not gotten as many chances to do so as she'd have liked. This morning he seemed willing to let her do as she wished, and she wasn't going to pass on the opportunity.

Her hands fluttered over the beard-roughed skin of his jaw, and she kissed a line from his lips to his neck, enjoying the rugged rasp against her lips. His pulse jumped wildly at his neck as her mouth closed over it and nipped lightly with her teeth.

"Are you seducing me, Serena mine?" he said in a near groan. "Has the slave turned master and temptress?"

She smiled and shoved, rotating his body until he lay flat on his back underneath her.

"I knew I shouldn't have left you untied," he murmured, though there was no true regret in his voice.

"Make love to me, Damon," she whispered. The need was strong in her voice. "Just us. No bonds. No games. Just two lovers enjoying waking beside each other."

He circled her body with his arms, yanking her to his chest. She fell, her mouth landing close to his. He claimed her lips, devouring them hungrily. There was no casual sipping, no easy give and take. He simply took, unleashing his passion in a kiss that left her shaken and bare.

There was no disguising his need, his urgent desire for her. Power rippled through her, arcing in the air, electric and sizzling. That he could want her so desperately, just her, not the slave, not the games or the elaborate schemes, took her breath away.

He rolled, taking her with him until she was tucked underneath him, her legs splayed out, him cradled to her body. His hands tangled in her hair, clutching at her slim neck as he guided her to his eager mouth.

"Does your back hurt you?" he gasped out.

She had to actually think, to try and remember why her back would hurt. Then last night came flooding back in a storm of passion and lust. Images of how he'd made her feel. The pain. The desire laced with the fury of her orgasm.

"No, it doesn't hurt. Please don't stop, Damon. You won't hurt me. You'd never hurt me."

"No, Serena mine. I'll never hurt you," he said softly as he reclaimed her mouth.

His lips slid from hers and down her jaw until he reached the sensitive lobe of her ear. He nibbled lightly then sucked it between his teeth. When he moved below to claim the tender skin of her neck, chill bumps danced and raced across her shoulders and tightened her nape.

She made full use of her hands, delving into his brown hair, enjoying the crispness of the strands as they feathered across her fingers. His gaze sought hers as he rose from her neck and then moved to her breasts.

There was something wild in his eyes. Where before he had seemed restrained, in control and patient, now there was an urgency, a deep wanting in those warm brown orbs that melted her heart.

"Come to me," she whispered. "Be with me. Serena. The person, not the fantasy."

He stopped, his body going still against her flesh. His gaze penetrated her, dark and forbidding. Propping himself on one arm next to her head, he touched his fingers to her lips as if to shush her. "You were never just a fantasy to me, Serena mine."

Her chest swelled and expanded with emotion that caught her off guard. Was she too caught up in the mess of fantasy versus reality? Was she having a hard time separating the two in her mind? Why was it suddenly so important that he want her and not the obedient sex slave?

He dropped his head and kissed her, long and sweet. His tongue danced with hers, touching, licking, loving her mouth deeply and intimately.

There was a reverence to his every touch, almost hesitation, as though he feared she would shatter under his caresses. Carefully he ran his hand over the curve of her shoulder. The backs of his knuckles grazed the soft skin above her breast and then slid over her nipple.

"Are they sore?" he asked as he stopped and thumbed over the point.

"A little," she admitted. "They're more . . . sensitive. They still tingle."

"Did you like the clamps?"

She nodded.

He leaned down and put his mouth over the taut peak. Warm and moist, his tongue flicked over the tip as his lips closed around the aureole. Her pussy tightened as he sucked in smooth rhythmic motions.

With his free hand, he reached between them, sliding his

hand between her parted thighs. He found her wetness, and his fingers teased over her opening. His cock lay rigid against the inside of her thigh, and he opened her then positioned himself so that his length was cradled in her folds.

He smiled when her eyes widened as he rubbed up and down, the plump vein on the underside of his penis pressing against her clit. His balls crowded her pussy entrance, and she remembered how they'd felt sandwiched between them when he'd fucked her ass.

She reached down, and he reared farther up on his knees to give her access. Her fingers slid through her curls so that his cock nudged the tips each time he came seeking through her folds. Up and down he rubbed, sucking in his breath each time she stroked the blunt crown.

Her juices coated him and transferred to her hand. She withdrew and brought her fingers up to his mouth in a saucy dare. He didn't hesitate. Taking her wrist, he held her fingers captive and proceeded to suck each and every one.

Not letting go of her hand, he leaned forward, forcing her arm to her side. He found her other one with his free hand and entwined their fingers before pressing them to the mattress on either side of her head.

He lay above her, his body pressed to hers, his cock between her thighs. He nibbled playfully at her chin, and when she laughed, he captured the sound as his mouth covered hers.

He rocked his hips, moving up and down until he found her entrance. He slid deep, seating himself far within her body. Then he stopped, holding himself tightly against her as he devoured her mouth.

She wriggled her hands, just enough to test how committed he was to holding her down. He released her immediately, and she touched him with greediness, her hands coaxing over his arms to his muscular shoulders and then to his back.

She loved the male roughness, the dips and curves of each muscle and the rigidity as she feathered over them. She loved feeling him flinch, as though her touch was intensely pleasurable to him.

He withdrew, sliding his engorged cock over aching, pulsing flesh. Then he rocked forward again, slow and easy. She sighed and wiggled her hips, impatient for the pleasure he would give her.

A smile curved his sensual lips, and his eyes gleamed as he stilled once more inside her.

"You're a miserable tease," she reproached.

"What's your hurry?" he murmured as he kissed her quick and light and then proceeded to pepper a line down her jaw to her throat.

"Mmmm." She arched into him, seeking those sinful lips, needing to feel them against her skin.

Thrust and withdraw. He set a lazy rhythm, his pace unhurried and relaxed. Each stroke sent her senses flaming, a slow crawl to completion. Like a rope swing in the heat of summer, starting slow, swaying in the wind, higher and higher, until it reached toward blue skies.

She closed her eyes, basking in his sunshine. His hands roamed freely over her body, cupping and molding, his touch light and seeking. Each caress told her more than words that she belonged to him. She was his and he knew her better than any other lover she'd ever been with.

When she felt his pace quicken, felt him swell within her, stretching her to her limits, she pulled his head down to hers. She fused their lips, pouring all that she felt into her kiss.

He lowered his body to hers, melding to her as he wrapped his arms around her. Their bodies entwined, he cupped his hips over her, thrusting repeatedly between her legs.

"Serena," he whispered as he buried his face in her hair.

Her breath stuttered across her lips like a hiccup. She flew higher on the swing until the sun bathed her face and she closed her eyes to its brightness. Warmth, sweet, honeyed warmth flooded her soul. Joy flickered across her heart as her orgasm swelled and then burst around her like flowers opening to the sun's rays.

"Damon," she whispered back, her voice choked.

They held each other tightly as their bodies quivered and shook in the aftermath of their lovemaking. He lay, warm and limp over her body, covering her like a blanket. She rubbed her palm absently over his back as he softened inside her.

Finally, he moved away, pulling her with him so that she was cradled in his embrace.

Neither spoke, and maybe they didn't want to ruin the moment with something as harsh and unwieldy as mere words. Serena contented herself with lying in his arms, listening to the soft pounding of his heartbeat so close to her ear.

CHAPTER 24

"*W*ake up, sleepyhead."

Damon's voice rumbled in her ear, and she moved her head in protest and snuggled deeper into the covers. He chuckled and smacked her affectionately on the ass. She winced as a tingle of discomfort hummed over her sore flesh. Almost as quickly a curl of pleasure simmered deep and she was taken back to the previous evening.

"Come on, Serena. Get up and get dressed. We're taking a trip."

She opened one eye to glance warily at him. "Are you always this obnoxiously cheerful in the morning?

He smiled. "It's no longer morning. You slept until noon. And good morning sex will do that to a guy."

"Good any sex will do that to a guy," she corrected.

"True, but then guys aren't known for their depth," he said with a sexy wink. "Now get up and get dressed. I've already packed a bag for you."

She sat up and wiped the sleep from her eyes as she blearily tried to focus on him. "Where are we going?"

"I thought we'd go see my mom," he said lightly. "It's been . . . a long time since I've seen her and it's time to go back home."

She scrambled from the covers and hooked her legs over the side. "Your mom? Where does she live? And, um, am I going as your slave or as a friend or what?"

He put his hands on her arms and squeezed gently as he hauled her to stand in front of him. He kissed her lingeringly then brushed a finger over her nose. "What do you want to go as, Serena mine?"

The question confused her, not for its lack of clarity. It was certainly direct and uncomplicated enough. But it was one of those questions that asked her to state intentions she wasn't sure of yet, and worse, asked her to declare them before she knew of his feelings.

Feelings?

She stepped away abruptly, desperate to put distance between them. Did she want him to have feelings for her? When the fuck had this gone beyond a simple fantasy to grandiose thoughts of a relationship?

It was hard to think of a relationship when the extent of their "courting" had consisted of bondage, spankings and ass fucking.

She nearly groaned aloud. So it wasn't quite that crude, and it reduced what had been an extremely satisfying sexual experience to something cheap and smutty.

"Serena?"

She glanced back up at Damon who looked at her with confused eyes.

"Is something wrong? If you'd prefer we not go, I can go an-other time."

She shook her head. "I'd love to," she said huskily. "Let me get a shower. I can be dressed in half an hour."

He leaned in to kiss her again. "Take your time. I'll pack the car."

They zipped down Interstate 10 in Damon's BMW. He drove with the practiced ease of someone well acquainted with the horrors of Houston traffic.

For the first couple of hours they rode in silence, Damon's gaze fixed on the road ahead. Occasionally she glanced at his profile, studying his tense expression. He'd seemed eager to visit his mother earlier, but now, as they crossed over the Louisiana state line, his jaw was firmly set.

Wanting to ease some of the strain, she tentatively reached across the seat for his hand. He glanced over and smiled, easing some of the lines at his brow.

Not wanting to pry too deeply into what may or may not be bothering him, she opted for general and light. She cocked her head to the side and smiled at him.

"Tell me something about yourself."

Amusement twinkled in his eyes and he seemed to relax.

"Like what?"

"Oh, anything. I'm all ears."

He rubbed his thumb over her palm while he gripped the steering wheel with his other hand.

"Okay. I like good wine, good food and beautiful women."

Serena snorted. "Tell me something I don't know. You're horribly spoiled. Tell me about your past lovers."

He coughed. "I'm not crazy. A guy should never talk about other women when he's in the presence of another one, particularly one he's currently having sex with."

"Come on, it's not like I'm your girlfriend," she said lightly. "How come you don't have a permanent slave to do your evil bidding?"

His expression sobered. "It's not that easy."

"No?"

He shook his head. "There are plenty of women who are into the fantasy. Not so much the reality."

"You mean like me," she said softly.

He stared over at her but didn't agree. He didn't have to. It was the simple truth.

"No one ever wanted to do it . . . permanently?" she asked. "Did you ask them to?"

"I only asked one," he said as he looked away. "The others . . . it was obvious it was a fling, and I was okay with it. I never wanted something permanent or I just didn't think it would work long-term."

"Except with one," she said.

He nodded.

"Did you love her?"

The corner of his mouth crooked up. "Maybe? She was the only woman I thought might be the one. You know the whole clichéd one in a million, the one meant for me. All that sappy bullshit you women read about in romance novels."

"Bitter much?" she asked with a raised brow.

He laughed, and his shoulders sank again as he relaxed. "You're fun, Serena. You don't let me take myself too seriously."

"Well, someone's got to keep you in line," she teased. "You could easily become too spoiled if left unchecked."

He grinned and squeezed her hand.

"So what happened with this woman? Did she just decide that the slave thing didn't work for her or what?"

He blew out his breath. "We enjoyed a very exciting sex life. She was into every imaginable kink. I couldn't believe my good fortune. She was into me, didn't seem too impressed with my money and wanted to please me. In turn, I wanted very much to please her. We talked about the kind of lifestyle I led and that it wasn't a game. It wasn't something I did randomly. She was on board with that. I wanted to marry her. I wanted to own her. I wanted her to own my heart."

"Oh boy," Serena murmured. It was on the tip of her tongue to say what a dumbass the woman had been for running from Damon, but then how big of a hypocrite would that make her?

"Yeah, you can guess the rest. One day she decided that belonging to me wasn't what she wanted. She wanted freedom, though I never tried to restrain her. Her time with me was mine, but I never tried to interfere in her outside interests. I knew that to make it work, we both needed time and space outside of an exhausting sexual odyssey."

Serena slowly nodded. "So she left."

Damon nodded. "And I let her go. She was my slave, the woman I loved, but she wanted freedom, and I couldn't do anything other than grant it to her."

It was her turn to squeeze his hand. "I'm sorry."

He smiled. "If I was still with her, you and I would have never embarked on our own odyssey."

"True. I guess I'm not so sorry after all. I do regret that you were hurt."

He reached over and touched her cheek. "Thank you for that, Serena mine."

"Did you call her that too?" she asked in a sudden flash of irritation.

Damon gave her a puzzled look. "Call her what?"

"Mine."

He slowly shook his head. "No. I've never used that particular endearment with anyone before. Does it bother you?"

"Only if you used it for all your women," she said honestly.

"No, just with you."

It was ridiculous that it gratified her to hear it, but she wouldn't lie outright and say it wouldn't have annoyed her if it was used so casually. She loved the endearment. Loved the way it made her feel. Special. Like she truly belonged to him.

"What about you, Serena? Why did you seek me out? Did your previous lovers not satisfy your hunger?"

She leaned back against the head rest and sighed. "It's hard to explain, really. I won't say my lovers were bad. They were all different. Some better than others, but they all satisfied my needs at the time. It was only later that I felt like something was missing, that I wanted something more but couldn't articulate what it was exactly.

"My lovers were everything I could ask for. Kind, generous. Willing to please. I guess we just didn't click long-term. One of them proposed, but the idea of spending the rest of my life with him turned me cold."

"I know how the poor bastard feels," Damon said ruefully.

Serena winced. "That probably sounded pretty close to home and not very tactful of me."

"No, at least you were honest, just like Tonya was honest with me. I can't fault either of you for that. It would have been worse if you had lied. In the long run, it would have been harder for everyone."

"I know," she said softly. "But part of me also wonders what might have been. If I made a mistake. If right now I wouldn't be happy in a marriage with children and someone I could grow old with."

"It's easy to play the *what-if* game, but if you had enough reservations to end the relationship early on, you were probably right. Settling is something I swore never to do. It's not fair to me or to the woman I'm involved with."

"I think you have some pretty solid views on relationships," she complimented.

He winced. "If that was so, I'd have a committed relationship of my own with maybe one or two rug rats underfoot. Although, I'm not in a hurry for children. I want time with my wife. I want her to myself, as selfish as that may sound."

"If you're selfish, then so am I. I'll make a confession, one I've never given anyone else."

"Oh, now I'm intrigued."

She laughed softly. "A bit ago, when I said that part about maybe now I'd have a husband and children. Well, the truth is, I've never been in a hurry for kids either. It's easy to say what I might have when there's no possibility of it, you know?"

"Yeah, I do know. So you're saying you don't want children?"

"Maybe? I don't really know. I guess I haven't met a man who made me think seriously about settling down and bearing offspring. I'm not convinced I'll be terribly good at it. And like you, I'd like some time with my lover. Just the two of us. I have such dreams about going places together. Seeing new and exciting things . . ."

She trailed off and looked self-consciously over at Damon. He smiled warmly at her.

"I think we have a lot in common, Serena mine."

Her body hummed with pleasure, and she squeezed his fingers. They did have a lot in common except the one looming obstacle. And it was a biggie.

She wanted a fantasy. He wanted the real thing.

With a resigned sigh, she turned to look out her window at the passing cypress swamp. It wouldn't do any good to allow herself to become too emotionally invested in Damon. They wanted different things. And she could never give herself so unreservedly to a man on a permanent basis.

CHAPTER 25

$\mathcal{D}$amon's mother was sitting in a porch swing waiting for them when they drove up in the late afternoon. Serena wasn't sure what she'd been expecting, maybe a sweet, silver-haired lady with an apron. Now she felt pretty silly when confronted with the gorgeous, young-looking woman who stood and beamed as Damon got out of the car.

She was wearing blue jeans and a T-shirt, and her hair hung to her shoulders. Not a single silver hair marred the deep chestnut color, so close to Damon's own. Where his eyes were a chocolate brown, his mother's were a sparkling green.

Damon walked around and helped Serena from the car then slipped his hand in hers as they walked toward his mother. She greeted them at the steps, opening her arms to Damon.

Her eyes glittered with tears as she hugged her son, and Serena felt her own throat tighten at the emotional reunion.

"It's so good to have you home, son," she said as she pulled away. Then she turned her gaze to Serena and smiled warmly. "I'm Josephine Roche, Damon's mother."

Serena smiled in return but before she could open her mouth, Damon put an arm around her shoulders and drew her close.

"Mom, this is Serena James."

"I'm so glad to meet you, Serena."

"I'm very glad to meet you as well, Mrs. Roche."

"Please call me Jo. It's what I'm used to."

"Mom, if you'll take Serena inside, I'll get our bags."

"I'd be glad to. Serena? If you'll come with me. I have tea made, and supper will be ready in half an hour. I made Damon's favorite. Sausage gumbo."

"So what will you and Serena eat?" Damon asked innocently.

Jo laughed then planted both her hands on Damon's cheeks and kissed him soundly. "I'm so glad you're here. You've been away too long."

"I know, Mom. I'm sorry," he said softly.

She smiled a little sadly and patted him on the cheek. "I know how hard it is for you."

He kissed her palm then pulled her hand away and squeezed before letting it go. "You two go on in. I'll be right behind you."

Serena followed Jo inside the sprawling southern home. The porch completely wrapped around and butted into a wooden deck in the back of the house. Serena stood at the window looking out over the bayou that snaked its way through the Roches' property.

"Great view, isn't it?" Jo asked beside her.

Serena turned to take the glass of tea that Jo offered and nodded. "Do you have alligators?"

Jo grinned. "A few. Damon used to go hunting them when

he was a teenager. Always swore he'd get one. He and his father spent many hours up and down these swamps. They caught plenty of catfish, but never any gators."

"You're not telling all my secrets are you, Mom?" Damon asked as he came to stand behind Serena.

He put his arm around her waist and dropped a kiss on top of her head. Serena tensed, not entirely comfortable with the display of affection in front of a woman she'd just met, but Jo smiled openly in delight.

"I thought we could eat out on the deck this evening. We can watch the sun go down and look for fireflies over the bayou," Jo said.

Damon stilled against her and she turned around to see a sad smile crossing his face. "Just like old times."

Serena glanced back at Jo, whose face reflected a sad poignancy even though she too smiled. She reached out and squeezed Damon's hand. "Yes, just like old times."

Then she turned and reached to squeeze Serena's hand. "Why don't you let Damon show you around while I set the gumbo back on to warm. I'll call you two when it's time to set the table."

"Still a slave driver, I see," Damon said.

"Damn right. I cook it. You can at least set the table and clear up afterward."

He leaned over and brushed a kiss across his mother's forehead. "With the way you cook, I'm getting the best end of the bargain."

"You always were a charmer. Just like your father."

The two exchanged sorrowful glances before Damon took Serena's elbow and urged her toward the triple-glass French doors that overlooked the deck.

"I'll take you to see my favorite fishing holes," he said as he opened the door.

Warm, muggy air stifled Serena's breathing as she followed Damon outside. It was a good hour before sunset, and the temperature was near its highest point of the day.

"My father built this," Damon said as he ran his hand along the cedar railing of the porch.

"It's beautiful." She observed him for a long moment before biting the bullet and taking the plunge. "I take it your father passed away?"

Damon slowly nodded. "Two years ago. He was fishing." He turned and pointed to a bend in the bayou. "Right over there. My mother found him slumped over. He had a massive heart attack and died on the spot. He never had a chance."

She touched his arm. "I'm sorry."

"He was the best," Damon said quietly. Though he didn't overtly acknowledge her gesture, he put his hand over hers and left it there.

"You haven't been home since?" she asked. He appeared to be so close to his mother. It seemed odd that he'd stay away so long.

A sad, weary look entered his eyes, dulling them to a drab brown. "No. I tried. But it was too painful. I got all the way to the driveway, and I turned around and drove back to Houston. Pretty cowardly."

He moved to the railing and rested both hands on the wood, leaning out over it as he stared over the cypress clogged bayou. "It hurt my mom. I knew it, but still, I couldn't make myself come back. I couldn't face being here without him."

"Why now?" she asked softly. Why with her?

"I don't know," he admitted. "I've missed my mom. I've needed to face her, this house. Needed to realize that my staying away doesn't alter the fact that he's gone. And maybe it seemed easier with you."

She inhaled sharply, unable to control her surprise at his statement.

He touched her cheekbone then slid his hand behind her head and pulled her toward him. She rocked against him as he tilted her upward to meet his kiss.

It was gentle, it was soft. In a word, it was exquisite. It shook her to her core.

"Thank you for coming with me," he whispered against her lips. "It means a lot."

She smiled as she drew away. "I'm glad you wanted me with you."

He took her to the banks of the bayou and they watched the catfish surface as if expecting to be fed.

"My mom feeds them every evening," he explained. "They're spoiled rotten."

They continued along the edge as it wound through the rolling terrain of his mother's property. A rickety dock was situated in the crook of one of the bends, and an old johnboat was tied up. It rocked gently with the ripples of the water. The green paint was faded and peeling. Stenciled with black paint on the side was *Roche*.

"My father's boat," Damon said. "It belonged to his grandfather. Old as Methuselah but it still runs. Mom takes it out every now and again just to keep it going."

"She misses him too," Serena said, remembering the sadness in her eyes.

Damon sighed. He turned to face the water and shoved his hands into his pockets. For a long moment he was silent. His lips moved as though he had difficulty forming the words.

"It was hard on her and even harder when I stayed away even though she understood."

He glanced down at his feet, and his shoulders sagged.

"It was selfish of me and it's something I regret. They were . . . they were so in love. They were high school sweethearts, and she married him when she was sixteen. Folks around here didn't give them a chance of lasting or ever amounting to anything, but they proved them wrong. He built this house for mom when she was pregnant with me. I grew up here. It's the only home I ever knew."

He smiled and glanced sideways at Serena. "My father made his fortune and retired early. He and mom were supposed to travel. Have fun. Live and love and enjoy life. He died just a week after they returned from a trip to Paris. It was where my mother had dreamed of traveling since she was a girl."

Serena blinked away the tears that stung her eyelids. "At least they got one last trip together before he passed," she said.

Damon nodded. "We all had some good times together. For so long it hurt to think about them, to remember life with Dad knowing he wasn't here anymore. But now . . . now it just feels good to remember."

She reached out, caught his wrist and pulled his hand from his pocket. She laced her fingers through his and tugged his hand to her side.

They both turned when they heard Jo calling to them. She was standing on the deck waving and motioning them to supper.

"Come on. The gumbo's not as good when it's cold," he said.

"Race you," Serena challenged even as she took off.

"Cheater!" Damon yelled as he pounded after her.

She would have beaten him to the steps, but just as she

made the leap, he plucked her from the air and spun her around in his arms. She shrieked in outrage and he responded by dumping her on the ground and following her down to tickle her unmercifully.

When she was wheezing for breath between peals of laughter, he finally stopped and hauled her up.

"Declare me the victor," he demanded.

"Never!"

She launched herself up the steps then turned around and did an imitation of Rocky, hands in the air as she danced back and forth.

"Little cheat," he grumbled as he walked past her to the table where his mom waited.

"Damon always was a poor loser," Jo said as she grinned at Serena. "He was always the most competitive child. Best at everything."

"And who did I get that from, pray tell?" Damon said dryly.

"Your father, of course."

Damon snorted and headed toward the door. "You ladies stay here. I'll be back with bowls and silverware. Want me to bring out the gumbo, Mom?"

"Please," she said. Then she turned to Serena. "Would you like wine or tea with your dinner?"

"I'll have whatever you and Damon are having," Serena said.

"In that case, it'll be wine. It's an indulgence of ours. Even during the two years he was gone, he'd call and I'd sit here on the deck and we'd share a glass of wine and talk on the phone."

"It sounds like you're very close," Serena said.

"He's my only child," Jo said by way of explanation.

Damon came back out with bowls and spoons then went

back in and returned a moment later with a steaming pot of gumbo.

"Get the rice if you don't mind. It's in the steamer. And snag the bottle of wine I have laid out," Jo said as Damon set the pot down.

She and Serena sat and when Damon returned with the rice, Jo served up the gumbo. Though it was hot and muggy, the gumbo, usually more suited for the cold of winter, tasted delicious.

After dinner, they sat back with a glass of wine and watched the lightning bugs pop over the water. In the distance crickets chirped and frogs croaked. The tree locusts added to the cacophony, but it was soothing to Serena. After so long hearing only the sounds of the city, she was lulled by the tranquility here.

"So how long have you two been together and how did you meet?" Jo asked, breaking the silence.

Serena stiffened and sent Damon a panicked glance. He took her hand under the table and squeezed reassuringly.

"We were introduced by a mutual friend. We've only been seeing each other a short time, but I'm hoping to convince her to keep me around for a while."

Jo smiled. "Smooth-talking bastard, just like your father. And they expect you to fall at their feet for their efforts," she said to Serena.

Serena laughed, her discomfort passing. "I expect they do. And I'll admit, it does turn my head. As I've told him before, he's no stranger to pretty words."

"Lord no. I swear all the Roche men have the lion's share of charm and charisma. Sometimes you just have to call bullshit, though." She winked at Serena as she said the last.

Serena chuckled as Damon rolled his eyes.

"If I have charm, it sure as hell never worked on you," Damon said to Jo. "And it damn sure never got me out of trouble."

Jo grinned. "You have your father to blame for that. By the time you came along, I was well acquainted with the Roche silver tongue and had built an immunity."

She turned to Serena. "What about you, Serena? Where are you from and what do your folks do?"

Damon looked curiously at her as well, and she realized that they'd never really talked about her. Or him for that matter, until the trip over. They'd been too busy talking with other parts of their anatomy.

She flushed slightly and looked away from Damon. "I was born and raised in Houston. My dad is retired from an oil company, and my mom still teaches school. I'm an only child as well."

"Ah, then you and Damon are both likely spoiled rotten," Jo said.

"I don't deny it," Damon said as he sipped at his wine.

"Good damn thing. I'd hate to be sitting close to you when that lightning bolt descends."

Serena laughed again, enjoying the easy rapport between mother and son. It made her miss her own parents, though it hadn't been that long since she'd last visited. It was easy to get caught up in work, become too busy to pick up the phone or stop in to say hello. After witnessing Damon and Jo's grief over losing Damon's father, she was going to make it a priority to see her folks as soon as she got back. Life was short. Damon's father's sudden passing was certainly a testament to that.

"My mom is great," Serena said, suddenly compelled to talk about her own parents. "I probably was spoiled, but she raised me to be independent. To think and do for myself. She was one of nine children, and the only one to graduate high school. She put herself through college and got her teaching degree. I was always so proud of her. She doesn't take any shit from anyone."

"Sounds like my kind of lady," Jo said.

"I think you'd get along well," Serena said with a smile.

"And what do you do?" Jo asked. "If you don't mind me asking."

"This isn't an interrogation, Mom," Damon said mildly.

"No, it's okay," Serena said. For a long time she had felt discomfort over explaining her business to other people. But the happiness she brought her clients quickly removed any unease she felt over the legitimacy of Fantasy Incorporated.

"I own my own business. I fulfill fantasies," she said.

Jo blinked in surprise. "What kind of fantasies?"

"Mom," Damon said in warning.

"Not the kind you're thinking," Serena said as she hid her smile. Not unless having her own sexual fantasy fulfilled counted.

"I create scenarios for people. A fantasy situation. For instance, one of my last clients had a dream of being a chef in a top restaurant in Houston. He didn't know how to go about it, wanted me to arrange the details, so I did."

"Oh, how fun! So it's like a play day almost," Jo said.

"Well, I suppose you could call it that. It's a chance to do something you might not otherwise get to do. My most recent client wanted to be a princess of her own cruise ship."

Serena's face tightened, and she regretted bringing Michelle up.

"I think that's wonderful, Serena. And how creative! I've never heard of another business like it."

"Thank you. I enjoy it."

Jo reached for her plate, but Damon stood and motioned her away.

"You ladies sit tight, and I'll put away the dishes."

"You raised a good man," Serena said with a sigh as he disappeared inside.

"Yeah, well, just don't let him think you know that," Jo muttered. "Because then they get impossible to live with."

Serena chuckled and leaned back in her chair, inhaling the night air. She glanced up at the sky, which was clear and dotted with the first stars. And she wished. Wished for the impossible. She wished for the fantasy to never end.

CHAPTER 26

*D*amon stood at the sink, looking out the window at his mom and Serena smiling and laughing like old friends. He wasn't sure why he'd chosen now to return home or why he'd asked Serena to come. It had just seemed right. Now that he was here, he was glad he'd come. He should have never stayed away, no matter how much it hurt. His mom had been hurting too, and she'd needed him.

His mom's questions about Serena pressed home just how little he knew about her. Yes, he'd run a background check. He knew cursory details, but he didn't know any of the stuff that mattered. What made her tick. What she dreamed. What made her happy and what made her sad.

And it bothered the hell out of him.

He'd make it his mission to find out every nuance of what made her the person she was.

Collecting a full bottle of wine and the opener, he headed back outside. Rich laughter met his ears as he opened the door, and he realized how very good it felt to hear his mom laugh again.

The two women looked up, warm welcome in their eyes. It felt damn good. He moved his chair closer to Serena then settled beside her. He flung an arm around her shoulders and pulled her into the crook of his arm.

"Are you enjoying yourself?" he murmured as his mom poured more wine.

"Very much so," she returned as she looked up at him, her blue eyes flashing from the glow of the interior lights.

"We won't be able to stay out much longer," Jo warned. "Mosquitos will eat us alive. The citronella seems to work for a bit after dark, but then it's like they converge in a feeding frenzy and no humans are safe."

"Ugh, I'm starting to itch just thinking about it," Serena said.

"They grow 'em so big here that Louisiana tried to make the mosquito the state bird," Jo said with a straight face.

Serena laughed. "In that case, I'll definitely be heading in soon."

Damon leaned close to Serena until his lips brushed her ear. He smiled when he felt the tiny shudder that worked up her spine. "Why don't we go in now? It's been a long day."

She turned to look at him, her smile lighting up the night. "I am tired."

He turned to his mom, who was already rising from her chair. "We're going to turn in, Mom. Thanks for supper. It was wonderful as always."

Jo leaned over and gently kissed his brow. "I'm just glad you finally came home, son." She smiled and smoothed a hand over his cheek just like she had done when he was a boy.

She walked toward the door and then turned back. "I'll

have breakfast served up around eight in the morning. You two can eat before you get back on the road."

As his mom disappeared inside, Serena looked at him questioningly.

"I told her we could only stay one night. I wasn't sure . . ." He dropped his gaze, feeling a little discomfited by his uncertainty.

"You weren't sure what?" she asked softly.

"I wasn't sure if I'd be able to stay," he admitted.

She smiled and leaned up to brush her lips across his. "I think you did wonderfully, and you made your mom so happy."

He squeezed her to him then stood, motioning her up with him. "Let's get inside and get ready for bed. I was hard on you yesterday, and you must be exhausted."

She trembled against him as they walked toward the French doors. He ran his hand over the curve of her bottom, remembering the glow from the crop the night before. She had reacted as he'd expected, wanting and begging for more. He couldn't remember ever seeing a more beautiful sight than her bound before him, her skin red and pink from the lash of his whip. She had offered herself wholly to him, and he'd been humbled by her gift.

He guided her down the long hallway to his old bedroom that his mom had made into a guest room. It bore no resemblance to the teenage retreat of his high school years. Instead, it was decorated tastefully in neutral colors with her own touch of sunshine.

"The bed isn't as big as mine," he said as he closed the door behind them. "Which means we'll just have to sleep closer together."

"And that bothers you?" she asked with a raised brow.

"Not on your life," he said as he pulled her into his arms.

He kissed her long and hard, releasing all of his pent-up hunger. Not being able to touch her the entire day, being so close and hearing her laughter, seeing her smile without being able to make love to her had driven him beyond his endurance.

"Take your clothes off," he ordered, his voice raw and unrecognizable.

As though sensing how close he was to the edge, she slowly peeled her clothing away, performing an erotic striptease that had him simmering with impatience. She'd called him a caveman, and in this moment, he felt like one. He was ready to tear every shred of clothing from her body, throw her on the bed and fuck her senseless.

The glimmer of gold came into view as her shirt fell away, and the band that he'd given her flashed. He touched it, tracing its outline with his finger.

"You belong to me," he said.

"I belong to you," she affirmed quietly.

He yanked her to him, crushing her softness against his harder frame. Somewhere between endless kisses and frantic sighs, he pulled raggedly at his own clothes, shoving until they were both naked.

Like this morning, he made no effort to subdue her or keep her from touching him. He wanted it and craved it with a fierceness he couldn't explain even to himself. Her hands stroked over his chest, a heated path that turned his insides molten.

His dick was hard, painfully so, and straining outward, bumping against the softness of her belly. And then her hands lowered, enclosing him in her silken grasp. He closed his eyes and groaned, whether in pleasure or pain, he didn't know. Didn't care. He only knew he wanted her to keep on touching him.

She pulled at his waist, urging him toward the bed. They tumbled together, her underneath until they were sprawled on the mattress in a tangle of bodies.

"Tell me what you want, Damon," she said as she stared up into his eyes. "I'm yours. I belong to you. I want only to please you."

He closed his eyes savoring the sweetness of her declaration. It was as if she knew just what to say, what he needed to hear.

"Open to me, Serena mine. Take me inside your body. For I belong to you as well as you belong to me."

Her slim thighs parted, and she opened to him as she wrapped her legs around his waist. He lowered his head to kiss her, to possess her mouth as he possessed her body. His tongue slid over hers as his cock sheathed himself in her feminine warmth.

"I could stay this way forever," he said against her lips. "You're so beautiful, Serena. I've never had another woman like you. I doubt I ever will."

The words sounded dangerous even to his own ears, but he couldn't call them back. He knew in the deepest, darkest corner of his soul that when it came time to let her go, it would kill him.

For now, he thrust, planting himself as deeply into her body and her heart as he could. Imprinting, claiming her. He forgot about her fantasies, that this was a kinky game built around forbidden desires. Right here and right now, he made love to her as he'd never made love to another woman.

He savored every gasp of pleasure, each sigh that poured

from her lips. He sipped and savored her sweet nectar as he rode her with delicious abandon.

When he felt his orgasm looming, he stilled within her, wanting to make it last as long as possible. He didn't want it to end yet, not before she found her own release.

Her hands fluttered to his cheeks, stroking over his jaw and touching his lips. He kissed each finger in turn as they rested against his mouth.

He didn't need to ask her if she was close. He felt the quickening of her body, her pussy clenching tighter around his dick. Her breathing ratcheted up and she became more frantic underneath him, twisting and writhing as she sought relief.

"Together," he whispered as he rocked against her. He thrust deeper and deeper, faster and faster until her features blurred in his vision.

He closed his eyes and threw back his head as he strained, fighting the fire that raged in his balls. His cock pulsed and swelled. Pressure built and expanded upward, racing to the finish line.

She went liquid around him, bathing him in her sweetness. And then he exploded within her. His hips twitched almost painfully with each jet of his release. He jerked and moaned before finally collapsing into her waiting arms.

She held him, her arms around his waist as she stroked his back. Her lips were pressed to his neck, and she kissed the spot where his pulse beat wildly.

He found himself opening his mouth to say words better left unspoken. Reluctantly he closed his lips and laid his head down on her shoulder.

Not wanting to smother her, he rolled slightly, keeping a tight grip on her so that she came with him. When they were both on their sides, she snuggled up tight against him, her body warm and soft. Sweet.

She was asleep almost instantly, but he stayed awake long into the night, content to hold her—and hold on to this moment for as long as he could.

CHAPTER 27

*J*ulie climbed out of her car outside of Faith's apartment and stood there for a long moment before finally starting toward Faith's door.

She wasn't used to being such a chicken shit, and she damn sure wasn't used to lacking in self-confidence. But this whole thing with Nathan had thrown her a serious curveball. Which was why she was going to do something about it. And hopefully Faith could help.

She knocked on the door and stood back, hands shoved in the back pockets of her jeans. The door swung open and Gray stood there looking inquiringly at Julie.

"Uh, hi, is Faith here?"

"Hi, Julie. Sure, come on in," Gray said as he smiled warmly.

"Sorry to barge in. I would have called but I was close and decided to just stop by," she said lamely.

"You're not barging in." He directed her toward the small living room and then turned his head toward the hallway. "Baby, Julie is here to see you."

He turned back to Julie. "Can I get you something to drink? I make some mean sun tea."

Julie nodded. "I'd love some. Thanks."

"You bet." He smiled again and headed for the kitchen. He nearly ran into Faith as she came down the hall. "I'm fixing Julie some tea. Want some?"

"Mmmm, yeah, sounds great," Faith said as she smiled up at Gray.

Julie looked up as Faith walked into the living room and sighed as Faith gave her an inquiring glance.

Faith sat down on the couch next to her and turned so she faced Julie. "Okay, so what's up? You have one of those looks that scares me."

Julie smiled weakly. "Actually I'm the one who's scared shitless."

"Uh-oh."

"Yeah, well, remember what you said about Damon helping you out with your, um, fantasies?"

Faith arched an eyebrow. "Uh-huh."

"And you sent Serena in his direction for her fantasy because he owns this sex club or whatever."

"Spit it out, Julie. What are you getting at here?"

"Well, I thought maybe he could hook me up. I mean, not personally, because Serena might kick my ass if I made a move on her man, and as hot as he is, he's not rough enough around the edges for my taste."

Faith's lips formed an O.

"But first . . ."

"I don't like the way you just said that," Faith said cautiously. "You're plotting."

Julie grinned. Faith was no dummy. "First I plan to show Nathan Tucker just what he's missing. Right before I leave him in my dust and move on to some hot, sweaty, monkey sex, which hopefully Mr. GQ can help out with."

Gray cleared his throat, and Julie looked up to see him staring at her with amusement.

"I don't suppose you'll forget everything you just heard?" Julie asked hopefully.

"Far be it from me to ever refuse a lady anything," Gray said as he set the glasses of tea on the coffee table. "But I feel compelled to lecture you about that damn sex club." He stood to his full height and stared sternly at her. "It's not a place you need to be wandering into."

Faith smothered a giggle with her hand and rolled her eyes at Julie. "It's not that bad," she defended.

Gray glared at Faith. "You're not ever going back there, so don't get any ideas about taking Julie. And Julie, I really don't think it's a good idea that you involve Damon in any sort of scheme. I'm not saying he isn't a good guy. He's been very good to Faith, and for that I'm grateful, but the members of his 'club' are another matter. Who the hell knows what you might be walking into."

"At least he didn't hear the part about Nathan," Julie muttered in a low voice to Faith.

Gray grinned. "Oh, I did, but I figure whatever he gets he deserves. Just wish I was a fly on the wall for the occasion."

Faith shooed him away with her hand. "Leave us to do our girl talking. I promise not to plan a raid on The House without telling you first."

"You damn well won't be going whether I know about it or not," Gray muttered. But he turned and walked back toward the bedroom after another glare in Faith's direction.

"And this is the guy who agreed to let another man fuck you?" Julie asked in disbelief.

"Julie! For God's sake keep your voice down," Faith hissed.

Julie held her hands up. "Just sayin'."

Faith shook her head. "Okay, so tell me what sort of fantasies you want Damon to help fulfill, and then you can tell me what you have planned for Nathan. And don't leave a word out."

CHAPTER 28

*S*erena leaned back in her chair and stared out the window of her office building. First day back at work after a week of being Damon's slave.

Slave.

It was a laughable term when she considered just what her experience had been. All the reading, all the mystery and fantasy. What she'd expected was a far cry from what she'd received.

Pampered. Cherished.

Maybe she'd expected true slavery. To be debased or degraded. Had she wanted that? Some of the scenarios she'd fantasized about embarrassed her now. Made her feel ashamed.

She reached back, trying to rationalize what drove her need to subject herself to a man's dominance. But the answers didn't come. And now that she was away from Damon, back in the normal realm of reality, she felt removed from her experience as if it had all been a dream.

The idea of going back to the fantasy seemed odd, as if the curtains had been pulled back, exposing the truth, shining light over a shadow.

Julie and Faith had both called, wanting to meet her after work for drinks and gossip, and obviously to get the dirt on Serena's week in captivity, if you could call a week of decadent pleasure and endless spoiling *captivity*.

Serena had cried off, saying Damon expected her home, and it was the truth. Why she still sat here at her desk as the evening progressed, with her cell phone turned off, was a mystery she wasn't moved to solve.

A part of her was tempted to call Damon and tell him she wouldn't be back, that the agreement was over. It would make her a flaming coward, not to mention she wanted to see Damon again. She wanted to be with him. And she owed him more than a brush-off over the phone.

She shoved away from the desk and stood. As her slacks adjusted and slipped down to cover the band around her left ankle, she frowned unhappily. For a long moment she stared at the place where she knew the cuff resided, now covered by her pants. She'd purposely not worn a skirt because she hadn't wanted the unusual piece of jewelry to be seen. The blouse she'd chosen was a half sleeve to hide the armband.

No one could possibly know what the jewelry signified, no one but her. But she hadn't felt comfortable stepping outside of the fantasy she and Damon had created, hadn't wanted to bring it to *her* world. It crossed a dangerous threshold.

Sex confused the issue. As trite as it sounded, when emotion entered the picture—and it had—sex was no longer just sex. Lust was no longer just lust. And fantasy was no longer just fantasy.

She knew this, cautioned clients about it on a daily basis, and yet here she was, up to her neck in a fantasy that blurred the line so much that even she had a hard time figuring out how much was real and how much wasn't.

She wouldn't lie to herself and vow that there wasn't any real attraction between her and Damon, or that she longed with painful ferocity for something deeper than casual sex and a fantasy role. But he'd made it clear what he wanted, and she'd been equally clear about her wants and needs.

Opposing destinations with a brief intersection.

That about described her and Damon.

She glanced at her watch and winced. She was postponing the inevitable. There was a decision to make. Either she went back to Damon or she called it off. But standing here being wishy-washy wasn't the answer, and it didn't get her any closer to the solution.

She collected her briefcase and her keys and reluctantly headed for the elevator. It was odd how strange the whole situation looked as soon as she removed herself from the fantasy. But while she was there, living it, wanting it and craving it, there was nothing but the moment. Nothing but the need for more.

Was this what addiction felt like? Wanting something that wasn't good for you and losing all objectivity in the process?

When she got into her car, she didn't immediately head for Damon's, nor did she go home. She drove. As much as it pained her to admit, she was scared. Scared of how easily she could lose herself if she allowed it. During the week she'd been with Damon, she'd found herself doing anything to please him. Without question, without hesitation, never offering argument.

It was frightening how easily she turned into someone else.

But more unnerving was the idea that maybe she hadn't so much turned into someone else as she'd embraced who she'd always been.

"No. This isn't me," she whispered. "And I don't want it to be."

Gripping the steering wheel a little tighter, she picked up the phone and dialed Faith's number.

A moment later, her friend's concerned voice came over the line.

"Where are you?" Faith demanded before Serena could even say hello.

"I'm in the car," Serena said calmly.

"Damon is frantic with worry. He said he's been unable to reach you and that you aren't at the office or your apartment."

"Shit," Serena muttered.

"Is something wrong?" Faith demanded.

Serena took in a deep breath. Just hearing that Damon was worried made Serena feel like an inconsiderate clod.

"Faith, I just have a question."

"Okay."

"Remember when you said that Gray told you he could never be involved with a woman who wasn't strong enough to submit?"

There was a short pause. "Yes, of course."

"Do you believe that?"

"What are you getting at, Serena?" Faith asked softly.

"I just want to know if you believe it. That it takes someone strong to give up ultimate power, to allow a man to take care of her, to make decisions for her."

"Yes, I do."

The conviction in Faith's voice moved her more than the actual words.

"Thank you," Serena said quietly. "I need to go. I need to get home to Damon."

"Serena, what's going on?" Faith asked.

"We'll talk later, okay?"

She hit the end button before Faith could offer further argument. For a moment, she held the phone in her hand, tempted to call Damon, but she wasn't at all sure what she'd say, and now, as if she'd known all along where she'd end up, she realized she was only a few minutes from his house.

She punched the power button to turn her phone off again and tossed it onto the seat. A few minutes later, she pulled into the drive of Damon's home and frowned when she saw several cars parked out front. She pulled up behind the last and cut the engine.

Leaving her briefcase and phone on the seat, she got out and walked to the front door. As soon as she hit the top step, the door flew open.

She raised her gaze to meet Damon's furious one. His eyes were nearly black, and anger tightened his lips.

"Where the hell have you been?" he demanded.

His words lashed over her, igniting her own helpless anger.

"I don't have to explain myself to you," she snapped. "Our agreement is for when I'm here."

He reached out and cupped her shoulder, yanking her inside the house. The door slammed behind her, and she winced.

"This has nothing, *nothing* to do with any agreement," he bit out. "It has to do with common decency. I was worried, Serena. I thought you might be on the side of the road somewhere, hurt and alone. Or in the hospital. Or in the fucking morgue."

She flinched at the raw edge in his voice. There was more than anger. There was true concern and frustration.

"You wouldn't answer your goddamn phone. I even sent Sam to your office and then your home and then back here so he could trace your possible route."

She closed her eyes against his censure because he was right. She'd been an irresponsible twit all because she didn't have a goddamn spine.

"I'm sorry," she said tiredly.

He held up his hand. His jaw ticked like he was trying to hang on to his temper.

"What happened?" he asked bluntly. "Where have you been and are you all right?"

This was one time when she wished she'd actually been in some sort of an accident just so she didn't have to tell him she'd been hiding. From him. From herself. From this combustible attraction between them.

"I was thinking."

"*Thinking?* You were thinking? And in all this thinking, it never crossed your mind that I might be worried, that you at least owed me the courtesy of a phone call to say you'd be late? Not as your *master*, Serena. Not as some guy who considers you a slave, but as someone who cares about you."

She closed her eyes as fatigue centered between her shoulders. When she opened them again, Damon was dragging a hand through his hair in a supreme gesture of agitation.

"Go and change into the clothes I've laid out for you," he said in a controlled voice. "Then return to the living room. We have guests."

He stared her down as if waiting for the word to cross her lips. He was forcing her into the decision she'd been wavering on the entire day. If she said no, she'd leave, and she wouldn't be back. If she did his bidding, she was committing to staying, to continuing the farce.

Neither option seemed attractive to her right now. What she really wanted was to be alone, and she could be alone if she just said no.

Instead, she nodded and walked past Damon toward the bedroom. He didn't touch her, didn't hold her back or say anything further. When she looked back as she entered the hallway, he'd already left the foyer.

She continued up the stairs, her fatigue and confusion growing with each step. When she got to the bedroom, she saw that Damon had laid out one of the exquisite dresses he'd purchased for her along with a matching black bra and panties, silk stockings and a pair of expensive heels. There was even jewelry to accompany the sophisticated look.

As she continued to stare at the clothing, she had a swift realization. Tonight she wasn't his slave. He was inviting her into his world. His real world, where he expected her to mingle with his guests. Normalcy. A step out of the roles they played, and yet, they only existed in the realm of her fantasy. A world *she* had created.

He was making it real. Fear raced up her spine. Fear and uncertainty. He was changing the rules and the parameters. How could he expect her to embrace his reality and then turn away? God, she didn't need it to be more real between her and Damon. If anything she needed the protection that fantasy and escapism offered. There was no chance of her losing her way when things weren't in reach.

But to expect her to interact with him as if they had a chance, as if things were normal . . . it was the height of cruelty.

Her head spun as panic and distress tightened every muscle. She couldn't attend as his date, some woman he had a relationship with. No, if she attended, it would be as his slave. There would be no breaching the walls of her carefully constructed fantasy.

CHAPTER 29

$\mathcal{D}$amon returned to the living room after taking several moments to collect himself. He'd been distracted the entire time he was entertaining his guests because he'd been worried about Serena. There were only so many times he could excuse himself to use his cell phone before it went from an inconvenience to outright rudeness.

When he'd heard her drive up, his relief had made him weak in the knees. That pissed him off almost as much as her thoughtlessness. And then he'd seen her pale face and enormous blue eyes, seen the fatigue lurking in the shadows. She'd said the words every man dreaded hearing. She'd been thinking.

He'd worried about her first day outside the fantasy they'd built in the week they'd been together, and rightly so. She'd already started pulling away, and there wasn't a damn thing he could do about it.

He tuned in to the conversation as two of the waiters he'd hired for the evening made rounds with trays of hors d'oeuvres and wine. The piano music, usually something he enjoyed, tinkled like broken glass on his nerves.

Part of him wanted to punish Serena for the worry she'd caused him. For a moment he'd considered telling her to undress and come to him nude with only the jewelry he'd given her adorning her skin. None of his guests would be shocked or surprised.

But he wouldn't embarrass her, had sworn that he'd never do anything to purposely humiliate her, and he damn sure wasn't into retaliation.

No, he'd deal with her punishment later. If she balked, if she said no, then it would end sooner than expected but the result would be the same whether now or three weeks from now. He couldn't keep her forever, and the haunted look on her face when she came to his door further drove that point home.

A chuckle echoed over the room, and Damon looked up to see the source of his guest's amusement. He stiffened when he saw Serena standing in the doorway, not a stitch of clothing on her gorgeous body.

She stared defiantly at him, her eyes glittering with challenge. Not responding to the obvious bait, he set his glass of wine aside and ignored her for a moment while he finished the conversation he was involved in.

He kept tabs on her from the corner of his eye. She stood quietly, but the longer she stood, the more ill at ease she became. When he was convinced she was about to turn and walk back out, he started across the room, his pace unhurried, his expression purposely unreadable.

"Serena," he said as he came abreast of her. "So glad you could make it. Everyone has been eager to meet you."

She glanced sharply up at him then twisted her hands nervously in front of her. An impulse decision she was already regretting, by the looks of things. He'd already tried to make things easy for her. He wouldn't do anything more.

"Come," he said, taking her arm. As they walked toward the people gathered, he leaned down to whisper close to her ear. "That's two punishments I owe you now. One for your inconsideration and one for your blatant disobedience."

Conversation ceased as everyone looked openly at him and Serena. Warm smiles framed his friends' faces, but it was for a fraud. They were glad for him when they shouldn't be. They thought he'd finally found a woman willing to commit herself wholly to him.

He introduced her around, and Serena's growing confusion was a tangible thing. Her brow creased, and it was obvious the smile she'd pasted on her lips was dangling precariously.

"Congratulations, Damon," Robbie offered as they approached one of his oldest friends. "Your woman is quite beautiful. You're lucky to own her."

Serena glanced back and forth between Robbie and Damon, her lips pursed. Then her gaze settled on the woman standing quietly by Robbie's side, and Damon saw the instant that understanding flashed.

She tensed and color swept up her neck and into her cheeks. Her mouth tightened and tears crowded her eyes. Damon didn't give her an opportunity to do much with the realization. Instead, he ushered her onward. She wasn't going to be thrilled when they came to the next person in line to be introduced. They already were acquainted. But she'd made her choice, and she'd have to live with the consequences.

As they walked toward the window where two men stood, one turned, and he felt Serena go rigid beside him.

"Micah," Damon said calmly. "I'd like you to meet Serena. I understand the two of you are already acquainted. Serena, you know Micah Hudson. He's a good friend of mine."

Micah flashed a smile at Serena and raised an eyebrow as his gaze swept over Serena's naked body.

Damon bent low so that his lips were a mere centimeter from her ear. His hand curled tightly around her arm even as his finger brushed across the band.

"I would have spared you this discomfort," he murmured. "You brought this on yourself by thinking to embarrass me in front of my guests. No one will blink an eye over your nudity. Every man here with the exception of Micah is accompanied by his slave. So you see, Serena mine, you've only succeeded in shaming yourself."

She trembled in his grip but nodded once in acknowledgment of his words. She gave Micah a quivery smile even as her chin jutted upward as she gathered her tattered pride around her.

"Of course I remember Micah," she said quietly.

"Serena, I must say you look lovely tonight," Micah said. "Damon is a lucky bastard."

"I like to think so," Damon said in a low voice.

He glanced sideways at Serena to see that she still held herself stiffly, her expression shuttered. She wasn't going to give an inch, but then neither was he. Better to confront the issue here and now because he wasn't going to waste the next three weeks building a dream with borrowed nails.

He straightened and looked at Micah. "Since you're the only one here tonight without a slave, I'd appreciate it if you would assist in the discipline of mine."

"What?" Serena spit out.

He turned and pinned her with his stare. "Care to make it three, Serena mine?"

Her lips clamped shut, but he could see her itching to say it, to blurt it out, to end it here and now. And so he waited. Expecting it.

To his surprise, her shoulders lost some of their rigidity. She closed her eyes and lowered her head.

"Serena?" Micah asked.

She slowly raised her head to look at him.

"Are you okay with this?" Micah asked gently. "All of this, I mean?"

Damon didn't take exception to the question or to Micah infringing on his relationship with Serena. Micah loved women. Period. He was protective of them, flirted endlessly with them, but at the end of the day, he'd take on just about anyone who was taking advantage of a woman. And right now, it was a question that Damon very much wanted the answer to himself.

"I hurt Damon," she said in a clear voice. "I was thoughtless when he's been nothing but considerate. And then when confronted by my actions, in my anger I tried to embarrass him. I accept his punishment."

"Even not knowing what it is?" Micah persisted.

"He won't hurt me," she said. The utter conviction in her voice carried across the room, and there were several nods of approval from his friends.

Micah glanced back up at Damon, evidently satisfied that Serena was acting of her own volition and didn't need saving. Damon's lips twitched with amusement.

"Would you have fought me if she'd said she was here against her will?" he asked Micah.

"Damn straight," Micah said with a chuckle. "If only so I could be the hero and carry her off into the sunset."

Damon turned formally to Serena and stared at her without emotion or inflection. "You've earned two punishments. One I will administer now in the presence of the people you've tried to offend. The other, which is for your lack of consideration for me, will be administered in private."

She faced him calmly and nodded her acceptance, but he could see her body trembling and the whiteness of her knuckles as she curled her fingers into tight fists.

"Follow me," he ordered as he started for the center of the room.

He motioned for Robbie to press the button that would drop the restraints from the ceiling. Serena's eyes widened when she saw the two individually suspended cuffs slowly descend.

When they were low enough, he took Serena's wrists and secured each, checking to make sure they didn't bite too harshly into her skin. Then he nodded at Robbie, who raised the cuffs until her arms were stretched over her head.

From one of the cabinets near the television, Damon took out a spreader bar with ankle cuffs. He secured her legs on either side, spreading her so that her heels left the floor. She was now completely vulnerable and helpless.

He couldn't help the surge of arousal even as the reason for her punishment weighed heavily on him. It would do no good to linger too long on his darker thoughts when such an enjoyable experience awaited him.

Serena was beautiful in bondage. Her absolute submission, her acceptance of his authority over her humbled him and made him hope again. Even as he cursed her for inspiring that hope.

Gathering her long, unbound hair in his hands, he carefully

placed the strands over her shoulder so they were away from her back. Then he walked around to face her, his hands at his belt buckle.

"Your punishment is one lash for every one of my guests you disrespected. That makes a dozen. For each of those people I get one for me in turn. That makes twenty-four total. I won't go lightly. You will give me pleasure and receive none in return. Is there anything you wish to say before we start?"

CHAPTER 30

o.

Serena knew it was the word Damon expected to hear. Did he want her to say it? Did he want to push her until she had no choice but to give up and call it quits?

No, there was something else in his eyes. He tried hard to hide it, but she could see it, a glimmer of . . . hope? He didn't want her to quit, but neither would he force this on her.

She locked gazes with him, hoping her eyes said more than words ever could. She shook her head wordlessly and braced herself for the pain and embarrassment of what lay ahead. It was hers. It belonged to her and she would own it with grace and humility.

He undid his belt and pulled it from his pants. In plain view, he carefully doubled it over and handed it to Micah, who once again looked questioningly at Serena.

She briefly closed her eyes but then reopened them and

nodded at Micah so he would know that she accepted this. Micah took the belt from Damon and circled behind her.

"You will look at me and only me," Damon said.

Her arms already ached from the strain, and her toes were numb from the awkwardness of being stretched so that her weight rested on the balls of her feet.

Again she nodded, just hoping he would get on with it. But she should have known better. Damon was nothing if not patient and exacting.

The first lash startled her. Her entire body jerked, and she cried out as pain burst over her back.

Strong fingers dug into her chin and forced it from her chest where it had fallen.

Her gaze found Damon, his stare hard and penetrating. "At me, Serena mine. Look at me. At all times."

She raised her chin from his grasp and steeled herself for the next blow. It came like fire. This time across her ass.

When she made no sound and kept her stare locked with Damon's, she saw approval spark in his eyes. It was obvious the last thing he wanted was for her to dissolve into a blubbering mass of hysterical female.

The next lash came quicker, across her shoulders where the skin bunched from her arms being stretched above her head. She closed her eyes and blew out her breath in a long whoosh.

Damon's fingers yanked at her chin, and she opened her eyes to see reprimand in his.

"Add another lash for her disobedience," Damon said to Micah.

She sucked in her breath and stared at him with hurt in her eyes.

"At me, Serena. Look at me. Every time you disobey me, I'll add another lash."

The next blow fell in the middle of her back, and she sank her teeth into her bottom lip, but she kept her eyes open and directed on Damon.

Micah spaced the lashes equally over her back and buttocks, careful not to put two in a row in the same spot. By the time he got to eleven, her entire back pulsed and ached with red hot intensity.

At twelve, Damon called a halt. Hope surged within her. Maybe she'd pleased him enough that he'd pardon her from the remaining thirteen he'd promised.

"The rest I want on her ass and only her ass," Damon said. "I want it red. Beautiful, like her. Alternate cheeks, but don't spare any effort."

Her body went rigid, and she sucked in her breath, her protest surging to her lips.

"It will only hurt worse if you tense," Damon said gently. "Relax, and it won't hurt as bad."

She took a long breath and forced her muscles into submission. Just as she wilted against her bonds, the first lash, stronger than before, streaked across her ass.

They came fast and furious, no break in between. Micah set a relentless pace, one destined to try the limits of her endurance. Locked into Damon's loving gaze, his strength bleeding into her, bolstering her, the pain diminished. What was given in punishment became intensely pleasurable, and yet she knew it was not meant to be.

The room became hazy around her as she slipped beyond the immediacy of her bonds, of the welts rising on her ass. A soft sigh escaped her, and she stopped mentally counting the loud smacks as they fell.

Damon was all she could see. His hand cupped around her chin, supporting her even in punishment. His gaze was hard but proud and she reveled in that pride.

Do this for me.

It was as if she heard the words aloud. As though he asked her to understand, to take it because he demanded it, because she wanted to please him.

And she did.

Sorrow bled through the pleasure. Regret that she'd disappointed him.

"I'm sorry," she whispered as the final lash descended.

Damon cupped her face in his hands and gently kissed away the tears that she hadn't realized she'd shed.

"Serena mine."

He said her name like a benediction, and his warm approval was all she felt in that moment. The pain diminished. Tension lessened in her arms, and the souls of her feet met the floor again.

Micah's hands touched the tops of her shoulders and pressed firmly down. At first she didn't understand what he wanted. She was still hazy, her back hypersensitive. Light shudders worked over her body at the slightest touch. Her skin was alive, crawling, edgy with unfulfilled need.

Damon was more patient this time as he waited for her.

"Down on your knees," Micah murmured close to her ear.

Her knees buckled instantaneously, and Micah caught her underneath her arms to keep her knees from hitting the floor.

In front of her, Damon loosened his pants, unzipping them with deliberate precision. Micah's hand tangled in her hair, forcing her head up just as Damon reached into his pants and pulled out his cock.

Damon stepped forward, his erection fisted in his hand. With Micah's hands at the base of her neck forcing her head back, Damon put his palm on her forehead and guided his cock past her lips.

Unlike at the auction, where he had to reprimand her for taking control, this time she was exhausted and let him use her mouth as he wanted.

Micah supported her neck while Damon thrust repeatedly to the back of her throat. Damon's words echoed in her mind.

You will give me pleasure and receive none in return.

But he was wrong. Her pleasure was tied to his.

She opened herself to him fully, her gaze seeking his. Damon's eyes glittered above her as Micah angled her back even farther so Damon was all but straddling her face.

He sank into her mouth until her lips met the crisp hairs at the base of his cock. For a long moment he remained there, still, his sac pressed firmly to her chin.

She struggled but Micah's hands tightened in her hair and Damon pressed harder. Her gaze flew up again, seeking his and she immediately calmed.

He withdrew, sliding his engorged cock over her tongue until the crown rested on her bottom lip. He reached down and cupped her chin as his cock was poised for reentry.

"The longer you resist, the longer I'll make this last," Damon said. "You're mine, Serena. Your body is mine. Your mouth is mine. I own you. I'm fucking your mouth because it belongs to me. I'll use it for as long as it pleases me before I come, and you'll swallow everything I give to you."

In response, she merely opened her mouth wider to show

him her submission. Immediately, he shoved forward, forcing himself to her very depths.

She controlled the urge to fight, to gag and to reject the cock so deep in her throat. It took everything she had, but she focused on Damon's eyes, locked on to the warmth and approval she found there, and she blocked everything else out.

As soon as she relented, he quit prolonging his orgasm and sped up his pace until he fucked her mouth as he would her pussy. Her cheeks hollowed and the sucking sounds filled the room as he smacked in and out of her mouth.

Precum spilled and coated her tongue as he swelled larger. Two men held her head. She was powerless and immobile. On her knees, her legs spread and bound, a cock possessing her mouth with relentless force. It was almost as though she were having an out-of-body experience, for as with the whipping, she slipped from the boundaries laid by her body and floated free, high on pleasure she didn't understand but embraced with her entire being.

Damon's face blurred but she felt him. His hands, his strength, his cock and finally the very essence of him. Male, primitive.

She drank greedily, determined that she would reject no part of his offering. In his hands, she found a comfort she'd never imagined. A security and safe haven that she would never know outside of his arms. She knew it, accepted it as an irrefutable truth.

"Serena."

She heard her name. Soft and mellow. From a distance.

"Serena mine."

Loving. Tender and approving.

A dreamy smile tugged at her lips, and it was then she realized that Damon had slipped from her mouth. Micah's hands had left her hair. Gentle hands were tugging her upward as fingers pulled at the bonds at her ankles.

Her legs shook, and she wobbled precariously, but she was caught against a hard chest. Whispered words melted over her ears. Damon's face came into focus. She blinked. Once and then twice.

"Go and kneel by my chair," Damon said in a low voice. "You'll remain there until our guests have taken their leave. I'll bring you food and drink once everyone else has been served."

Numbly, she stepped forward. Though Damon let her walk alone, he followed close behind, and she knew he wouldn't let her fall.

As she sank to her knees on the soft pallet by his chair, a soft moan escaped before she could call it back. The warm, heady flow of pleasure faded and was replaced by a pulsating ache across her throbbing back and buttocks.

Awareness of her surroundings flooded back as she watched the activity in the room return to normal. She was largely ignored save for the occasional curious glance thrown her way.

She held herself rigid, determined not to disappoint Damon further in front of his friends. Her jaw ached from being set so hard, but she'd allow no sound of discomfort to escape her.

How could she have gone from such indecision just hours earlier to complete and utter acceptance of Damon's demands? Did distance change her perspective? Did proximity blind her to all reason?

What had possessed her to goad Damon as she had done? At the time she'd been angry, lashing out, more over her own indecision and frustration than anything Damon had done. Now she just felt foolish.

And she still had one more punishment to suffer.

Her shoulders sagged, not in fear, but in regret.

Across the room, Damon stood with Micah and one other man. They conversed in low tones, occasionally stopping as others joined. Damon was comfortable with these people. He smiled easily and gestured with his hands.

A flush crawled over her cheeks when, at one point, she obviously became the conversation piece because they all turned to glance at her. One man gestured toward her and smiled broadly at Damon. Damon's expression changed rapidly, becoming dark.

It didn't take a rocket scientist to figure out what the man had wanted.

She lowered her head, refusing to look at those observing her any longer.

"Your shame becomes his."

Serena's head came up to see Robbie standing a foot away holding a drink as he looked over at Damon.

"Hold your head up so that he can hold his up. Give him pride."

She resisted the idea of this man telling her anything, but neither did she want to cause Damon any more embarrassment than she already had.

Her gaze slid coolly over Robbie's face before she nodded briefly in acceptance of his dictate.

Evidently satisfied, he walked away to join a beautiful woman across the room. Was she his slave? His touch was possessive as he slid his hand up her back and then around her waist. She smiled welcomingly at him, and he bent down to nuzzle at her ear. There was clear affection between them even if her posture was submissive.

The next hour was a test of her staying power. Her back

ached, her legs ached from kneeling. Her spine was stiff from her position, and she wanted nothing more than to lie down and curl into a ball.

Damon had largely ignored her, sparing her only an occasional glance before he returned to his guests. There was laughter and conversation, and for the most part, Serena ceased to exist.

Then the call for dinner was given, and if Serena thought being on display in front of everyone had been difficult, the sudden quiet of the empty living room was worse. The guests filed into the dining room, and she could only hear them in the distance.

She could get up and walk out. Nothing was keeping her here. She could go to the bedroom and crawl into bed or she could simply walk out, get into her car and go home. To her apartment, back to her life. Fulfilling other people's fantasies. Selling them lies and half-truths. Shades of gray, pocket dreams and a day in the sun.

But still she knelt there, determination driving her relentlessly. It was no longer about her and her fantasy. If she left, if she walked away, her failure became Damon's. He didn't deserve it when he'd only given her what she wanted.

Is this what you want?

It came to her as a whisper, a soft ribbon threading its way through her consciousness. It was a question she couldn't answer. Or maybe she didn't want to answer it.

She lost track of time and was startled when the guests began to trickle back into the living room. Damon approached, holding a plate. Without saying anything, he settled into the chair beside her. With a gentle hand, he directed her head until she rested on his lap.

A sigh of contentment, of weariness and relief, expelled from the innermost part of her body.

He fed her, small bites, coaxing them past her lips. Occasionally he stopped to offer her a drink from the glass at his side.

There was a calmness and intimacy to his movements. He didn't just feed her mechanically. He touched her frequently, short little brushes across her cheek, or he'd smooth a strand of hair from her face. When wine gathered at the corner of her mouth, he wiped it away with his thumb and then licked at the pad.

She closed her eyes as her cheek rested against his leg. He didn't make any further attempt to feed her more. Instead, he simply stroked her cheek. As he spoke to those around him, his fingers slid into her hair and to her nape where he gently massaged.

She was very nearly asleep when she heard Damon say goodbye. Her eyes opened sluggishly, and Damon carefully pushed her head away as he rose. She wobbled and then steadied herself as she watched him see his friends out.

Soon there was only her and Damon. He stood at the doorway of the living room, staring at her. In that moment, she wished she could read his thoughts, wished they were broadcast on his face, but he was expressionless.

Nervous apprehension fluttered deep in her stomach when she remembered that he'd promised her a private punishment after his guests had left.

She swallowed as he finally made his way over to her. He stopped a short distance away and simply held his hand down to her. She reached up and slid her fingers across his warm palm. He pulled her to her feet and then turned her in the direction of the bedroom.

They walked in silence, her dread growing with each step.

The bedroom was dark as they entered, but Damon made no move to turn on the light.

"Do you need to use the bathroom before bed?" he asked, startling the silence with his deep voice.

"No," she said quietly, not sure he'd see her head if she shook it.

He left her a few feet from the bed and went to pull back the covers. When he was finished, he turned and took her hand. Unsure of what he wanted or what he would do, she let him guide her to the mattress. But then he merely eased her into bed and pulled the covers up over her as her head settled onto the pillow.

Without a word or gesture, he simply turned around and walked out, leaving her there in the dark.

For a long time, she lay there, waiting, expecting. Fatigue settled into her limbs, but she fought the veil of sleep, waiting for Damon to return.

Loneliness ate at her. She wanted him there, even if it meant her punishment. She wanted him to return and settle it so they could go back to the easy companionship they'd enjoyed during the week she'd devoted solely to him. She wanted to tell him she was sorry.

She watched the clock, flinching as each minute passed. After an hour, desolation covered her like a fog. Where was he?

She curled into a ball, gathering the sheets around her in an attempt to comfort the coldness that invaded her. As tired as she was, as much as she fought the urge to sleep, it wasn't right. He hadn't bound her. He hadn't come to bed.

As she huddled there in the dark, alone with longing that nagged insidiously at her, bleak realization came. *This* was her punishment, and it was worse than the lash of his belt.

CHAPTER 31

$\mathcal{D}$amon sat in the armchair that faced his bed, watching
Serena sleep as dawn seeped through the window over his shoulder. He'd slept little, opting to work late into the night. He'd
caught a few hours on the couch in his office before coming
here so he could be with Serena when she woke.

Her face was turned to him, and he could see the evidence
of old tears on her cheeks. The idea that he'd hurt her with his
desertion didn't make him feel better. The punishment was
necessary. She was teetering between the two worlds, one of
her making and one of her choosing. But it didn't soothe him to
know he'd caused her pain. Her pain was his pain. Her joy was
his joy.

He . . . loved her.

He shook his head in denial though there was no one to see
it. An intelligent man learned from his mistakes. He'd already
loved a woman he couldn't hold on to, only he hadn't known it
until too late. From the beginning he'd known he couldn't have

Serena, and it should have been easy to keep his emotions sepa-
rate from their arrangement.

Should have been was just another way of saying he'd
fucked up.

He dragged a hand through his hair and tilted his head up
to stare at the ceiling. What the fuck was he going to do for the
next three weeks? Continue living a lie while he gave a little
more of himself away in the process?

He lowered his head until he once again found her soft outline nestled in his bed. His bed. His woman. What he wouldn't
give for it to be real.

Three weeks. He could take what she offered or he could
have nothing at all. Were three weeks worth having knowing
she'd walk away after they were over? She was close to walking
now. He'd seen it in her eyes even as he hoped with everything he had that she'd stay.

All or nothing was bullshit. It never worked out that way.
Life was all about taking what you could get when you could get
it and surviving when it wasn't enough.

Yeah, he'd take the three weeks, because when it was over, it
would be all he'd have of her to hold on to. The memory of
when, for a time, she was his.

Serena woke from a drugged sleep, her eyes heavy and swollen.
For a moment she simply stared out the window, as she realized that she was still alone in bed. Then her gaze flickered to
the chair next to the window, and she blinked when she saw
Damon sitting there, angled to the side.

He was asleep.

She threw off the covers and her feet hit the floor as she

hurried from the bed. Ignoring the soreness of her muscles and the tingling of her back, she flew across the floor.

She came to a halt in front of him, her hands outstretched to touch him. But she remained still as she simply drank in his appearance.

He looked tired, his hair rumpled and the shadow of stubble on his jaw. He was wearing the same clothes he'd worn at the party the evening before. The same clothes, minus the belt he'd used on her back.

There was a vulnerable look to his face in sleep. An opportunity to see his expression unguarded. Slowly, she sank to her knees between his legs and laid her head against his thigh.

He stirred, and she took his hand in hers, lacing their fingers together. And then she brought his hand to her lips and kept it there.

"Serena," he whispered.

Though it was hard, and she feared what she'd see in his eyes, she raised her head to meet his gaze. She didn't like to think of how she appeared, so open and unguarded, her feelings and uncertainty so evident, but she owed him this.

"I'm sorry," she said in a low voice. "You didn't deserve how I treated you yesterday. You've been so good to me, Damon."

He raised his hand to cup her jaw, and he rubbed his thumb tenderly over her cheek.

"You sound as though you're saying good-bye," he said, and she was surprised to hear a note of sadness in his voice.

"I would think you'd want me to leave. I'm not proving to be a very good slave," she said wryly.

He stroked her face, his fingers feathering over her cheekbone. "I want you to stay, Serena mine. I want it more than anything."

"Then I'll stay."

The resolve in her words shook her. They sounded so final when she herself was so uncertain. She didn't want to make a promise she couldn't keep. They had a contract, for God's sake. One that could be withdrawn if one or more of the parties desired. This wasn't supposed to be personal. It was business.

"What are you thinking?" he asked. "A shadow crossed over your face, and you suddenly seem so sad."

She sighed and rubbed her cheek against his palm. "This wasn't supposed to become so . . ."

"Involved? Emotional? Painful?"

She nodded. He'd used just the right words. How else to describe the rawness and the ache that had nothing to do with the kiss of the belt. "Maybe we shouldn't continue . . . this," she said.

"I won't make the decision for you," Damon said. "I want you to stay but I can't and won't make you."

"I want to be here," she said as she swallowed back the throb in her voice.

"Then you should stay."

"You make it sound so simple."

He tugged at her chin and rubbed his thumb over her bottom lip. "It is simple. If you want to stay, then don't go."

"I feel as though I've lost something. Some part of myself. But I don't know what, so how can I have missed it?"

"And what have you gained?" he asked softly.

She stared at him with wide eyes, his question hitting her hard enough to knock the breath from her. Gained. Lost. Wasn't life a never ending process of both?

She looked down, unsure of what to say. He turned his wrist to glance at his watch and then made a sound of regret.

"You're going to be late if you don't shower and dress now, Serena mine."

She laid her head down on his lap for a long moment as his fingers trickled down her hair. Then she nodded and pushed herself to stand in front of him. And waited.

He brought her hand to his lips and kissed it. "Go now, Serena. I'll see about your breakfast while you get ready for work. I'll be in the dining room."

CHAPTER 32

"You can't avoid us forever, Serena. Don't think I won't show up at your office and drag you out kicking and screaming if I have to," Faith said when Serena answered her office line.

Serena sighed and put her palm to her aching head. She shifted forward in her seat because whenever she brushed across the leather, it irritated her still-sensitive back.

"I'm busy, Faith. Trying to catch up after being away from work for a week."

Faith snorted. "You're avoiding me and we both know it. Be glad it's me calling and not Julie."

"Yeah, well why isn't she?" Serena asked. "Not like her to miss out on an opportunity to be nosy."

"She's too busy plotting."

"I don't even want to know," Serena said. And she didn't. She was simply too tired and had too much on her mind to worry about whether or not Julie was ever going to make a move on Nathan. She said as much to Faith.

"I think she's giving up on Nathan. Well, after she carries off her scheme to show him what he's missing out on."

Serena rolled her eyes, amused despite the heaviness weighing on her.

"You should probably know, she plans to approach Damon."

"*What?*"

"Not personally and not until after your month is up," Faith said quickly. "She wants him to set up a fantasy for her."

"For the love of God," Serena muttered. "He's not a freaking pimp."

"Says the woman who went to him for the same thing?" Faith pointed out.

"You're not endearing yourself to me right now, Faith."

"If it makes you feel any better, both Gray and I tried to talk her out of it. For different reasons, mind you. I don't have a problem with Damon's establishment, just Julie's motivation. Gray hates The House and I think he's afraid Julie will drag me there with her," she finished with a laugh.

Serena didn't want to think about the end of her time with Damon or that Julie would be going to him for help. Who was to say he wouldn't volunteer for Julie's fantasy?

Guilt nagged her even as she thought it. Nothing Damon had ever said or done made her think he approached sex so casually that he'd jump from her bed to her friend's. And speaking of friends . . .

"Faith, about Micah."

"What about Micah?" Faith asked.

"Do you and he . . . well, do you and he and Gray have an agreement?" God, how the hell was she supposed to put this anyway?

"Why are you asking?" Faith asked softly.

Fuck me.

"He saw me naked. Damon didn't plan it that way, mind you. Was my own fault. But then he sort of participated in my punishment, and well, afterward, I remembered that you and him . . . that is, you and him and Gray . . . Well, I just felt bad about it."

"Serena, there is nothing between me and Micah except deep friendship. I love him dearly, and yes, we had sex. Once. There is no agreement. Gray would have a coronary if someone suggested it. But now, you know you're going to have to tell me all about this punishment Micah participated in, because it sounds freaking hot."

Serena groaned. "Look, can we do this some other time? You've made sure I'm alive and well, and I really do have work to catch up on, and I sure as hell don't want to be late tonight and cause Damon the same grief I caused last night."

"But are you well?" Faith asked quietly. "I didn't get the impression that things were okay yesterday. I'm worried about you, Serena. I've worried about you from the start of this. And I'm worried about Damon. I don't want either of you hurt."

"I don't want us hurt either," Serena said quietly. "But I'm afraid it might be too late."

"Oh, Serena." Faith's unhappy voice filtered over the line. "Do you want me to meet you for lunch?"

"I really appreciate you trying to help, Faith. Really, I do. But this is something I have to work out on my own."

"I understand, but I need to say one last thing. If you can't give Damon what he wants, what he needs, then let him go."

Serena stared at the phone for a long time after Faith hung up. Let him go. It sounded so easy. And it should be. Who the hell formed an attachment after only one week?

Okay, it had been longer than a week. But not much, and it was still too soon to feel so deeply for another person.

But that wasn't what was important. They wanted different things, and not insignificant things like favorite foods or different brands of toothpaste. Damon wanted a woman like Serena had pretended to be for the last week, and he wanted her on a permanent basis.

"Serena?"

Serena looked up to see Carrie standing in her office doorway. She frowned. Carrie had been crying.

"What's wrong?" she asked sharply.

"Mrs. Tasco just called."

"Did something go wrong with the cruise?" Serena asked.

Carrie's eyes filled with fresh tears. "No, in fact, it was perfect. Mrs. Tasco said she'd never seen Michelle so happy. They were scheduled to return to port today. Michelle died in her sleep last night."

Serena went completely still. Her chest hurt as pressure increased.

"They just wanted to say thank you," Carrie said in a choked voice. "They said Michelle's last hours were so full of joy and wonder. The princess party you arranged was the highlight of her life."

"Find out when funeral arrangements are being made," Serena said. "Send flowers."

Carrie stood there, her expression one of surprise. "That's it? That's all you have to say?"

"Just do it, Carrie. And if that's all, I'm really busy right now."

Carrie spun around and stalked from Serena's office, slamming the door behind her. For a long moment, Serena stared at the closed door. Then she dropped her head to her desk, burying her face in her arms.

Her shoulders shook uncontrollably as the tears came. She was fooling herself. What she gave her clients wasn't real. It wasn't even a substitute for real. She dealt in games and deception.

She could give a little girl the trappings of being a princess, but she couldn't give her what mattered most. A long, healthy life with parents who loved her.

Damon was wrong. Dreamers did die. They died every single day.

Damon was sitting in his chair when Serena walked in the door that afternoon. He laid aside his laptop and looked up, prepared to call her over. His welcome died on his lips when he saw her pale, strained face.

She dropped her briefcase by the door and kicked off her shoes almost mechanically. Then she walked slowly toward him, her eyes thick with grief. She looked as though she'd been crying, but she was completely dry-eyed now.

He got to his feet and crossed the room to meet her. As soon he got close, a small cry erupted from her lips and she threw herself in his arms. He gathered her close and held her as sobs cracked from her lips, falling harshly on his ears.

He guided her to the couch, half carrying her and half assisting and then sat, pulling her down onto his lap. "Serena, tell me what's wrong. Are you hurt? What happened?"

She buried her face in his neck and held him tightly, her fingers digging into his skin. Her sobs continued to spill out and so he simply held her, until finally she quieted and lay limply against his chest, her strength drained.

"Serena?"

She tensed and drew in a slight breath, and her body felt small and fragile against his. Dread tightened around his throat because he couldn't help but know what she was going to say.

"I'm leaving, Damon," she said in a hoarse, quiet voice. "I tore up the contract. The agreement is done. You're free."

He went still. The pain of her announcement shocked him with its ferocity when it shouldn't have. He knew it was coming, and yet he felt each word like a serrated edge over his heart.

"Why?" he demanded.

She started to pull away, almost violent in her movements as she sought to free herself from his embrace. But he wouldn't let her up. No, she would face him and give him the reason, damn it. He wouldn't make it easy for her when this was the hardest thing he'd ever had to confront.

He gathered her wrists in his hands and held them close to his chest. "Why, Serena? You owe me that much."

"I owe you no explanation," she said in a cold voice. "Either party can terminate the contract at will."

"I don't give a *damn* about the fucking contract. This isn't about a piece of goddamn paper, Serena. This is you and me and what we've shared, and I deserve to know why you're throwing it away."

"I can't live a lie any longer," she whispered. "It hurts. Everything I do is a lie. It's not real. It can't be real. I can't give people what they truly want or need and you aren't any different. I can't give you what you need, Damon, so I'm letting you go."

He stared at her as the garbled explanation fell from her lips.

She pushed herself away from him again, and this time he let her go.

She turned to go but before she took a step, he said her name. She hesitated but didn't turn around.

"I love you, Serena."

This time she stopped. He could see her shoulders trembling, see her fingers ball into fists at her sides.

"Stay," he said softly.

Slowly, she turned around, devastation written on her face. Her mouth tightened and her throat worked up and down as she swallowed.

"No," she whispered.

And there it was. The one word she'd never said. The one word he'd told her would free her. His pain was stunning and fierce. The finality of it rolled over him until he could barely stand it.

Her hand flew to her mouth and she made a sound, a wounded, pained sound that an animal might make. And then she ran.

CHAPTER 33

$\mathcal{S}$erena knew she was pushing herself too hard, she knew she was avoiding her friends, and she knew without a doubt that she didn't have a prayer of ever getting over Damon.

She was a coward, a bitch, and she was heartbroken.

She hadn't attended Michelle's funeral. Carrie was livid and had called her heartless. Serena didn't deny it. If she had any sort of a heart, she wouldn't have strung Damon along making promises she couldn't keep. Oh, she hadn't overtly made any promises, but she'd bought into the whole fantasy. Lost herself in something that wasn't real. She'd wanted it and wanted it badly.

No, going to the funeral wasn't something she could handle, but still, she found herself walking slowly toward Michelle's headstone as the evening shadows lengthened.

Newly dug dirt lay atop the small mound and a huge assortment of flowers decorated the area. Serena's gaze fell on the shiny stone, still so new, where Michelle's name was engraved.

Tears welled when she saw that below her name her parents had added an inscription.

Always our princess.

Serena knelt and carefully leaned over to place a tiara at the head of the grave.

"If there is any justice, you're reigning in heaven with a pink princess gown, a diamond tiara and a purple scepter," Serena whispered. "I'm so sorry I couldn't do for you the one thing that mattered most."

"But you did."

Serena whipped guiltily around and saw Mrs. Tasco standing there, tears shining on her cheeks.

"I'm sorry," Serena murmured as she stood. "I didn't mean to intrude." She started to walk away, but Mrs. Tasco touched her arm as she got close.

"Please, don't go."

Serena hesitated, torn between the need to be away before she succumbed to the tears boiling at her eyes and the pain she saw reflected in a mother's eyes.

"I heard what you said, and you're wrong. There was nothing anyone could do for Michelle's health. God knows we tried. We saw countless doctors, tried treatment after treatment, but we knew . . . we knew she didn't have long. What you did was give a little girl who had known so much pain and sorrow a reason to smile, to laugh, to be happy, even when she knew she was dying. For that, Miss James, you will always have my undying gratitude."

Her voice broke on a sob, and she covered her mouth with trembling fingers.

"I can never repay you for the sight of my daughter's face lit up like a million suns as she danced at her coronation ceremony aboard the cruise ship. Or for the look on her father's face as he whirled her around the dance floor."

She enfolded Serena in her arms and hugged her tightly as sobs racked her frame.

"I'm sorry for your loss," Serena whispered, knowing it wasn't enough, that it would never be enough.

"Thank you. Thank you from me and her father both. We'll never forget what you did for our daughter."

Serena tried to smile and failed. Mrs. Tasco squeezed her hand and then slowly moved past her and away from the grave site.

A slight breeze blew the tears dry on Serena's face and none replaced them as she stared back at the tiara sitting in front of the stone.

Realization and death of dreams. Life. She could spout the bullshit about how things were cyclical but it wouldn't bring her any peace, and it damn sure wouldn't make her feel better about a little princess who wanted so little and gave so much.

Exhausted and heartsick, she began the walk back to her car. Though it was warm and muggy with barely a breeze to break the oppressive heat, Serena hugged her arms close to her body and put her head down as she walked along the manicured pathway of the cemetery. Her fingers lay over the arm band that Damon had given her, hidden by her sleeve. She hadn't taken it or the ankle bracelet off. She couldn't bear to.

When she reached the parking lot, she dug into her jeans pocket for her keys, and when she looked up, she saw Julie and Faith standing by her car.

They didn't wait for her to react, say hello or go away. They converged, flanking her and wrapping an arm around her waist and shoulders.

"Gray said he and Connor would get your car on their way home," Faith said as she herded Serena toward her vehicle. "You're coming with me and Julie even if we have to knock your ass out."

When she didn't even offer an argument, Julie gave her a worried look. "You look exhausted, Serena. When was the last time you slept?"

"I haven't." She closed her eyes to prevent the tears from coming. "Not since I left Damon."

Faith sighed and shoved her gently into the front seat.

"Where are you taking me?" Serena asked mildly as Faith slid into the driver's seat.

Julie leaned up from the backseat. "Well we could call it some hokey bullshit like intervention, but I prefer to call it us kicking your dumb ass."

Serena laughed, but it sounded harsh and ugly. She leaned her head against the seat as warm tears left salt trails down her cheeks.

Julie squeezed her arm as Faith backed out of the parking lot. They drove in silence, and Serena kept her eyes closed, not wanting to see the pity or concern in her friends' eyes. She still had no idea where they were going but if it involved food and sleep, she could certainly deal.

She fell asleep and when she woke again, Faith and Julie were pulling her out of the front seat. As she staggered to her feet, the smell of salt and an ocean breeze wafted gently through her senses.

"Where are we?" she asked as she tried to blink the fog from her eyes.

"Beach house," Julie said.

Serena frowned as they mounted the steps to the large house.

A single light shone from the porch, warm and inviting. "Whose house?"

"Does it matter?" Faith asked in exasperation.

"Guess not," Serena muttered. "As long as it has food and a pillow."

"I'd say it's about time you started talking about eating and sleeping. You look like you haven't had either in a week," Julie said.

Serena sighed. She'd lost count of the days. It didn't matter.

Faith unlocked the door, and they walked inside. Julie went back out for their bags while Faith plopped Serena down on the couch with instructions to stay.

"Yes, Mom," Serena mumbled.

They fussed, bullied, pinched and prodded until she ate every single thing they put on the plate they prepared for her. She dreaded the end of the meal because she knew that was when they'd start in with the demand for answers. But to her surprise, they bundled her off to bed.

"Get some sleep, Serena," Faith urged. "We'll be here when you wake up. You're done running yourself into the ground."

Serena nodded to acknowledge she'd heard, but she was already going under.

Julie glanced over at Faith and held her finger to her lips then angled her head toward the door. They walked outside and shut the bedroom door before returning to the living room.

"I need to call Damon," Faith said. "He's been worried sick about her."

"And Gray. He wasn't crazy about you coming down here without him," Julie said.

Faith shivered. "I wasn't so crazy about it myself but at least it's not the same beach house. Damon sold the one where Gray was shot."

"Do you think we're doing the right thing?" Julie asked. "I can't decide, and yet I know we couldn't stand by and watch her self-destruct. Hell, Faith, what are we going to do when she wakes up? I don't have the answers."

Faith paused in the act of taking out her cell phone. "Honestly? I don't think Serena is going to get better until she and Damon are together again."

"Did I mention that I hate meddling friends?" Julie grumbled. "I hate *being* one even more. It was her decision, Faith. We can't make her go back to Damon."

"I told her to give him up," Faith said painfully. "I should have stayed out of it."

"Oh, shut up. Serena didn't leave Damon because you told her to, and if she did, she's a bigger dumbass than I thought."

Faith leveled a glare at her. "You know, Julie, it's amazing Serena and I haven't cut your throat. If I were you, I'd sleep real light tonight."

"Call your man and then call Damon. I don't think I've ever seen a man so worried over a woman. Made me all gooey inside."

"Let's just hope this works," Faith said as she punched the keypad of her phone.

CHAPTER 34

$\mathcal{S}$unlight speared her right through her eyeball as soon as Serena cracked one eyelid open. With a groan, she turned so that the sun was out of her face. Her gaze fell on the clock and she saw it was straight-up noon.

Every muscle in her body grimaced when she tried to move so she just lay there listening to the distant sounds of the gulf. A seagull's cry echoed right outside the window followed by another and still another.

Peace. Such an elusive, sweet creature. It mocked her at every turn.

Faith and Julie waited outside that door and Serena wasn't ready to go yet. She burrowed deeper under the covers, sleep still lurking close on the horizon. It was tempting to retreat and sleep until she forgot, until the pain and sadness went away. But she'd already proven herself the world's biggest coward.

With a sigh, she swung her legs over the side of the bed and stood. She registered that she was still in yesterday's clothes about the time she saw the jeans and T-shirt lying on the dresser against the wall.

Apparently she should add breaking and entering to the list of crimes that Julie and Faith were accumulating. They'd obviously raided her apartment before abducting her and carting her off to the beach.

A smile softened the strain around her lips. They were the best. They'd drag her back into the world kicking and screaming, they'd listen to her cry and bitch and wail, but then they'd tell her to shut the fuck up and get over it.

She collected her clothes and headed for the bathroom that adjoined the bedroom they'd stuffed her in. After a quick shower, she almost felt human again. She dressed and then ducked back in her room to get the light windbreaker she'd worn the night before.

Her hand found the arm band again, and she traced the outline through the jacket sleeve. She closed her eyes, determined not to give in to the grief hurtling through her mind. She steadied her composure and then shuffled down the hall, ready to face her kidnappers.

The living room was quiet and empty, but as Serena glanced out the glass doors leading to the wooden deck overlooking the ocean, she saw Faith and Julie sprawled in loungers, drinks in hand.

She squared her shoulders, sucked in a breath and headed for the door. As soon as she slid it open, Julie and Faith both sat up and turned to look at her.

"Well, you look better," Julie said bluntly. "Not that you look great, but definitely a step above hammered horse shit."

Serena smiled wryly. "Thanks, Julie."

Faith got up and took her arm and immediately herded her

toward a lounger. "Sit," she insisted. Then she turned to Julie. "Get her some juice and something to eat. Then we'll make her talk."

Serena laughed and marveled at how weird it sounded. "Will there be pain involved?"

"Only if you clam up on us," Julie said as she headed inside.

Serena took the lounger Julie had vacated and leaned back, directing her face into the sun. Warmth spread over her skin, but oddly, she still felt cold on the inside.

"What happened, Serena?" Faith asked quietly.

"I stopped trying to sell rainbows and wishes."

"What the hell does that mean?"

"It means I'm through dealing in fantasies, Faith."

"But what about your business? Your clients? Serena, you've made so many people happy."

Serena closed her eyes. Except for her. In that she'd failed miserably and hurt a good man in the process.

"Okay so what did I miss?" Julie asked as she came back out. She plopped a plate on Serena's lap, forcing her to open her eyes again. Then she held out a glass of juice.

"Apparently Serena is done with Fantasy Incorporated," Faith said darkly.

"Say what?"

"I'm selling the business," Serena said calmly.

"But why?" Julie demanded. "This was your brainchild, your baby."

"Not anymore," Serena said softly. "Someone else can take over and do the same. It's just not for me anymore. I'm tired of . . . fantasy. It's not real. Nothing was."

"Okay, are we talking about your clients here or are we talking about you and Damon?" Faith asked.

Serena's hands trembled around her glass of juice, causing it to slosh precariously close to the rim. She sat forward and placed the glass on the leg rest of the lounger and set her plate down on the deck. "Damon deserves someone who isn't playing games," she whispered. "Someone not out for fantasy and cheap thrills."

Faith sighed. "Serena, you only gave it a week. Then you ran like the hounds of hell were after you."

Serena dropped her head and put her hands over her face. "I love him, Faith."

"Whoa, back up," Julie interjected. "I was with you up until that part. You love the guy—after only one week, mind you—but instead of sticking around to see how things work out, you dump him? Makes perfect sense to me."

"You don't understand," Serena said as she raised her head again.

Faith leaned forward on her chair and took Serena's hand in hers. "Then make us understand, Serena. Because you're obviously miserable. You've been avoiding us. You're not eating. You're not sleeping. And Julie's right. You look like hell warmed over. It has to stop."

"How do you stop loving someone?" Serena asked. "I don't even know if it's him I love or if I'm in love with the fantasy he gave me. Do you see my problem now? And how am I supposed to believe he loves me when I never gave him the real me, the real Serena? He loves a fantasy. He loves the ideal I sold him."

Faith expelled a long breath. Even Julie had nothing to say for once. Finally Faith scooted in closer to Serena and looked her hard in the eye.

"Are you sure you didn't give him the real Serena?" Faith

asked gently. "Is the thought of what he wants so abhorrent to you?"

"It was a game," Serena said. "A role I played, a role he played."

Faith held up her hand. "Whatever you may think about your actions, let me assure you that Damon never played a role. What you saw, what you got, was Damon. He doesn't play games. Yes, he entered into the agreement but it was because you wanted what he could give you. He didn't have to act, Serena. That's the real Damon."

"Look, I appreciate what you guys are trying to do. Believe me. But I don't want to talk about it. I don't want to rehash it because that's all I've done for the past week. I just want to forget."

Even as she said it, a cold chill snaked through her veins, and she clutched the jacket tighter around her. Maybe she was coming down with a bug. God knew she hadn't been taking care of herself worth a damn.

Damon would have taken care of you. He would have never let you get so run-down.

She closed her eyes and shook her head. It wasn't Damon's responsibility to take care of her. It was hers.

"Can you forget?" Faith asked. "Really? Or are you instead going to screw up the best thing that's ever happened to you because you're afraid?"

Serena gave her friend a startled look. "Afraid?"

"Yeah, afraid. Afraid that if you put your faith, your well-being, your entire self in Damon's hands, that he'll let you down, that he'll screw up."

"Serena, if that's the case, then you'll never have a relationship with a man," Julie said with a sigh. "Believe me, I know. I'm not sure that fear ever goes away. We're women. We're conditioned to fear betrayal, I think. Or at least it feels that way."

"It's not that," Serena said quietly. "Damon wouldn't hurt me. I know that. I'm afraid I can't be what he needs. I'm afraid I'll hurt *him*."

Faith sighed. "Shouldn't you let Damon decide whether or not he wants to take the risk?"

Serena had no answer for that. The question discomfited her because it was too close to the truth. She'd taken the decision out of Damon's hands entirely.

She buried her face in her hands. She was so damn tired. She wanted to sleep for a year.

Faith squeezed her leg and got up from her chair. Serena glanced up to see her check her watch and exchange glances with Julie.

"We've got to run to the store to stock up on supplies," Julie said. "Why don't you stay here and hang out in the sun. We won't be gone too long."

Serena nodded. "Thanks, guys. Really."

Faith leaned down to hug her. "We just want you to get better."

"If you had a rewind button, that would be cool," Serena said with a crooked grin.

Faith looked at her with serious eyes. "Would you really go back and erase what you had with Damon if you could?"

Serena stared out over the water, watching as the waves rolled into shore and then retreated. "No," she said honestly. "I wouldn't trade that week for the world."

CHAPTER 35

$\mathcal{D}$amon pulled up to his beach house and cut the engine. As he got out, he saw Julie and Faith coming down the steps of the house. They looked grim and worried.

Faith came to him immediately and gave him a hug. "She's not doing well, Damon. She needs you."

Did she? He sure as hell needed her. He wanted her. But he had no idea what Serena wanted.

"Where is she?" he asked quietly.

"We left her on the deck," Julie said tersely. "She's a mess. She's talking about selling her business. It's like she's given up."

Damon closed his eyes. Had he done this to her? Made her so desperately unhappy?

"Go to her," Faith said softly. "Convince her, Damon. She's so afraid."

He almost laughed. Afraid didn't even come close to describing his feelings. He was absolutely terrified. Terrified that he'd fail, and that he'd leave without her.

"We're gonna go," Julie said. "Call us if you need us, okay?"

"Thank you," he said to them both. "You're good friends to Serena. She's lucky to have you. If I have my way, she'll be leaving with me."

He watched as they got into Faith's car and drove away, and then he turned back to stare at the beach house. Faith had told him on the phone that Serena was exhausted, hadn't eaten and looked like hell. He wanted to walk in, turn her over his knee and spank her ass for not taking better care of herself, but that wasn't going to win him any points in his pursuit.

Instead he was stuck walking on tiptoe until he could find a way to persuade Serena that she belonged to him and they belonged together.

He squinted against the sun and mounted the steps. He let himself in the front door and headed for the back deck. When he got to the glass doors, though, he didn't see her in the lounger.

He opened the doors and stepped out, scanning the beach. His pulse leaped when he saw her, standing in the distance, her back to him as she stared out over the water.

He crossed the deck and made his way down the wooden walkway over the dune and then stepped onto the beach. As he neared her, he slowed his pace.

There was a fragility to her stance. Her arms were hugged tight around her body, and she was huddled in a jacket as though the wind blowing chilled her to the bone. Her hair whipped like streaks of midnight, and then she turned, ever so slightly, and he caught a hint of her profile, the softness of her face and the sad set of her lips.

Faith was right. She looked tired. She looked worn out, but she was still beautiful.

Serena mine.

He didn't know whether he should stay where he was or go to her or wait for her to turn and see him standing there. The waiting was agony as he readied himself to fight a battle he wasn't prepared to lose.

And then she turned, and those beautiful, expressive eyes widened in shock.

Serena stared in bewilderment at Damon, who stood just a few feet away. He was dressed for a day in the sun. Khaki shorts, polo shirt and brown sandals. Sunglasses were shoved to the top of his head, messing his hair slightly. He was heart-stoppingly gorgeous, and he stood there watching her, his liquid brown eyes bright with concern. But he was here.

Joy, pure and unfettered, flooded her body until she feared she'd fall to her knees. She swayed and threw her hand out only to catch air as she tried to steady herself.

He stepped forward to catch her, but she righted herself and blinked away the shock of seeing him so close after so many days.

"What are you doing here?" she asked faintly.

"I came for you."

A shiver worked over her body.

He frowned, concern brightening in his eyes. "Are you cold?"

"I've been cold since the day I left your house," she whispered. She wanted to cry. But more than that, she wanted to be warm again.

He held out his arms, and she walked into them, unable to

deny the comfort of his embrace. He tucked her head under his chin, and she laid her cheek against his chest. She closed her eyes as his warmth bled into her.

Slowly the ice began to melt. A low throb began, and sweet relief whispered delicately through her veins.

He lowered them both onto the sand, arranging his body around her as he positioned her between his legs. He kept firm hold of her, absorbing the trembles of her body as the cold gradually eased, and she could feel the sun once again.

"What happened, Serena mine?" he asked against her hair. "Why did you leave?"

She buried her face in his neck and tried to keep the tears at bay. "She died, Damon," she said hoarsely. "Michelle, the girl I told you about. She died during the cruise I arranged for her."

Damon stroked her hair, offering her comfort with his touch. He was calm and methodical, no urgency to his actions. No question. Just acceptance. Did he have acceptance enough for both of them?

"I'm sorry," he said huskily. "I'm so sorry, Serena. Why didn't you tell me? Why didn't you let me help you? Why leave?"

For a long moment she lay there, unable to form a response around the knot in her throat. She knew her thoughts weren't logical. Maybe she'd always known she was chasing a fantasy.

Damon waited. He sat there quietly, just holding her as she collected her courage.

"I thought that if I could give her her dream, it would be enough to save her. That if I could make magic for her, I could save her."

"Oh, sweetheart," Damon said, his voice cracking as emotion throbbed in his throat.

"When she died, I realized that nothing I'd done made a difference. None of it. She got a few minutes to be a princess, and her parents have a lifetime to live without their daughter.

"My clients still have to go back to their normal lives. They enjoy a brief respite and nothing more. I realize now how cruel it is. To give someone a taste of paradise only to yank it away? I can't think of anything worse.

"I never knew, would have never known if I hadn't tried to fulfill my own fantasy. It was then that I realized that there are worse things than never living your dream or never indulging in a fantasy. It's far worse to get a taste and know that it isn't real, will never be real, and then go back to your regular life *knowing* what it's like to have perfection and that you'll never have it again.

"Some things . . . some things are better left in the realm of fantasy," she said faintly.

"I think I understand what you're saying," he said.

She pulled slightly away so she could look into his eyes. "Do you? Then you know why I can't . . . why we can't . . ."

He shook his head. "I said I understood what you were saying, not that I agreed."

He lifted a hand to her face and trailed his fingers over her temple and to her cheekbone. They shook as he moved them to her lips.

"I have a lot I want to say to you, and I want you to listen to every word."

She nodded slowly.

"Good. Now, I understand that you're afraid. I understand that the volatility of our attraction, of our relationship, frightened you. It scared the shit out of me as well."

Her eyes widened.

"Don't look so surprised, Serena mine. You knocked me for a friggin' loop."

He leaned in and brushed a light kiss across her lips before withdrawing again. "Somewhere along the way, you decided that the Serena who gave me the gift of herself couldn't possibly be real. That not only was she not real, but she could never be what I wanted and needed. And so, you decided that in order to do what was best for me, you were going to leave me. Never mind the fact that you never once consulted me in the matter. Pretty messed up, wouldn't you say?"

"It's not that simple," she argued, remembering that she'd said the exact same thing to Julie and Faith not long ago. She glanced away, no longer able to meet the burning intensity of his eyes.

"Serena, look at me," he said gently.

He didn't prod her, didn't tug at her chin as he had so many times before. But she turned back anyway, unable to resist his softly spoken request.

"It's as simple or as complicated as we make it. Me? I'm a simple kind of guy. I love you, and I hope to hell you love me or that maybe you can love me, given a little time and persuasion on my part.

"You, on the other hand, are as complicated as they come. You twist yourself in knots until you don't know which end is up. You try to convince yourself that you can't be what I want or need, but you've never asked me what I want. Or what I need. Because if you had? I would have said only one thing. You."

She opened her mouth, but nothing would come out. He wiped his thumb over her lip as if removing the obstruction.

"Don't you have anything to say to me right now? Like that you're sorry for running out on me, or that you're sorry for worrying the absolute hell out of me, or that I had to make your friends kidnap you so I could see you again?"

He took a deep breath as though he was gathering his own brand of courage.

"Or that you love me just a little bit?"

She stared at him for a long moment, trying to match his courage, trying to form the words and work them past the knot in her throat.

"I do love you," she finally whispered.

The look of absolute joy, the crushing relief that flooded his eyes, took her breath away. His hands shook so badly against her face that he had to take them away to prevent them from bumping her skin.

She put her hands to his face this time, needing the contact and needing him to understand that loving wasn't the be all, end all in the equation.

"I think I love you," she amended. "I want to love you. I just want to be sure of who it is I love, and I want you to be sure of who it is *you* love."

"You're going to need a translator for that, Serena mine, because you lost me at the *I think I love you* part."

"You were very honest about what you want in a relationship, Damon. I was honest about what I wanted out of my fantasy. You said you'd never settle for less. And I'm frightened of the person I became during that fantasy."

"Why does she frighten you, Serena?" he asked softly. "Why do you think that this part of who you are can't be reconciled with all the other facets of your personality?"

"I lose all sense of myself when I'm with you," she blurted. "You're an addiction, Damon. I can't stand the thought of disappointing you. I'd do anything for you, and that scares the shit out of me. It's like as soon as I get near you, I have this overwhelming desire to please you, to do anything you ask of me. Do you understand that?"

"I understand it because I live it every day that I'm with you," he said. "Do you think that I don't burn to please you? That I don't live in fear of disappointing you, that I'm not afraid that I'll let you down or fail to protect you? It's hell, Serena. But it's also the sweetest pleasure I've ever known."

She stared back at him, stunned by his declaration. It mirrored her own feelings, her fears and panic. He described the jagged line she trod with him so very well.

"What if there comes a day that I can't give you what you ask for?" she choked out. "What about when the fantasy dies and that person who'd do anything to please you ceases to exist? What then?"

He put a finger to her lips. "I'll never ask for something you can't give, Serena mine. I only want what you freely offer. I only want you. With me, belonging to me. Me protecting you, cherishing you, honoring you with my every breath, with my body, my soul and my heart. What we have isn't fantasy. You may have convinced yourself that it isn't real, but it doesn't get any more real than what we've shared."

Her heart ached so badly that she feared it was going to swell right out of her chest. How could she make him understand that what she feared the most was disappointing him? Of seeing the love that shone so brightly in his eyes fade and die because she couldn't be what he wanted?

"There's nothing to say that we have to rush into this," he continued. "All I want is a chance. Time. You with me. Us working together."

"And if I disappoint you?" she asked. "If I decide I can't be what you want? What then?"

He smiled and shook his head. "Stubborn, hardheaded woman. Haven't you heard a word I've said? Serena, you can call yourself whatever you damn well want to. I've never liked the word slave, as Faith will attest. That was your word, your label. You once asked me what you were to call me and I told you Damon. Just Damon. So why can't we be Damon and Serena? Two people in love. We can work on everything else."

Hope fluttered and uncurled, rising toward the sun from its cold haven in her soul. Her pulse sped up, as against her will, she looked ahead to what could be if she took a chance.

"I'm sick to death of the word *fantasy*," Damon said. "If I never hear it again, it will be too soon. I'm real. You're real. Our love is real. Our attraction is real. Those welts on your pretty ass were real."

His hands moved to her arms, and his fingers collided with her arm band through the material of her jacket. He stilled and glanced up at her, the question in his eyes. Then he carefully tugged at the sleeve of her jacket until he had her halfway out of it.

The gold band gleamed in the sun, bright against her pale skin.

"You kept them on," he said softly. "You left and yet you still wear the gifts I gave you. My mark of possession."

She raised her hand to touch the intricate design, tracing one of the lines until she bumped into his hand. "I couldn't bear to take them off," she admitted. "It seemed so final."

He put his other hand on the opposite arm and pulled her gently to him. Their lips touched, reverently, light and seeking. As her body pressed close to his, she could feel the tension rolling through his body, and it was then she realized how afraid he was.

"What's this about you selling your business?" he asked in a quiet voice as he pulled away.

There was no censure or reproach, no disappointment. Just loving concern that made her throat swell and ache. She dropped her head only for him to cup her chin and tug gently until she faced him with watery eyes.

"I can't do it anymore," she whispered. "I can't sell false dreams."

His gaze softened, and the look he gave her was so full of understanding that she had to swallow back the tears.

"You're raw right now, and you're hurting," he said gently. "I think you should give yourself time before you make any decisions about your business. Spend some time with me, Serena mine. Give me—us—a chance. Let me take care of you. Let me cherish you the way I want to cherish you. Then, when you're ready, you can decide about Fantasy Incorporated. There's no hurry. You and I have all the time in the world."

The tears that had so threatened and stung her eyelids slid silently down her cheeks. "I'm so afraid," she whispered. But at the same time, the heavy weight, the burden she'd been carrying around, lifted and took wing. She felt lighter and freer as hope unfurled.

He pulled her away just far enough that he could look into her eyes. "The only way you could disappoint me is by giving up on us, because all I ever want you to be is mine."

She stared at him for a long moment, taking in the loving sincerity in his voice. And then she smiled through her tears. "I certainly never *want* to disappoint you, Damon."

"Then say yes," he said, his voice urgent and hoarse. "Say you'll come home with me."

She curled her arms around his neck and raised her lips to his. For the first time, her fears subsided. Renewed hope, alive and strong, surged hotly through her heart.

"Take me home," she whispered.